A RYAN DONOVAN MYSTERY, BOOK #1

WICKED NEMESIS
—— OF THE ——
HUNTED

TRACEY L. RYAN

LUMINARE PRESS
WWW.LUMINAREPRESS.COM

Wicked Nemesis of the Hunted
A Ryan Donovan Mystery, Book #1
© 2023 Tracey L. Ryan

All rights reserved. No part of this book may be reproduced,
scanned, or distributed in any printed or electronic form without
the prior written permission of the author/publisher.

*This is a work of fiction. Names, characters, places, and incidents either
are the product of the author's imagination or are used fictitiously and any
resemblance to actual persons, living or dead, businesses, companies, or locales
is entirely coincidental.*

Printed in the United States of America

Luminare Press
438 Charnelton St., Suite 101
Eugene, OR 97401
www.luminarepress.com

LCCN: 2022922574
ISBN: 979-8-88679-126-6

*In memory of Mario
who will be eternally missed
not only for his Italian cuisine but
also for his entertaining stories
and kind heart.*

Buon cibo e buoni amici.

CHAPTER 1

The sound of the waves playfully dancing with the pale sands of Nassau's Cable Beach echoed throughout the beachside villa. A gentle ocean breeze flowed through the open balcony doors of the second-floor master suite. As a result of the villa's expert design, the balcony looked like it was kissing the indigo water on the expansive horizon.

The early morning glow painted warm hues of orange and yellow against the light blue canvas of the sky in the Bahamian paradise. Most of the resort's guests were still in a deep slumber, allowing the sounds of nature to create a relaxing symphony. Ryan Donovan found dawn to be the most magical part of the day, no matter the location. The anticipation of new beginnings had always tantalized him.

Ryan, dressed in only black boxer briefs and a deep tan, embraced the day. Overlooking the pristine beach, which resembled a lush light-beige carpet below him, he inhaled the salty air. The sun glistened off the crystal-clear water while Ryan stretched his arms over his head, trying to wake up his sleeping muscles. It was Ryan's last day in this tropical sanctuary—a well-deserved break from the disturbing reality that had consumed him over the past year.

The two-story villa was nestled in a private section of the large oceanfront resort and boasted million-dollar views of the Atlantic Ocean through floor-to-ceiling windows. Inside the five-star dwelling was an open floor plan infused with natural light and enough room for six people. The Bahamian color scheme enhanced the relaxing vibe of this little piece of heaven with soft blues and cozy neutrals.

Slowly, Ryan made his way downstairs to the patio and the private plunge pool. Stripping off his briefs, he waded into the refreshing water. Completely submerged in the cool liquid, the blood flowed through his veins, awakening all his senses.

His time alone lasted fifteen more minutes until Anita's arrival. Just like she had done every morning since Ryan arrived, Anita meticulously set up her portable massage table on the secluded patio. She always placed the table facing the ocean and completely obscured from the prying eyes of other guests.

With water gliding down Ryan's sculpted body, he strode over to the table and positioned himself face-down as was the routine. Once Ryan was situated, Anita ran a towel over his body to absorb any remaining water droplets. Anita rhythmically rubbed eucalyptus-infused massage oil into her hands in preparation for the task in front of her. The light scent of the eucalyptus intoxicated Ryan, putting him in a trance.

Anita's fingers penetrated deep into Ryan's muscles while his thoughts drifted to days gone by.

Hunter Logan, CEO of Ares Logan Industries, was Ryan's best friend and current employer. They had known each other for more years than Ryan could recount. Even when they lost touch for several years while Ryan was off playing secret agent and Hunter was conquering the business world, they were able to pick up where their friendship left off without skipping a beat. And when Hunter offered his best friend the chance to leave the clandestine world of spy games, Ryan decided it was an opportunity he couldn't resist.

Surprisingly, it had not taken Ryan long to settle into the role of chief of security for one of the world's largest conglomerates. While Ryan acclimated to the next chapter of his evolving story, he was surprised by how many of his past skills would need to be utilized in the corporate world.

Although Hunter had his fair share of women over the years, Ryan always knew Emma Sharpeton was the one who got away from Hunter many years earlier. Emma wasn't only beautiful but also smart and determined. She started her own company fresh out of college, with a little discreet help from Hunter, and quickly became one of Boston's rising stars. Ryan knew the first time he had met Emma she could be fierce as a jaguar and gentle as a lamb, making her the perfect match for Hunter.

A heartfelt smile subconsciously formed on Ryan's chiseled face when his thoughts shifted to the fairy-tale ending and murderous mayhem that he, Hunter, and Emma had been thrust into unwillingly. After surviving the firestorm in the normally quiet, small town of Hardwicke, Hunter had not wasted any time in proposing to Emma. Ryan never knew Hunter had been carrying the stunning three-carat emerald-and-diamond engagement ring in his jacket pocket the night Hunter's world changed forever. Hardwicke had been a turning point for the three of them on many levels.

Anita continued to work her magic while Ryan relived the past year in vivid detail. Summer had faded into autumn with its crisp air and golden tones—the perfect time of year for a wedding in New England. Hunter and Emma decided on a private ceremony for immediate family only. The nuptials were held inside the thirty-story atrium at the Ares Logan headquarters next to the koi pond. Like the Boston Children's Gala held in the same location several months prior, the space was decorated with warm white twinkle lights in the trees, adding even more charm to the enchanting event. A white fabric runner led up to a trellis covered with pale pink and yellow roses that served as the altar.

Emma's two best friends—Hannah and Morgan—were the bridesmaids. The groomsmen consisted of Emma's brother, Robert, and Ryan. Victoria, Emma's mother, flew in from Arizona to walk her only daughter down the aisle.

Ryan remembered watching Emma struggle with her emotions while walking down the aisle. Although a time for tears of joy, Ryan noticed the corners of Emma's eyes glistened with a hint of sadness. Most little girls dream of their wedding day and their father walking them down the aisle. Ryan knew this was something Emma could only imagine since her father's murder several years prior.

Hunter and Emma lost their fathers tragically— Philip Logan in a plane crash in South America along the Amazon and Craig Sharpeton in a targeted hit-and-run car accident. Another revelation the threesome had uncovered during their nightmare over the last several months—Craig's car accident was not truly an accident but, instead, ordered by Philip to silence a loose end in his deranged mind.

Ryan tried to focus on the magic of that day instead of the sins of the past. The golden rays of the afternoon sun had filtered through the immense glass structure, creating an angelic illumination.

Hunter almost fainted when he saw his radiant bride walking down the aisle. Ryan had never seen his friend so electrified and nervous at the same time.

The women in the wedding party wore floor-length, pale lavender sheath gowns with a cowl neckline. The men sported dark Armani suits with complimentary lavender-striped silk ties. Victoria had selected a classic floor-length dress in pale yellow, with long sleeves and a flared skirt. The star of the show was Emma in her elegant ivory, fitted gown, with a pleated waistline and beaded cowl that hung softly down the back. The dress had a gentle flair on the bottom to provide a hint of a train. Droplets of sunlight glistened off the beads as Emma continued down the aisle to her destiny.

Ryan was thankful the ceremony was succinct and not overdone. He was never one for the pomp and circumstance weddings usually provided. The wedding couple opted to write their own vows, which eloquently summed up their relationship. Once the formalities were completed, the justice of the peace declared them married, prompting Hunter to pull Emma into an epic kiss.

The reception was held at Mario's Ristorante, a favorite of Hunter's. Mario surpassed expectations once again with the décor and multiple courses of mouthwatering Italian cuisine. The tables were decorated with warm white twinkle lights and pale pink roses in Murano glass vases. Just when the guests finished one course, the next surreptitiously appeared in front of them. Following tradition, Hunter and Emma fed each other a slice of white cake with buttercream frosting. Emma felt mischievous and smashed part of the slice into Hunter's face, causing the small crowd to erupt in laughter. Hunter playfully grabbed Emma and passionately kissed her, transferring most of the frosting to her pristine face. The party was in full swing when Mario cleared a small space for dancing. He even stole a dance with the blushing bride.

The next morning, Hunter whisked off his wife for three weeks in the mystical lands of Ireland and Scotland. The couple decided on a driving tour of both countries, staying in quaint villages and majestic castles along the way. Ryan insisted two security guards accompany them, which Hunter was less than pleased about. The greatest fear Ryan had was that danger still lurked in the shadows. There was still a multitude of unanswered questions surrounding the cancer-prevention drug research and the murderous plot to obtain it.

Anita could feel Ryan's muscles tighten when darker memories started to infiltrate his mind. The memories flashing through Ryan's head were like a trailer to an upcoming action-adventure movie.

Philip Logan's depraved obsession with Emma when she was a teenager, calling her a "whore" and "trash."

The shock that Hunter had a half-sister, Ashley, who was the result of a dalliance between Hunter's mother, Katherine Logan, and Hardwicke's police commander, Chief Dyson, and subsequently given up for adoption.

Ashley portraying herself as a lost kitten and cleverly inserting herself into Hunter's and Emma's lives.

The stalking and terrorizing of Emma by Ashley to get to Hunter, with the help of her accomplice, Greg Smythe.

And the undeniable danger surrounding the cancer-prevention formula for anyone involved.

Before his mind could delve deeper into the abyss, Ryan heard Anita whisper something into his ear while she finished his massage and simultaneously undressed. As part of their week-long routine, Anita helped Ryan off the table and into the outdoor shower where she continued to stimulate his senses.

Ryan suspended his walk down memory lane to focus on living in the moment.

CHAPTER 2

Ryan gazed out the window of the Ares Logan private jet while it flew over the turquoise waters of the Bahamas. Once the jet climbed to its cruising altitude, Ryan leaned back in the leather seat and closed his eyes.

Dark clouds overtook Ryan's subconscious as he slipped into a state of unconsciousness. He couldn't help but feel uneasy. Ryan was going back to not only a plethora of unknowns but also the thought he wasn't any closer to discovering the key pieces of the puzzle.

This uneasiness conjured an image of Ashley for Ryan. Little did Ashley know she would be the one to pay the ultimate price for the unrealistic chance to obtain the cancer-prevention formula. Ryan, if he believed in this sort of thing, could almost entertain the idea the cancer-prevention formula was cursed. To their knowledge, four deaths could be directly linked to the quest for the formula: Craig Sharpeton, Philip Logan, Ashley, and Chief Dyson.

The first two deaths—Craig and Philip—happened several years earlier. As part of the investigation into who was tormenting Emma, the trio discovered Emma's father had been employed at Ares Logan's pharmaceutical division. As the primary researcher on a covert project, it was Craig's responsibility to unlock the secrets of the mysterious plant that Philip found in the Amazon by happenstance. Once Emma's father identified the true potential of the bright pink plant, Philip decided it was time to get rid of any witnesses. After Philip secured what he assumed was all the research, he hired a group of Russian thugs to cause the accident that killed Craig in Hardwicke.

Hunter's father also paid for his past sins when his plane crashed in the Amazon searching for more of the plant. Although the wreckage was located, Philip's body was never found. Given the Amazon is the largest rainforest in the world covering over two million square miles, it was a miracle the plane was even found. There were abundant challenges for the search team trying to locate the plane crash, including dangerous wildlife and extraordinarily little sunlight due to the dense vegetation. No one was ever able to determine what happened to Philip's body.

Was it taken by a deadly green anaconda or one of the indigenous tribes in the area? Ryan wondered. The only reason the search team even found the plane wreckage was because it was suspended in the air toward the top of the trees, nose down, so part of the tail was slightly visible in the lush canopy.

Then, more recently, the standoff at the Logan estate in Hardwicke ended with two more deaths—Ashley and Chief Dyson. Emma and Katherine were kidnapped as part of the wild plot to lure Hunter into a trap to exchange the drug formula for their lives. Witnessing the tragic death of her true love and being confronted with her past was more than Katherine's mind could handle. After being taken to one of the top hospitals in Boston, it was suggested she be relocated to a psychiatric facility specializing in her type of long-term care since her catatonic state hadn't improved. Katherine was flown shortly thereafter to Ocean's View Psychiatric Hospital in Cheticamp, Nova Scotia.

Hunter had been hesitant to place his mother in a facility hundreds of miles away. Through scrupulous research, Hunter confirmed this facility was the best in the world for dealing with his mother's type of mental and emotional trauma. Although Hunter had a tumultuous relationship with his mother for much of his life, he still loved her and would do anything to help her. Hunter had felt obligated to arrange Ashley's funeral because she had no other living relatives, and he chose to have her cremated. The ashes were scattered on the Logan estate in Hardwicke, which provided a sense of irony. Ashley had spent most of her adult life desiring to be part of the Logan family and now she was forever part of the estate in death.

Ryan's memories continued to venture down a gloomy path. Turmoil surrounded the cancer-prevention formula and the seeds that might make it a reality. Although not privy to the inner workings of this diabolical game, the final stage was clear to Ryan.

The cancer-prevention research was progressing toward the next phase with clinical trials expected in the next six months. One challenge the team continued to have was the trouble of overcoming the replication of the seeds. The researchers hoped to develop a synthetic substitute for the actual seeds since they didn't possess the genuine plants. All attempts to grow more plants from the seeds recovered at Emma's family's house in Hardwicke failed. Hunter understood the brilliant pink plants were indigenous to the Amazon but only his father knew the actual location. With Philip declared dead, the whereabouts of the plants were another mystery that would need to be solved.

Ryan's focus centered on unraveling Ashley's fiendish plan. The little voice in his head kept telling him to keep poking the hornet's nest. While Hunter was preoccupied with Emma in the enchanting land of kings and queens, Ryan continued with his quest to find answers, even while soaking up the sun and salty air.

The same questions kept consuming Ryan's mind.

Who had financed Ashley's adventures?

How was Ashley able to establish a clinical lab in an undisclosed location?

Who was behind the high-priced yacht surveilling them in Chatham?

What was the connection to the Russian thugs responsible for Emma's and Craig's car accidents in Hardwicke?

Who was paying Greg Smythe for his unique skill set?

How was Greg able to disappear without a trace?

And how did anyone beyond Emma and Philip know about the callous names Philip previously called Emma?

Ryan knew from his years of experience with clandestine operations to start any investigation by following the money—it typically provided clues to solving the larger mystery. Ashley and Greg's escapades required large sums of cash, and Ryan couldn't locate any sort of money trail directly leading back to either of them. Ashley had a little under two thousand dollars in a money market account plus an insignificant portfolio of stocks. Her adoptive parents left her the house in Hingham, which she kept, and nothing else of any real value.

Since Katherine didn't know about Ashley's true identity until the debacle in Hardwicke, Ryan surmised Katherine wasn't the person financing the scheme. At one point during the ordeal, Ryan speculated there was a chance Katherine bankrolled the plot. Ryan was grateful this had turned out not to be true for Hunter's sake.

The lack of answers nagged at Ryan, and he feared a serious threat was still looming unless the puzzle pieces could be assembled to his satisfaction. Ryan hypothesized that finding and identifying Greg Smythe was likely the key to identifying the real architect of the lethal cat-and-mouse game.

Ryan was jolted back to consciousness when the landing gear deployed, and the plane slowly began its descent.

Stretching his arms above his head as best he could, Ryan tried to shake off the lethargic feeling that had overtaken his body. In the distance, he could see the iconic Boston skyline under a partly blue sky when the plane emerged from the cotton-like cloud bank. Part of him longed to be back on the private Bahamian beach without any responsibilities, only pure relaxation.

Hunter's personal driver and bodyguard, Jared, met Ryan in the small terminal at the private airport. The men nodded to each other and walked in silence to the Mercedes. As Jared expected, Ryan threw his bag in the back seat, then joined him up front.

During the standoff in Hardwicke, Ryan learned firsthand what a valuable asset Jared was. With expert precision, Jared fired a single bullet directly into the center of Ashley's forehead. She was dead before she hit the floor. Ryan hadn't failed to notice Jared's cool demeanor before and after the incident. Even his own pulse was throbbing during that moment while Jared seemed perfectly calm.

Hunter never told Ryan the complete story regarding Jared's background, and Jared's personnel file contained only the basics. Ryan always assumed Jared had at least some military or police training for Hunter to have personally selected him as his driver-plus-bodyguard prior to Ryan joining the company. And now, Ryan was even more curious but opted to leave it alone until it was necessary to delve deeper. All Ryan needed to know was Jared could do what was necessary in a crucial moment.

Jared broke Ryan's train of thought. "Nice trip, Ryan?"

"Yes. It was very relaxing. Have you been to the Bahamas, Jared?"

Jared pulled out of the parking lot and merged into minimal traffic heading toward downtown Boston. "I've been there a few times. The view from the air always mesmerizes me with the varying degrees of blue ocean below."

"It is amazing. Anything of interest happen while I was gone?"

Wicked Nemesis of the Hunted   15

Ryan inquired even though he knew he would have received a phone call or text if there was anything of importance.

"Not that I'm aware of. The Logans arrived safely in Boston yesterday morning. I think Mrs. Logan added quite a lot to the local economies in the UK," Jared stated, allowing himself a small grin.

Ryan let out a laugh. "I'm not surprised! Glad that they made it back safe and sound. Is Emma completely moved into Hunter's penthouse?"

The residence where Emma and Hunter now called home was what Ryan would describe as magnificent. The floor plan was completely open with floor-to-ceiling windows offering incredible views in every direction. Hardwoods repeated throughout, the furnishings were in pale tones, and simple aesthetics separated the rooms.

The see-through gas fireplace added a divider between the dining and living room areas. Off the dining area existed an expert kitchen that any chef would be overjoyed to cook in. There was also a bar area that replicated a London pub. The penthouse included two well-appointed washrooms—one on either side of the space, a small pantry off the kitchen, and a gently winding staircase leading up to the second floor.

Although Ryan had only been up there a few times, the second floor carried the same design elements as the first floor. Ryan remembered the primary bathroom being something of a master-piece, with a shower that could fit five people and jets coming out of the walls to wash every nook of someone's body.

"I believe Ms. Sharpeton—I mean Mrs. Logan—still needs to move a few things over to the penthouse."

Jared resumed concentrating on driving through the tight city streets.

Ryan caught a glimpse of Jared checking all mirrors every twenty seconds—something only a seasoned professional would subconsciously do. Once again, Ryan's curiosity was piqued.

The view out the passenger-side window showed brick, concrete, and steel. It was a stark contrast to the palm trees and sandy beaches Ryan saw earlier in the day.

Jared gave Ryan a brief wave as he drove away from the modest apartment building where he dropped him off. The building was red brick and built at the turn of the century as a furniture warehouse. When the manufacturing companies moved out of Boston, this was one of many buildings converted into retail and living spaces. Ryan occupied a one-bedroom apartment on the top floor—his own version of a penthouse.

After numerous relocations in his previous job, Ryan never gave much thought to his living arrangements or material things. He learned to live with only the necessities and not waste time on extravagance. Although he loved Hunter's penthouse, it just wasn't in his DNA to own something so lavish. He was content with his seven hundred and forty square feet of space which combined modern and old city charm.

Part of the charisma was the exposed brick walls. The apartment boasted a small galley kitchen, one bathroom, and enough living space for a single man who worked more hours than the time he spent there. Ryan rarely entertained except for a handful of one-night liaisons whom he didn't allow to spend the night.

Upon entering the humble apartment, Ryan turned off the state-of-the-art alarm system. He noticed how the sun naturally brightened the space. A quick scan of the surroundings confirmed to Ryan everything was in proper order. He rolled his suitcase into the small hallway containing the bathroom plus the closet hiding the washer and dryer.

The refrigerator revealed the desperate need for groceries when Ryan opened the door to grab some bottled water. Ryan admitted to himself he sometimes wished he had someone like Hunter's housekeeper, Pauline, to clean and do errands for him.

Grabbing his wallet, Ryan decided to venture to the family-owned market on the corner where his building was located. He could get the essentials until he was in the mood for a full expedition to the grocery store.

Upon entering the Kern Family Grocery, Ryan was greeted with a big wave from the proprietors. Chuck and Kelly had owned the market for as long as Ryan had lived in the neighborhood. They were salt-of-the-earth type of people who loved their community and would do anything to help a neighbor.

While Ryan put his items on the counter, Chuck asked, "Where did you jet off to, Ryan? You're looking very tan."

"Just got back from the Bahamas and saw there wasn't an ounce of food in my apartment. What's new around here, Chuck?" Ryan asked as the two newest members of the Kern family arrived to greet him.

The two mini-Labradoodles, Harper and Finley, nuzzled against Ryan, waiting for a scratch on the head. Ryan obliged with a smile.

"Same old stuff. It's been fantastic weather. Kelly and I thought you might have been away this past week when you didn't pop in for your morning coffee." Chuck continued to pack up Ryan's groceries in a brown paper bag while Kelly brought an armful of toilet paper from the back storeroom to restock the empty shelf.

Ryan saw the total on the register and handed Chuck his credit card. "Back to the grind tomorrow. I could have used another week in the sun." Ryan's eyes brightened thinking about the warm ocean breeze.

Wicked Nemesis of the Hunted   19

Chuck handed Ryan's card back to him along with the bag containing two boxes of ziti, two jars of marinara sauce, milk, orange juice, bread, protein bars, and a six-pack of Guinness bottles. Ryan grabbed the bag with one arm and waved good-bye to the owners with the other.

The tepid sunlight hit Ryan as soon as he exited the store. A sense of serenity washed over him on the short walk back to his unpretentious dwelling. The leaves were starting to gently turn from deep green to an array of harvest colors. The smell of autumn filled the air. Although still warm, the change of seasons had officially arrived.

Once Ryan was back in his private lair, and the groceries were put away, he flopped on the couch dreading his next task—laundry. When his phone vibrated, Ryan took it as a sign from the heavens the laundry could wait.

Looking at the caller ID, Ryan answered cheerfully, "Hey, bro! How was the honeymoon?"

The British accent on the other end responded, "It was amazing! Ireland and Scotland were more than we could have imagined. Watching Emma experience them for the first time was incredible." Hunter's excitement protruded through the phone.

"That's great, Hunter. I knew you would have a fabulous time."

Ryan had traveled extensively throughout Europe as part of his previous occupation, including Ireland and Scotland. Someday Ryan hoped to experience it without the fear of being shot or killed.

"How was your Bahamian retreat?" Hunter asked with a snicker, knowing his friend more than likely had met at least one female companion.

"Very relaxing," Ryan responded, not delving into any specifics.

"The lack of information tells me there must be a woman involved or many women. I'll have to get the details from you later as my lovely wife is in the next room."

Ryan laughed into the phone. "Is Emma all moved into your palatial penthouse?"

Hunter lowered his voice. "How many shoes can one woman have? I mean, seriously! And knick-knacks. You wouldn't recognize my place anymore, Ryan. It went from orderly to a jungle of female trinkets overnight." Hunter moaned.

"Welcome to married life, my friend." Ryan chuckled.

"Perhaps you should get married, and then you can comment," Hunter responded playfully.

"No way! That's too dangerous even for me." Ryan opened a bottle of Guinness and took a swallow.

"I was thinking we could grab breakfast at the office around eight a.m. to catch up. Robert will join us later in the morning." Hunter's tone quickly turned to business.

Ryan caught how Hunter purposely wanted their meeting to be just the two of them. "Sounds good. I will meet you in your office and there better be coffee."

"I wouldn't dream of not having coffee for you. I may even splurge and get you a muffin." Sarcasm permeated through the phone.

Ryan could hear banging in the background. "Everything alright?"

"Emma is unpacking more boxes." Hunter let out a sigh and reminded himself this was all worth it.

"Okay, I'll see you in the morning. Give Emma a hug for me. And, Hunter, I really am happy you both had a wonderful time," Ryan replied genuinely.

"Thanks, Ryan." Hunter disconnected.

As the black liquid glided down Ryan's throat, he contemplated the multitude of reasons Hunter wouldn't want Robert included in the conversation. The only logical explanation was the unsolved mystery surrounding them like a mist in the Scottish Highlands. There wasn't much use in speculating; Ryan knew he would just need to wait until the morning to find out what was on Hunter's mind. Given there were no other reasons to help Ryan procrastinate, he begrudgingly started on the daunting task of laundry.

CHAPTER 3

The far-reaching rays of dawn infiltrated Ryan's apartment, gradually alerting him it was time to begin the day. Ryan started each morning with one hundred pushups and one hundred sit-ups. Once completed, he grabbed a protein bar, then headed to the shower to get ready to re-enter the world of corporate security.

The hot water ran over Ryan's darkened skin, reminding him of Anita. He imagined her massaging him in the outdoor shower at the beachside villa—specifically, the one morning she allowed Ryan to practice his own massage techniques on the most delicate parts of her own bronze-colored body. Before he could fully relive this fantasy, Ryan turned off the shower and dried himself. Reality was minutes away, and Ryan knew he needed to focus.

Ryan parked the corporate Mercedes in his designated space inside the Ares Logan garage. Within minutes, Ryan was in the elevator heading up to Hunter's office on the top floor of the rose-hued glass structure towering high above Boston's concrete jungle. He knocked and then walked into the office without waiting for approval.

The smell of dark roast coffee filled the air of the expansive office. Ryan took a deep breath, and a bright smile filled his face. Hunter shook his head at the theatrics from his long-time friend while he leaned back in his leather chair.

There was a time not long ago when Hunter couldn't be sure if Ryan and he would get back to being best friends. Hunter was relieved they were able to overcome the mental anguish from the wicked game they had been drawn into. It took the catastrophic escape in Hardwicke for Hunter to realize he could not imagine his life without Ryan deeply rooted in it.

"As his highness requested, there is fresh coffee and an assortment of breakfast pastries." Mockery oozed from Hunter.

"I expect this every morning. This needs to be written into my contract." Ryan stuffed a cheese-filled pastry in his mouth in one bite, dropping specks of crumbs on the hardwood floor.

"You may want to try using a napkin next time. *And*, you do not have a contract," Hunter responded matter-of-factly.

"I think I should consider getting a contract." Ryan's response was garbled with food.

Hunter tried to relieve the tension in his neck as he got up from his desk and headed over to refill his Royal Doulton coffee mug. The aroma awakened his senses. "With the wedding over and both of us back, I would like to get an update on the precarious situation we were dealing with before the festivities."

Ryan knew Hunter would never let the whole Ashley-and-Greg tirade go and for good reason. "Which aspect of the 'situation' are you referring to?"

"Any aspect! Do we know *anything* more than we did a few weeks ago?" Hunter thought about it and helped himself to a raspberry pastry.

"Here is what I know, which is the same as what you know. The person we know as Greg Smythe has disappeared into thin air. There hasn't been a single trace of him or anyone remotely fitting his description since he miraculously escaped police custody in Hardwicke."

"How can that happen?" Hunter felt unsettled.

"It really isn't difficult. We already know he was using a fake name. He just needs new bogus credentials and a simple disguise. Something as simple as dyeing his hair and growing a beard will be enough to stay hidden in plain sight. We also know Greg was hired to do this job, so he more than likely isn't in it for the long haul. There are a few probable scenarios.

"One, Greg is enjoying his payday on a beach in Mexico. Two, his employer wasn't happy the job imploded, and Greg is now fish food in the Atlantic. Or three, Greg is still on the job." Ryan knew Hunter wanted concrete answers as much as he did, but there just wasn't any to give right now.

As Hunter had done on so many occasions, he looked out at the Boston Harbor displayed in front of him. The sun once again glistened off the water like diamonds.

"Alright, so Greg Smythe, or whatever his name is, is a dead end. What about the money? We know Ashley certainly didn't have this kind of cash."

"I'm still looking into the money aspect. I was able to find a lab in Morocco that might be the one Ashley rented to try to finish the cancer-drug research. I won't bore you with the reasons why I think this lab has promise compared to thousands of others out there.

"Hunter, you know I will not rest until I fit all these pieces together." Ryan paused before continuing. "I am still not convinced we are out of danger. Someone paid Ashley and Greg to play their parts. This person went through a lot of trouble and, need I remind you, almost succeeded. They didn't expect us to survive the nightmare in Hardwicke." Ryan's solemn tone hung in the air.

Hunter continued to gaze at the boats in the harbor while Ryan's words infiltrated his brain. "I understand what you are saying. I also know you will check under every rock to uncover who did this…or is doing this. One thing I don't want is for Emma to find out about our suspicions," Hunter conveyed.

"That is your call, buddy. My two cents— wouldn't it be better if she knew?" Ryan felt Emma was entitled to know, given she was a pawn in the game as much as the two of them.

"She is so happy and relaxed now. I want her to stay that way until we have some credible information. I was really praying this would all be over by the time we returned from the UK. I have had a talk with Emma regarding security. She knows, due to our wealth, we must take extra precautions she wouldn't be used to."

"And how did Ms. Independent Emma react?"

"It took a bit of convincing, but she ultimately understood."

Ryan visibly hesitated.

"Just spit it out, Ryan." Hunter looked down at his semi-warm coffee.

"We never discussed Jared's expert precision in Hardwicke."

"No, we did not. What's on our mind, Ryan?" Hunter asked while he tried to quickly prepare his answer.

"I have never asked about Jared's background. And you have never offered any details. After the fiasco in Hardwicke, I admit I am more intrigued now than ever."

Wicked Nemesis of the Hunted   27

Hunter shrugged. "Jared came highly recommended by a business associate of mine prior to you joining. His credentials were top-notch. Expert marksmanship, as we both witnessed first-hand. No immediate family. Not sure what else you want to know that isn't in his employment file, which I'm sure you have already read."

"Nothing else, I guess." Ryan let it go for now.

Ryan grabbed another cheese-filled pastry before he headed to his office. "We *will* get to the bottom of this. This can't haunt us forever," he remarked when he left Hunter's office.

The substructure below the busy streets of Boston contained one of the most highly trained security teams in the country. Ryan hand-selected every person in his domain from analysts to the more clandestine surveillance team that stayed hidden in the shadows of the corporate conglomerate. Most of the people employed were former law enforcement at both the local and federal levels or had military backgrounds. His one secret weapon, as Hunter always referred to her, was a genius hacker and systems analyst who could find out anything about anyone.

The team hardly noticed Ryan walking through the area to his windowless but comfortable office. All the typical tasks were happening—newly hired personnel were being vetted, security cameras were being watched, and cyber-security analysts were monitoring potential threats to the collection of companies under the Logan umbrella.

Before sorting through the pile of folders left on his desk, Ryan decided to call Detective O'Reilly of the Boston Police Department to see if he may have made any headway on the situation.

"Detective O'Reilly," answered the gruff voice on the other end of the phone.

"Hi, detective. It's Ryan."

"Hey, Ryan. How are things in the ivory tower?" The detective assumed he would be hearing from Ryan eventually to check on the progress of the open case they shared.

"Just got back from a week in the Bahamas and wanted to see if there were any developments."

"Gee, must be nice to be lounging in the sun!" The detective bellowed. "Unfortunately, nothing new to report. I hate to say it, but we have hit a dead end. No pun intended."

With a small sigh, Ryan responded, "I figured as much. Just wanted to talk to you before I put more of my people on it."

Ryan had built a good relationship with Detective O'Reilly over the last year and knew the detective would have notified him if there were any substantial developments.

"I get it. I wish I had better news for you. It's like this Greg Smythe guy vanished into thin air. We always knew that was not his real name, but the last sighting we had of Greg was of him being put into the police cruiser in Hardwicke. People just don't disappear without a trace…or at least I never thought so until now." Detective O'Reilly leaned back in his squeaky chair and rubbed his eyes.

"I honestly never thought Greg Smythe would be this good. Alright, let me see what my team can conjure up. I'll keep you in the loop, detective."

"Please do." Detective O'Reilly paused. "Ryan, do you think this guy still poses a threat?"

"I wish I could say a definitive 'no,' but I'm just not sure. Typically, guys like Greg finish a job, change their identity for the next one, and move on." It was now Ryan's turn to pause. "The job with Emma, Hunter, and the cancer drug was never actually finished, which makes me edgy. And to top it off, we don't know who financed the whole endeavor. I just don't like unanswered questions." Ryan's stomach started to tighten.

Detective O'Reilly let out a deep breath. "Okay. I will do what I can to help. Be safe."

Ryan knew he had more resources at his disposal than Detective O'Reilly but silently wished the Boston police would have been able to find something while he was relaxing in the sun.

Just as Ryan was about to take a swig of the now lukewarm coffee he brought downstairs, a sealed, nine-by-twelve, plain white envelope caught his eye. It was set aside from the various other files and paperwork left on his desk, which piqued Ryan's curiosity.

The word "confidential" was stamped across it, which intrigued Ryan, given everything they did was private. A smirk formed on Ryan's face when he saw a handwritten note attached. The note was from his secret-weapon analyst, which gave him a speck of hope.

Inside the sealed envelope were several eight-by-ten pictures from what looked like the Hardwicke police cruiser's dashboard camera. The initial few images showed Greg Smythe sprinting away from the chaotic scene into the darkness.

One picture showed Greg directly in front of the police cruiser, unhandcuffed, with his head turned slightly to the right toward where all the action was happening at the Logan estate. Subsequent frames revealed Greg moving further down the road and either looking to his right or left. Ryan scrunched his eyes trying to find any relevance in these images and, after a few minutes, gave up. The last four photos contained the information Ryan was looking for and not something he had anticipated.

The pictures revealed Greg meeting a mid-size, nondescriptive black helicopter in the field approximately a half mile down the unlit, two-lane road from the Logan estate. The first image was of the helicopter hovering about fifty feet off the ground with what looked like a rope ladder deployed. The next

Wicked Nemesis of the Hunted   31

one was of Greg reaching for the ladder, followed by him climbing up for his escape. Finally, the last photo displayed the helicopter and its passenger rising above Hardwicke, heading in a westerly direction.

Gathering the photographs off his desk, Ryan repositioned them in sequential order on the conference table. It looked like a typical action movie unfolding in front of him. He half expected Bruce Willis or Dwayne Johnson to show up in the pictures, dangling off the rope ladder from the helicopter. Based on his experience, Ryan thought the helicopter looked like an AS532 Cougar. This was used by both civilians and the military due to its size and power. Generally, it was the go-to helicopter for search-and-rescue missions with added radar search equipment.

With a range of approximately three hundred and eighty miles, this would give Ryan a search radius to start with. These helicopters weren't cheap to rent or buy, so Ryan hoped to be able to find some sort of paper trail. The Kevlar yacht flashed in Ryan's mind. Once again, an expensive mode of transportation was being used, which fascinated him.

Ryan decided to text Hunter this added information, knowing it would trigger either a phone call or personal visit. As Ryan predicted, fifteen minutes later, the doorway to his office was overtaken by Hunter's bulky frame.

"So, you think you found this weasel's escape route?" Hunter snidely inquired.

"Seems that way. Come, take a look." Ryan moved out of the way so Hunter could get the full effect of the images before him on the conference table.

Hunter carefully inspected each photo, with Ryan watching him intently. After several minutes, Hunter rubbed his eyes. "Wow. This was all caught by the dash camera in the cruiser?" Hunter was mildly confused as to why no one alerted them of this earlier.

"Yes. None of us expected to see this. Just happened the police cruiser was parked in the ideal spot to capture all this footage. We may be able to learn even more by viewing the actual video. I'm working on having that sent to me." Ryan never divulged his methods of obtaining any data to Hunter.

"Well, this explains how Greg was able to leave Hardwicke without anyone seeing him. Hardwicke is such a small town. I always wondered how none of the townspeople saw a stranger wandering around the streets. Do we know if the Hardwicke police reviewed this video? Seems a bit convenient if you ask me."

Ryan shook his head. "I have no idea but will see what I can uncover."

The same thought occurred to Ryan. Understanding Hardwicke lost its police chief that night,

Ryan wondered if the dash camera video was mistakenly overlooked or purposely hidden.

"Now the million-dollar question: Do we know who owns the helicopter or who paid for it?" Hunter rubbed his temples.

"Not yet. We have a radius to work within since we know the typical range for this type of helicopter. That should narrow it down a bit, but I seriously doubt Greg—or Ashley, for that matter—would have put this expense on their credit card. The more plausible possibility is the helicopter may have been borrowed or stolen. In which case, there won't be any way to trace it unless there was a police incident report filed."

Ryan wished he were swimming in the turquoise waters off Nassau.

Hunter sat in one of the chairs in front of Ryan's desk and put his head in his hands. For a minute, he closed his eyes and transported his thoughts back to the Emerald Isle, with its rolling green hills, formidable castles, and more sheep than he ever imagined. He wondered if this would ever end, and if so, how it would end. Everyone involved thought Hardwicke was going to be the grand finale—how wrong they all were.

"Let me know what else you find out." Without waiting for a response, Hunter rose and headed back to his top-floor sanctuary.

Ryan called his secret-weapon analyst to obtain a copy of the video plus start the search for the mysterious helicopter. Once delegated, Ryan sat at his desk contemplating this latest piece of the puzzle. He made a mental note to reach out to Detective O'Reilly when more details were uncovered. At least they now knew Greg didn't vanish into thin air.

With all the commotion in Hardwicke that fateful night, any townsperson would assume the helicopter was part of the overwhelming law-enforcement presence. With most of the police preoccupied at the house, it was not surprising the helicopter went undetected, Ryan inferred. After the shootout at Hunter's family estate and Greg's subsequent escape, additional officers were called in from the state police and FBI to search for the fugitive, not knowing at the time Greg had already flown away to an unknown destination.

Ryan thought about the helicopter escape. Was it planned for both Greg and Ashley or only one of them?

And if only one of them, which one? Ryan pondered.

The assumption could be made it was for Ashley, given her ruthless leadership over many months to plan and execute the scheme. She clearly viewed Greg as an incompetent employee, based on comments Ryan overheard between the two at the Logan estate that tragic night.

Or was Greg the true mastermind and Ashley only led to believe she held the upper hand? Ryan silently considered this, leaning back in his chair with his arms clasped behind his head.

Wicked Nemesis of the Hunted   35

Ryan slogged through the remainder of the day. It felt like he was trying to walk in quicksand. To try to get a new perspective on the evolving situation, he decided to head to the onsite gym.

At the gym, Ryan nodded to a few of the regulars and hopped on the treadmill to do a quick five-mile run. Right when he was about to finish, his phone began to vibrate, signaling a text had arrived. Ryan slowed the machine and his body down.

The text from his surreptitious analyst read, "Found something. Call me."

Ryan debated whether to grab a quick shower before heading back to his office. The debate ended when Ryan got a whiff of himself as he toweled off the sweat protruding from his bronzed skin.

Fifteen minutes later, freshly cleaned but still damp, Ryan hit the speed dial on his cell phone after he entered his office. "What did you find?" Ryan never wasted time with pleasantries with his analyst.

"I came up with a few viable options. First, I researched all the airfields and businesses that would even have an AS532 Cougar helicopter. Then I tried to narrow it down after estimating the distance the helicopter would have to fly to get to the pickup location in Hardwicke.

"The next part was a bit trickier. To find potential destinations, I came up with the following scenarios: they would return to where the helicopter originated from, or Greg would be dropped off at a different location, and then the helicopter would fly back to its origin. Although I did not include the possibility of refueling before they continued in the analysis, I will investigate that next to see if there are any records out there."

"I agree with your approach." Ryan had not considered the refueling option.

"Boston is surprisingly only sixty-eight miles from Hardwicke by car and, given the amount of corporate activity in the area, it is a feasible point of origin. Same with Albany and New York City. Remember, these are the maximum ranges, so the helicopter could have come from someplace only twenty-five or fifty miles away."

"I understand." Ryan appreciated the possibilities could be endless.

"I think we should start with the following three companies. The first—Finny's Helicopters in Waltham. These people have been sanctioned by the FAA several times for not following the rules. It also looks like they may not be completely truthful with their financial records, meaning their bank statements show a business about to go under, but they have all kinds of brand-new equipment." She waited for Ryan to react.

"It certainly sounds like they wouldn't ask questions if the money was right," Ryan agreed, sounding hopeful.

"Next on the list is T$ Charters outside of Albany. Same deal with them."

"Okay," Ryan replied.

"And, finally, Gresham Executive Helicopter in Newark. The registrations of the helicopters are not jiving with state records, which leads me to believe they didn't purchase these legally," she stated, even-toned.

"You mean this is a helicopter chop shop?" Ryan had never heard of such a thing.

"I can't be completely sure, but that is my guess." She waited patiently for Ryan to respond.

Ryan took a deep breath and exhaled. "Thank you. Let's focus on these three companies as you suggested. Do your typical research on them. Send me whatever you find out." Ryan felt as if he were on a merry-go-round and could not get off.

"Will do. I will also send you the video shortly. I am reviewing it now to see if there is anything else I can find." Ryan's analyst hung up and a faint smile formed on her face.

Ryan began to pace around his office, trying to assimilate this latest information. He knew the odds of finding the helicopter company that helped Greg escape were slim. Ryan agreed with the logic it would need to be a company not completely reputable—a respectable company would have taken one look at the police activity that night and kept going.

An hour passed without any further progress by Ryan or his analyst, so Ryan decided to head home for the day. Once he was back in the sanctity of his apartment, Ryan called Detective O'Reilly with the information they had been able to uncover.

"Evening, detective."

"Hi, Ryan. What's up?" The detective's voice was cautious since he had spoken to Ryan just yesterday.

"My team was able to find out some interesting information, which I wanted to share with you. The good news is Greg Smythe was *not* abducted by aliens. Did you know one of the Hardwicke police cruisers caught his escape on its dash camera?" Ryan was sure this tidbit would entice the detective.

"No, I did *not* know that." The detective leaned forward on his desk, titillated.

"I will send you the video when I have it. This was not something any of us considered. Greg was picked up by a helicopter in a cornfield down the street from Hunter's house."

"Wait. What? Did you say this guy had a helicopter waiting for him?" Detective O'Reilly almost spit out his department-issued black coffee.

"Well, we know the helicopter was prearranged to pick someone up. The jury is still out whether it was supposed to be for both Ashley and Greg or just one of them." Ryan could not hide his trepidation.

Wicked Nemesis of the Hunted   39

"I would love to find out exactly who the helicopter was arranged for," Detective O'Reilly responded, sitting back in his squeaky chair and looking up at the water-stained ceiling.

"Me too. We are working on it. I wanted to make sure you were aware because my team has identified the type of helicopter. It was an AS532 Cougar, so based on its fuel range, we have also come up with some disreputable companies that may handle these types of requests." Ryan tried to stretch his body to release some of the tension growing in his muscles.

Before Ryan could go any further, the detective interjected. "Let me guess. One of the companies in question is Finny's Helicopters in Waltham."

"Interesting you would mention that one. It's at the top of our list. There are two others—one outside of Albany and another in Newark—that are of similar shadiness," Ryan replied, trying to hide his surprise.

"There have been rumors about Finny's for quite a while. I think they have been sanctioned by the FAA several times for being stupid. No one has been able to get them on the bigger stuff though." Detective O'Reilly started to tingle with the thought that this might accidentally lead to bringing down a known criminal enterprise.

"What do you mean by 'bigger stuff'?" Ryan had a feeling they were on the right track.

"They are suspected of money laundering and drug trafficking plus other various criminal activities. From what we know, the owner does not seem to be affiliated with any groups in particular. If you have the cash and a valid referral, he will do the job with no questions asked," the detective indicated.

Ryan perched himself on the edge of the couch and ran his hand through his hair. "Definitely sounds like the type of people we are looking for. I am still going to have my team investigate the other two companies just to be safe. But I think Finny's Helicopters is now our primary focus. Is there really a Finny running the operation?" A glint of hope surfaced for Ryan.

"The original owner has since retired to Arizona. His son now runs the business. The father never did any jail time, but the kid had some scrapes with the law when he was a teenager—vandalism, trespassing, and public drinking. There are rumors Finny senior was connected to organized crime, which would make sense given the type of business he was suspected of being involved in. The apple does not fall too far from the tree with the son.

"I will pass along your information to the organized crime division. I know a few of the senior detectives—good guys. They may have some additional intelligence on Finny's operation I could share with you."

"Just don't let them know how you came across the information. It might be better if you called the Hardwicke Police Department to see if they can send you a copy of the video—if you catch my drift." Ryan did not want Detective O'Reilly to cross the same lines he was accustomed to.

"Gotcha. Consider it done." The detective was both uneasy and anxious at the prospect this situation was far from being resolved.

"I will let you know if we are able to discover anything else interesting. Take care, detective." Ryan felt slightly better now than earlier in the day.

"You too, Ryan."

While excited at the prospect of closing down a long sought-after criminal enterprise, Detective O'Reilly wished this chapter ended with the incident in Hardwicke and did not like the idea that it could be creeping back into his city.

Ryan texted his analyst to relay the update from Detective O'Reilly and contemplated texting Hunter. He imagined Hunter was eating dinner with Emma, still reveling in their marital bliss. Instead, Ryan decided to call his former colleague and friend, Frank MacDonald.

Frank was one of Ryan's former clandestine teammates who now worked for the DEA. Ryan briefly recollected the ultra-secret missions they were part of to save the world. If the American people ever knew the actual number of threats against the country, they would never leave their houses, Ryan admitted.

Standing at six foot four, with solid muscle and bald, Frank was built like a house. When his phone rang, Frank grunted. "What?"

"Nice to see you haven't lost your sunny disposition, old timer," Ryan joked.

"Well, if it isn't my old pal, the corporate suit." Frank dropped his head back and let out a laugh.

"How are things going?" Ryan inquired genuinely.

"You know, same old thing. Glad you and Hunter survived the shootout in Hardwicke. I read the report. So much for your cushy mundane corporate security gig," Frank answered, speculating Ryan had not called solely to catch up.

"I know what you mean. And this is the reason for my call. I'm thinking you might have some information that might help in my investigation," Ryan acknowledged, knowing if anyone could help it would be Frank.

"Last time I checked, Ryan, you were out of this business," Frank stated flatly even though his curiosity was aroused.

"Well, it seems I keep being sucked back in," Ryan said, trying to sound aloof.

"What, specifically, do you need?"

Ryan recapped what he had learned up to this point for Frank, who listened without interrupting.

"I am thinking that if this company is into drug

Wicked Nemesis of the Hunted   43

trafficking, they are on the DEA's radar."

Frank paused. "Yes, they are on our radar. All I can tell you is it's an ongoing investigation. We have someone deep undercover inside their operation, and I can't compromise them."

Ryan was not surprised by Frank's admission. "I get it. I don't want to jeopardize anything you have going on. Hoping to be pointed in a general direction that could help me find Greg Smythe. My guess is Greg isn't part of this group. Only used them as his ticket out of town."

"He would have needed a recommendation from someone they trusted for these guys to even consider taking the job. It's not like they advertise their services on social media. Where has the money trail led you?" Frank was edging onto thin ice.

"If I could follow the money trail, I would. But since Greg Smythe, for all intents and purposes, does not exist, it makes it a bit challenging." Ryan struggled to hide his desperation.

"I hear you, brother. I also know you need to answer every question, or you won't rest. Could be one of those times to just let it go," Frank reminded Ryan.

"I need to make sure there still isn't a bullet with Hunter's and Emma's name on it…and mine for that matter," Ryan responded truthfully.

"I understand." Frank took a deep breath before he continued. "Here's some trivia for you. Did you know Waltham is only about fifteen miles from Logan International Airport?"

A smile formed on Ryan's well-defined face. "Thanks, my friend. Stay safe out there. I owe you one," Ryan said, more relaxed than when the call started.

"I believe it's two you owe me. Do not forget the stellar work I did locating that yacht in Chatham. Be safe."

Frank hoped Ryan comprehended the dangers lurking. The guys who Greg Smythe was apparently associated with were ruthless, especially if they thought information about their operation had been leaked.

Ryan was grateful for the information Frank passed along. Without compromising an ongoing investigation, Frank was able to confirm Greg more than likely went to Logan Airport. The challenge now was trying to figure out what Greg's destination was.

From Logan, Greg could have gone anywhere in the world. This was something Ryan's team would have difficulty tracking down since they did not know the alias Greg was now traveling under. The only way they could narrow it down was through facial recognition but even that would prove near impossible. Thousands of people went through the airport daily. Ryan theorized that even with the most robust software, it was still a needle in a haystack. And this was only if Greg was flying commercial. If he used a private charter, the possibilities were almost endless. It was doubtful an accurate flight plan would have been filed.

Knowing there was not much else he could do, Ryan headed to his small kitchen to prepare dinner: ziti with marinara sauce and a beer. He knew he needed to get back into a healthier routine with his diet and exercise but tonight opted for convenience.

For the first time in a long time, Ryan felt completely alone in his apartment. Talking to Frank made him wish for the insane days when he was helping rescue the world from evil. With Hunter now married, he had lost his wingman for nights like these.

CHAPTER 4

The morning glow of another picture-perfect New England autumn day permeated the apartment as Ryan lay awake in bed. The action movie in his mind carried on in an endless loop.

The shootout.

The helicopter.

The airport.

Greg had quickly become Ryan's nemesis. Doubt crept into Ryan's mind—he worried he had lost his edge and wasn't as good as he used to be. Greg was like a chameleon, able to change his look and identity as the job required. The mere thought of this infuriated Ryan. The code name given to Ryan by his former employer was "the chameleon." No one ever saw him coming, making him the ultimate lethal weapon.

After stopping in the cafeteria for his usual blueberry muffin to accompany the dark roast coffee from Kern's Family Grocery, Ryan closed his office door for added privacy. Before calling Hunter, he slowly savored the coffee while memories of sunrises and warm sand beneath his feet occupied his mind.

With his belly full and the caffeine slowly working its magic, Ryan called Hunter.

Hunter answered on the third ring. "I assume you are enjoying your usual blueberry muffin?"

"Why, yes, I am! And it's delicious. How is the sweet Emma?"

"As lovely as ever, but I'm guessing that isn't the reason for your call—to check up on my wife."

"I have some news. But before you get too excited, it is only a small piece of the mounting puzzle."

"Give me ten minutes and I will be down. I just need to sign a few contracts for Robert."

"I will be here waiting patiently," Ryan responded sarcastically before disconnecting.

While Ryan waited for Hunter, he wandered around his office thinking about Greg and the potential places he would go. There were several countries without extradition treaties with the United States, so any of those would be plausible. Unfortunately, Ryan didn't think that was the case.

From everything he had witnessed over the last year, Greg was arrogant and liked to flaunt his perceived superiority—the higher the risk, the more Greg enjoyed it. Ryan knew from his years of undercover work Greg had all the markings of a sociopath.

There was no doubt in Ryan's mind Greg's early years had disturbing parts—no one wakes up one day and decides to become a hired stalker and killer. Plus, Greg's talents were more than a typical contract killer—he got involved with his prey—which Ryan knew made him different. It was like watching a cat sadistically play with a mouse before it went in for the kill.

Examining Ashley's motives after the fact had been easier for Ryan than trying to understand what drove Greg's decisions. Ashley was driven by greed and revenge. The actual mastermind of this game knew her well-hidden background and used it to fuel the fire burning inside her. She had been the perfect pawn in the sinister chess game. Her tunnel vision surrounding the grandiose pot of gold at the end of the Logan rainbow played right into the carefully orchestrated scheme.

Ryan's thoughts drifted back to what made Greg tick. The more Ryan focused on Greg's psyche, the more he was convinced Greg may not be quite done with this job. Given Greg's psychological traits, Ryan believed Greg might be compelled to complete the job whether his employer wanted him to or not.

Before Ryan could dive deeper into the murky waters of Greg's mind, Hunter strode into Ryan's office. Hunter glanced around before taking his usual seat in front of Ryan's desk.

"So, you think you have a lead?" Hunter immediately jumped into the topic of conversation.

"As I said on the phone, it is another morsel in the lengthy trail of breadcrumbs that have been left for us to follow."

Hunter nodded.

"With the help of a couple of people who shall remain nameless, it looks like the helicopter took Greg to Boston. But let me fill in some of the blanks for you because I know you're about to ask."

Hunter nodded again without emotion.

"We identified three potential helicopter charter companies based on several factors. I won't go into details. The most promising one at the top of the shadiness list is Finny's Helicopters out of Waltham. They have been on both Boston police and DEA radars for quite a while. Neither agency has been able to get anything concrete to shut them down, though." Ryan paused to see if Hunter made the connection.

"I am guessing you confirmed your hypothesis with Detective O'Reilly and your buddy, Frank?"

Ryan smiled. "Yes. Both agreed Finny's felt like the right one to focus our attention on. The caveat is there is an ongoing investigation, so we need to tread lightly. And to be honest, I really don't care what Finny's is or isn't doing. I just need to know if there is a connection to Greg and what that connection is."

"I tend to agree. Do we know if there *is* a definitive connection?" Hunter leaned back in the chair and crossed his legs.

"We do—in an unofficial capacity. I am fairly certain, based on reliable information, the helicopter took Greg to Logan International Airport. After that, it is anyone's guess."

"Well, you were correct—this *is* only another morsel. Geez, this is like a scavenger hunt." Hunter let out a sigh.

"With each crumb of information, we're inching closer." Ryan hesitated and inhaled deeply. "Although I am not convinced Greg has left the country."

Hunter blinked rapidly in disbelief. "*What*? Why would he stick around? He could have hopped on a plane going anywhere in the world from Logan Airport."

Ryan anticipated Hunter's reaction. "You need to understand this is pure speculation on my part and based on years of undercover experience. Going undercover teaches you how to get into the mind of your adversary. Trust me when I say Greg has all the traits of a sociopath.

"Greg is manipulative, lacks empathy, and is callous. We both witnessed that firsthand and it only increased as the game progressed. Impulsiveness and risky behavior are also part of the behavior pattern—both of which, it is safe to say, Greg possesses."

Hunter ran his hand through his perfectly styled hair. "Let me guess. It's this impulsiveness or risky behavior leading you to believe he didn't make a run for it."

"Yes. Plus, the authoritarian and dominating side of his personality." Ryan looked directly at Hunter. "I don't only think he hasn't left the country…I don't think he's left *Massachusetts*."

Hunter shook his head. "*What*? That makes *no* fucking bloody sense whatsoever."

"Think about it. From all I told you about Greg being the definition of a sociopath, would someone like him run for the hills or palm trees?" Ryan waited for Hunter to absorb this.

After a few seconds, Hunter admitted, "Probably not."

"Hunter, I believe Greg *needs* to finish the job he was hired for. I don't think his personality will just let him be relieved he escaped unscathed and hide out on some tropical island."

"I sense there is more to this than what you are telling me."

Over the years, Hunter had become adept at reading Ryan. He never had to have his guard up or hide his true self from Hunter as a result.

"I think Greg is still being paid by someone to either finish the job or move to the next phase. Whatever that might be."

"How did I know that was going to be your

answer?" Hunter scoffed.

"I also am not sure Greg knows who his employer really is."

Hunter gave Ryan a puzzled look. "Not sure if I follow."

"Many of these hired killers use brokers who handle the back-and-forth communications to protect all parties involved. These brokers are confidential liaisons and all transactions funnel through them. The client with the problem contacts the broker. The broker then reaches out to a specialist with the appropriate skills. Then proper arrangements are made. Communications are routed through a series of secure channels, like burner phones. And the broker never knows the identity of either party—each is given an identification number, which is used for all transactions. The two original parties never meet, and neither is in direct contact with the other. The money usually goes through untraceable bank accounts in the Cayman Islands or some other place without the typical questions. Think of it as an insurance policy."

"This is making my head spin." Hunter rubbed his eyes hoping to infuse some clarity.

"*And*, I think the game may have changed. I am not saying we are completely out of danger, but I am not sure the endgame is to kill us."

"Well, that is a comforting thought," Hunter replied sarcastically.

"Let me clarify. If we get killed in the process, then we become collateral damage. My instincts are telling me all this still revolves around the cancer-prevention drug." Ryan slumped in his chair.

Hunter rose and started to pace around the office like a caged lion. "I guess it would make sense. That was the jackpot Ashley was after."

"Here's my theory on Ashley—someone did their homework and found the perfect player in the narrative they created. Ashley spent her life in the shadows of the great Logan family and thought she was owed a significant piece of the proverbial pie."

Ryan still wondered how someone was able to find out about Ashley's past.

As if reading Ryan's mind, Hunter contemplated, "I still don't understand how this unknown person was able to find out about Ashley. My mother did an unbelievable job of keeping this secret buried deep."

"I know. It's one of the things troubling me. Someone had intimate details of your family and was perceivably biding their time to put this plan into motion."

Ryan refrained from saying aloud the direction this pointed to.

Hunter strode to the door. Before opening it, Hunter turned to look at Ryan. "If I didn't know any better, I would say this has my father written all over it."

54   *Tracey L. Ryan*

Without another word, Hunter walked out of the office and disappeared in the direction of the elevator.

Ryan's chair squeaked slightly when he leaned back and stared at the once-white ceiling tiles like he had done so many other times when searching for answers. Thoughts similar to Hunter's regarding Philip plagued Ryan. The idea Philip somehow survived the plane crash in the Amazon did not seem plausible, although the fact remained no bodies were ever found.

Ryan had always assumed the local predators had a feast after the plane crash, until just a few minutes ago. *Could Philip have survived the crash and come back from the dead to claim what was his?* Ryan deliberated.

To get through the rest of the workday, Ryan needed to compartmentalize the idea Philip was still alive and, subsequently, the puppet master for the elaborate plan that consumed him, Hunter, and Emma over the past year. Ryan knew Greg was, nevertheless, the most relevant key to solving the mystery—if he could find him.

Exploring more of Ashley's past might provide additional answers, Ryan admitted. Without a second thought, he texted his analyst to give her the approval to continue looking into Ashley's background. Ryan knew there had to be answers leading someplace else besides Philip reaching out from the grave.

The remainder of the day was mundane for Ryan except for an issue that caused slight concern. There was a thirty-second period where all video cameras on the top floor had shut off. Normally Ryan would consider it a blip in the Wi-Fi except these were anything but normal times. Although Ryan thought the Ares Logan headquarters was virtually impenetrable, he also knew having a false sense of security could lead to deadly consequences.

Ryan called Hunter's office to confirm nothing odd had happened. Hunter verified it was business as usual on the top floor, although he peeked out the windows just to make sure the mysterious helicopter that carried Greg away was not looming overhead.

With both men satisfied it was just another day at the office, Ryan had his technical team investigate why the cameras on that specific floor went blank for multiple seconds. Ryan also had the technicians examine the intricate camera systems at the other Logan buildings, including the covert lab where the cancer-prevention research was being conducted. If other locations had the same issue at the same exact time, or at some other time during the day, Ryan knew it couldn't be a coincidence.

Ryan's attention drifted back to past operations in faraway countries. *Could the camera glitch be a decoy or a test run for an ominous cyber-attack? Or was he seeing threats where none existed?* Ryan speculated.

Before Ryan could pace around anymore in his office, his phone started singing the theme from *Top Gun*. A smile spread across his face when he saw the number.

"Hello, my lady."

Emma always giggled when she heard Ryan's greeting. "Hi, Ryan. I hope I'm not disturbing you."

"Not at all. I heard you had a wonderful time on your honeymoon. It's beautiful over there, isn't it?"

"I loved it! I was trying to convince Hunter to buy a country cottage while we were there, but he didn't go for it. Hunter said he had enough rainy days to last him a lifetime when he was going to boarding school in England. The compromise was I could redecorate the penthouse here," Emma said smugly.

"Ah, so that is what he was talking about the other day. He mentioned you had been adding some personal touches to the place."

"Even though Hunter has a beautiful penthouse, it was very masculine and, let's face it, sterile. I just warmed up the joint," Emma joked with a hint of sincerity.

Ryan could not help but chuckle. "Just you being there warms up the joint. I am sure you did not call to ask me for decorating ideas. How may I help you, lovely lady?"

"I am calling to formally invite you to our first dinner party at the penthouse. My mother is flying in from Arizona, and Robert will be there as well."

"Sounds fantastic. I wouldn't miss it for the world." Ryan accepted with a smile.

"Wonderful! This Saturday at six p.m. We will start with cocktails and light appetizers. Dinner will be served around seven."

"Great! Thank you for inviting me." Ryan knew how lucky he was to have such good friends—the family he always wanted.

"It wouldn't be a party without you, Ryan. See you on Saturday." Emma's enthusiasm filtered through the phone.

"See you then, my lady." Ryan disconnected and a warm sensation penetrated his soul.

CHAPTER 5

The rest of the week moved slowly for Ryan as his frontal lobe worked overtime trying to fit the puzzle pieces together. None of his regular sources had any additional information on his quest to find Greg. It was like searching for the proverbial needle in a haystack which frustrated him.

Ryan decided to compartmentalize the ugliness and focus on happy thoughts for the weekend. The task at hand for Friday evening could be scarier than some of the missions he had survived—Ryan needed to find a housewarming gift for Hunter and Emma. Since Ryan was a minimalist, this was not something in his wheelhouse.

What the hell do I get the couple that literally has everything? Ryan asked himself.

An idea suddenly popped into his head for a unique gift. Ryan sent a text to a local artisan to confirm they had what he was looking for and let them know he would be arriving at their Connecticut studio in approximately two hours to pick it up.

The item Ryan selected was waiting for him already gift-wrapped. He admitted it was the perfect blend of sophistication and uniqueness.

A slight wave of anticipation ran through Ryan as he thought of the upcoming dinner party. For one night, Ryan could relax and enjoy the company of his friends whom he considered family. It was the brief distraction he needed.

Ryan arrived promptly at six p.m. the next day as the hostess had requested. Emma greeted him at the door dressed in a cream-colored, cashmere, scoop-neck sweater accompanied by black trousers and black sandal wedge shoes. Ryan immediately noticed how Emma naturally filled her role as a wife without giving up any of her most enduring qualities.

"Good evening, my lady." Ryan bowed to Emma.

A girlish giggle escaped from Emma. "Hi, Ryan. I am so glad you were able to make it tonight."

"Wild horses couldn't keep me away. Plus, I wanted to see how you transformed Hunter's masculine man cave into a heartwarming home." Ryan chuckled, causing Emma to giggle again.

Hunter strode over to Emma and casually wrapped his arm around her waist while he brushed her temple with his lips.

"Emma, I told you not to laugh at Ryan." A sly smile formed on Hunter's face, and he winked at Emma. "Come into what is now Emma's house…

which used to be my house." Hunter clapped Ryan's shoulder and led him into the living room.

Ryan subconsciously scanned his surroundings as he did with every room he entered. Sitting on the couch were Victoria and Robert. Both rose when they saw Ryan enter.

Before Ryan could speak, Victoria wrapped him in a hug and whispered "thank you" into his ear before kissing him on the cheek. Ryan blushed slightly at the sudden affection from Emma's mother.

Hunter had made the decision, which Emma and Ryan agreed with, not to tell Victoria or Robert the full story of their Hardwicke caper. The trio felt it could potentially put Victoria and Robert in more danger than just being immediate family.

They knew it would be difficult to keep it entirely quiet given the immense media coverage across the country. Hunter's public relations team was able to withhold many of the personal family details from the news and downplay the incident. Since it was an active police investigation, the various law enforcement agencies involved also did their part in only allowing minimal information to be released.

The focal point of the news reports had been the deadly shooting of Ashley and Chief Dyson plus the subsequent fugitive hunt for Greg. When Victoria saw the location, specifically the Logan estate, her first call was to her daughter. Emma handled her mother's barrage of questions eloquently without divulging the truth. Ryan was amazed at how easily Emma had effectively managed her mother.

Emma spun a tail how Ashley had been the one Greg had kidnapped as part of an elaborate ransom ruse to try to get money from Hunter since she was Hunter's half-sister. Ryan and Hunter powerfully played the roles of heroes in this fictional version of events. Victoria had expressed her eternal gratitude to the gentlemen, knowing it could have been Emma, not Ashley, who had been killed. The threesome never spoke about how spot-on Victoria was.

A glass of Jameson was handed to Ryan, jolting him from the reflective moment.

"Thanks, Robert. How has it been at Authentic Financial?" Ryan asked and took a long sip of the smooth amber liquid.

"Living the dream! Things have settled down nicely since the acquisition. We have done some restructuring—more like shifting some people around. Overall, it has been good. How about you? How was your vacation?" It was now Robert's turn to slowly sip his own Jameson.

"Vacation was great. Lots of sun and sand— what more can you ask for?" Ryan let more of the velvet liquid glide down his throat.

Before any more conversation could take place, Emma called the group into the adjacent dining area to begin their multicourse meal.

Pauline, Hunter's housekeeper and cook, prepared three courses for the group: Caesar salad with homemade croutons and dressing, prime rib with garlic butter, accompanied by oven-roasted potatoes and asparagus, and Boston cream pie for dessert.

Knowing this was the first official dinner party for the group, Pauline added extra touches to the table setting as well. The dark mahogany color of the table was offset by light fall colors for the linens, which accented the white Lenox place settings. Warm white twinkle lights were placed down the center of the table like Hunter's and Emma's wedding. Each guest had an assigned seat marked by a bottle of their favorite wine.

After the three courses were devoured, the guests were invited to the living room to enjoy after-dinner drinks. Ryan was not completely sure he would be able to get up from the chair and walk the fifteen feet to the other room.

After the others started to leave the table, Ryan felt a gentle nudge.

"Would you like me to carry you to the other room, Ryan?"

He looked up to see Pauline standing behind him, with her hands on her hips and the slightest hint of a smirk on her otherwise stern face.

Knowing Pauline could do as she suggested, Ryan pushed his chair back. "No, ma'am. Once again, you outdid yourself, Pauline. I still think you should marry me." Ryan produced a bright grin and winked at Pauline.

Pauline responded by swatting the back of Ryan's head as was the tradition in their little game. "As I have told you, Ryan, you couldn't handle a woman like me." Pauline tilted her head back and let out a belly laugh before she began to clear the table.

Laughing out loud, Ryan joined the others for Irish coffee. He took a few moments to soak in the sense of family that filled the room. Everyone was smiling and carefree for the evening—the way it should be.

Hunter noticed Ryan surveying the group and walked over to where he was standing.

"I know what you mean," Hunter responded to the look on Ryan's normally resigned face.

"What?" Ryan asked, grimacing.

"We could have lost all this," Hunter stated.

Shaking his head in affirmation, Ryan replied, "Yes, we could have, but we didn't. *And* we won't. Not on my watch."

Before the men could continue, Emma glided over with coffee in her hand. "If I didn't know any better, I would say you both were plotting and scheming over here."

"I was plotting when would be appropriate to give you two a housewarming gift. Wait here. I forgot it in the car." Ryan dashed out the door before Hunter and Emma could respond.

"Where the bloody hell does he think I'm going? I live here," Hunter said, amused.

In record time and slightly out of breath, Ryan reentered the penthouse with a beautifully wrapped gift in hand. The silver, foil-wrapped box with a matching ribbon securing it was placed in front of Hunter and Emma on the coffee table.

A warm smile emerged on Emma's face before she wrapped her arms around Ryan.

"You don't even know what it is yet," Ryan commented.

"I don't care. It came from you and that is all that counts," Emma said warmly.

Hunter shook his head and untied the ribbon, leaving the box for Emma to open. Like a small child on Christmas morning, Emma took no prisoners. She ripped off the wrapping paper vigorously and tore open the box. Her hands grasped the prize inside and held it up for the others to see.

Emma's delicate hands were wrapped around a one-of-a-kind reclaimed wooden serving bowl from Walden Hill Woodworks. Her fingers traced the smooth edges of the cherry wood before handing it to Victoria to fawn over.

"It is beautiful, Ryan. Thank you!" Emma gushed from across the room.

Hunter rolled his eyes slightly, which Emma caught and responded to with a scolding look.

Wicked Nemesis of the Hunted   65

"Yes, thank you, Ryan. I needed another bowl," Hunter returned playfully.

The festivities began to wind down just before the strike of midnight. Given the array of alcoholic beverages Ryan had consumed, he decided to leave his car in Hunter's garage and take a ride share the short distance back to his humble dwelling. Ryan wasn't sure if it was the alcohol or the family vibes from the evening that warmed his soul. Or why he felt a calmness wrap around him.

CHAPTER 6

Just as he has done hundreds of times after unlocking the door to his apartment, Ryan immediately entered the code for the sophisticated alarm system. Within a split second, Ryan comprehended he did not hear the standard countdown beep of the alarm when the door opened causing the hairs on the back of his neck to stand up. Ryan swiftly ran through each of his movements prior to leaving for the evening in his mind to see if he may have forgotten to set the alarm.

Fairly certain he had engaged the alarm before departing, Ryan cursed himself when he recalled he left his Glock locked in the gun safe. There was nothing of significance to use as a makeshift weapon in the short hallway that led to the kitchen and living area. He wondered if he would be able to make it to his gun safe in the bedroom before the intruder decided to introduce himself if he was still in the apartment.

"Oh, Ryan, for heaven's sake, you don't need to search for a weapon. I came here unarmed as a measure of good faith." A sultry female voice protruded from the otherwise silent living room.

Ryan tensed when he recognized the voice.

A voice he had not heard in over fifteen years.

A voice that still rattled him to his core.

A voice that resurfaced memories he had buried deep in the past, or so he thought.

Cautiously, Ryan moved to the edge of the dimly lit living room. Sitting before him on the couch was a female silhouette surrounded by the moonlight filtering through the windows. Even in the minimal light, her distinct features were unmistakable.

"Aren't you happy to see me, love?" Her words hung in the air.

Ryan inched closer, attempting to survey the situation unfolding before his eyes.

"I won't bite, Ryan. Well, not unless you want me to."

Her voice stirred more than memories for Ryan. Memories he preferred to leave forgotten in the past.

Ryan scoffed while he made his way to the kitchen and grabbed a Guinness from the refrigerator. After popping the top of the cold beer bottle and swallowing hard, Ryan sat in one of the deep-cushioned chairs next to the couch.

"It's been a long time, Sue. I won't bother asking how you got in here," he uttered through clenched teeth. His hands were wrapped so tightly around the beer bottle that Ryan thought he might break it with his bare hands.

"We had the same training, love. Or has your cushy corporate job turned your brain to mushy peas?" A hint of an English accent slipped out.

"I remember…vividly. Why are you here?" Ryan was seething.

"I am getting the distinct impression you are still angry at me over our last encounter."

"Out of sight, out of mind, my dear."

Sue slowly crossed her long, toned legs, which protruded from her short black flared skirt, and leaned back on the couch. Ryan could not help but notice every inch of her bare legs, which he knew was the point. His eyes traveled up her body, remembering each feature in rich detail until he was staring into her mocha-colored eyes.

For an instant, Ryan recalled fifteen years ago and the mission he wasn't sure his team would survive. The small team of three operatives had only one objective—to retrieve intelligence regarding potential terrorist targets in the United States. The assignment was given the green light after months of research by a few key operatives on the ground in a desert land halfway across the world.

Ryan, Frank, and Sue were sent in to recover the data and bring it back to Washington, DC, for further analysis. It should have been a routine assignment until it wasn't. By the time the team was extracted, Ryan ended up shot, Sue was missing, and an informant had been killed.

The mocha eyes looked at him with wonderment. "Remembering the last time we saw each other?" A sly smile formed on Sue's face.

"I was recalling I got shot," Ryan stated curtly. "And you were the one who shot me. Something like that leaves an impression."

A small sigh escaped from Sue. "Let's not be melodramatic. You weren't seriously injured. I made sure I did not permanently damage any part of your exquisite body," she countered, meeting Ryan's eyes.

"That is *not* the point." Ryan could not believe he was having this conversation.

"I know," Sue acknowledged.

"Once again, *why* are you here?" Ryan let out a huff of frustration.

"No need to get your knickers in a twist. I have been sent to help you—just like in the old days."

Sue knew it would not be easy to convince Ryan of her intentions. The trust between them died fifteen years ago.

Ryan threw up his hands. "What could you possibly think I need help with?"

Sue needed to tread lightly. Her orders were to assist Ryan but not necessarily divulge the true nature of her latest mission. "There is the case of your missing suspect, Greg Smythe."

"And what would you or your employers know about that?" A twinge of panic rose in Ryan.

"Ryan, you of all people should understand we know a lot about a lot of things. If you don't think the agency has not been tracking you all these years, then you're more naïve than I thought." Sue crossed her legs the opposite way, hoping to distract Ryan.

Ryan was unfazed by Sue's amateur attempts at distraction. "Trust me, I know they tend to keep tabs on their former employees."

"I have always trusted you, Ryan." Sue began to enjoy the game she and Ryan were playing, reminding her of the past.

"Poor choice of words on my part." Ryan sneered.

Ryan was tired of this cat-and-mouse game. Years ago, he found it enticing. Now he found it irritating.

"Ryan, what I can tell you is that your Greg Smythe has caught the attention of certain people in my organization at an international level. I've been given the approval to share relevant information with you in the effort to apprehend him."

"And what is considered 'relevant information'?" Ryan asked, knowing exactly what this meant.

"Anything we seem fit to share with you. Remember, Ryan, you are on the outside looking in now," Sue replied in a slow, taunting tone.

"I may be on the outside looking in, but it seems as if your team can't do this without me. Especially given you are not supposed to be operating on US soil. Funny, you are now knocking on my door. I am not some junior agent or civilian who could be easily swayed by your bullshit, Sue. Now, if you don't mind, I would like to get some sleep."

Taking her cue from Ryan, Sue slowly rose from the couch and adjusted her skirt.

"Very well, Ryan. I will say goodnight…for now. You know better than anyone that when the agency wants something, they usually get it. Here is the number I can be reached at. I look forward to speaking with you again very soon."

Sue placed her business card on the coffee table and left the apartment.

Ryan finally relaxed when he heard the door close and the elevator in the hallway chime. Before Ryan could think about sleep, he changed the alarm code and dead-bolted the door.

Feeling more secure than a few moments prior, Ryan peeled off his clothes as soon as he entered the bedroom. Before he crawled into bed, Ryan pulled back the covers to make sure Sue had not slipped a poisonous creature between the sheets. Ryan then checked the closet and under the bed before allowing himself the opportunity to sleep.

Thoughts of long-ago missions plagued Ryan's dreams. The tenacious trio, consisting of him, Sue, and Frank, each brought unique expertise to the team, creating a false sense of being indestructible. Their success rate was one of the highest in the agency, although it came at a heavy cost. The team had lost several people along the way, given no mission was foolproof and without risk.

The dreams led Ryan down the grim path from their last mission together. Unbeknownst to him and the team, it was an ambush that had been set up by a double agent. The building where Ryan, Frank, and Sue were sent to retrieve a laptop containing encrypted data was destroyed by a remote-detonated bomb. The three agents narrowly escaped and found themselves in a town controlled by their enemy.

In the distance, Ryan could hear the helicopters sent to extract them. Before backup could reach the three operatives, a firefight broke out. Little did Ryan comprehend at the time that the next moments would be life-altering for him.

The three agents managed to make their way to safety but not before Sue told Ryan and Frank to continue to the helicopter. Sue accidentally dropped the satchel holding the laptop the team recovered a few hundred feet away. The next few minutes replayed in slow motion for Ryan.

Ryan yelling at Sue to leave the laptop.

Ryan clutching her arm to force her toward the waiting helicopter.

Sue breaking free from Ryan's grasp and pointing her weapon at Ryan.

As the bullet was fired from the chamber of the gun, it generated a slight breeze. At first, Ryan didn't know he had been hit until he tried to move his arm and it went limp. A searing pain permeated through his right forearm where the bullet traveled front to back. The next few moments were a blur for Ryan. His emotions ran on overdrive—anger, hurt, and fear. Frank grabbed Ryan by the collar, and they dove into the helicopter waiting for them. The last memory Ryan had of Sue was watching her run toward the town with the satchel in her hand.

Ryan woke in a cold sweat, thinking he was still on the helicopter. It took a few moments for him to grasp he was in his Boston apartment...alone. He also now understood why he had been unnerved by Greg's escape in a helicopter. Another coincidence with his new nemesis.

CHAPTER 7

D awn slowly broke through the onyx sky, illuminating Ryan's sanctuary. Staring at the ceiling for more than two hours, Ryan rewound and replayed the events of last night in his head. Including the new questions plaguing his logical brain.

When did Sue arrive in Boston?

Who was Sue working for?

What did Sue really know about Greg Smythe?

Where had Sue been all this time?

Sunday was a low-key day for Ryan. He would tend to any household chores, like grocery shopping and cleaning. Sometimes, depending on his mood, Ryan would hit the gym or at least lift weights in his apartment.

Ryan knew today would be different. He needed to find out all he could regarding Sue and what she was up to before this snowballed into a full-blown avalanche. Reaching for his phone on the night-stand, Ryan texted his expert analyst. If there was any hope of finding any scraps of information, she was the only one who would be able to do it.

Ryan texted Frank next. Frank was there when the incident happened and had a good understanding of what made Sue tick—something Ryan thought he knew in another lifetime, though he was unsure of anything involving Sue in his current state of mind.

While Ryan let the steamy water of the shower wash away the current encounter with his former colleague, two texts arrived.

In the first text, his analyst confirmed she would begin trying to uncover Sue's deepest secrets after she returned from brunch with her mother on Newbury Street. Ryan smirked when he read this. It never occurred to him she would have family locally. For some reason, Ryan always assumed Sue was a loner because she preferred to stay in the shadows.

As he toweled off his sculpted body, Ryan grasped this was another aspect he was wrong about. So much for his expert profiling skills, Ryan huffed.

Once dressed in vintage dark jeans and a Rolling Stones T-shirt, Ryan sat on his couch to read and follow the instructions on the second text.

The phone was answered within ten seconds.

"What?" replied the gruff voice on the other end.

"You were the one who told me to call you, remember?" Ryan countered.

"So, you had a late-night visitor? A not-so-welcome blast from the past," Frank teased.

"It was a bit unnerving to find her casually sitting on my couch after all these years, I will admit. I honestly thought she was dead." Ryan relaxed.

"No such luck there, pal." Frank's cautious tone permeated through the phone.

"I have my people looking into the who, what, where, and when. Not confident they will be able to unearth anything of importance. You know she was an expert at covering her tracks." Ryan grumbled.

"That's an understatement. Why was she there? Or, let me rephrase, why did she *say* she was there?"

Frank, like Ryan, did not believe in coincidences. Sue mysteriously reappearing after so many years, conveniently at the same time as the Greg Smythe situation, made Frank just as apprehensive as Ryan.

"She claims she is here to help me. I didn't know I needed any help." Ryan forced a laugh.

"Hmm. Normally I would say it is intriguing but not with Sue. She never cared about helping anyone but herself." The bitterness surfaced in Frank's voice.

"I know, Frank. Believe me, I haven't forgotten what she did," Ryan responded tersely.

The betrayal was like a cut that refused to heal for Ryan. It had faded over time, but the scar remained.

"I remember you telling me you tried to find her after we got out of that hellhole. I didn't want to push you, but, perhaps, now is a good time to tell me what you found." Frank prodded.

Wicked Nemesis of the Hunted 77

"Unfortunately, I couldn't find out a whole lot. As you know, Sue was suspected of being a double agent, but no one was ever able to prove it. It wasn't like the agency was going to admit they trained a ticking time bomb."

The last thing Ryan wanted to do was relive the nightmare but understood it needed to be done.

"I never told you, but I also had a few contacts back in the day do a little snooping. Same thing—nothing conclusive but plenty of speculation," Frank confirmed.

Ryan sighed. "I'm guessing I will hear from Sue sooner versus later. Granted my profiling skills are a bit rusty these days, but she came across as being anxious. Did you know that she has a British accent?"

"What?" Frank asked in disbelief. "She is an American"

"It slipped out when she was trying to convince me I needed her help. Was only for a second, but the accent was undeniably there. *And* she knew she slipped up."

So many scenarios were swirling in Ryan's head, and none of the potential outcomes were good.

"The plot thickens. Let me put some feelers out. Not sure I will be able to do any better than your team, but it couldn't hurt."

Frank was intrigued and even more suspicious about the timing of Sue's unannounced arrival in

Boston. This was all too convenient in Frank's mind.

"Thanks, man. I appreciate your help. I will keep you posted on what I learn. Stay safe."

"You too." Frank paused. "Ryan, keep your wits about you with Sue. She is a viper as we both found out the hard way."

"I know." Ryan disconnected and sank back into the comfort of the couch in almost the same spot where Sue was sitting several hours earlier.

Ryan was showered and dressed without anywhere to go. The only errand needing to be done was grocery shopping, which Ryan had put off long enough. He hoped by doing something as mundane as picking up food would spark some ideas on how to deal with both of his problems—Greg's disappearing act and Sue's reappearing act. Ryan shook his head—this had all the makings of an illusionist show on the Vegas strip.

Balancing several plastic grocery bags in his hands by the handles and hoping none would break, Ryan hesitated before unlocking his door. The memory of the prior night came into full view.

Ryan slid the key into the lock, then slowly opened the door. Within two seconds, the beeping of the alarm signaled that it was safe to enter his apartment. Ryan quickly put the grocery bags on the floor so he could punch in the alarm code. Not realizing he had been holding his breath, Ryan exhaled.

"Why does this woman still put me on edge?" Ryan asked aloud to the empty apartment.

Listening for a brief second, half expecting someone to respond, Ryan made his way to the kitchen to start unpacking his provisions for the week.

The rest of the day trudged along for Ryan. He managed to sit through several football games, including the New England Patriots. Ryan's mind floated to the past where clandestine operations and intrigue consumed his life.

Dusk gently fell upon the city of Boston like a cashmere blanket. Ryan made his way from the couch to the kitchen to find something for dinner. Cooking was never something Ryan enjoyed. He knew enough so he would not starve, but never understood how people spent hours preparing a meal that was devoured in a matter of minutes.

Ryan finally decided to heat up the rotisserie chicken and broccoli casserole he picked up from the deli section at the grocery store. While his dinner was in the oven, Ryan started reviewing his conversation with Sue again. The plethora of unresolved issues between him and Sue was an understatement, and Ryan could not have this interfering with his sanity or current job. He needed to find a way to get her out of his head—for the final time.

Before Ryan could follow his unsavory thoughts any further, "Wicked Game" by Chris Isaak flowed through the kitchen from his cell phone. Checking his caller ID, Ryan wavered when he saw the number on the screen.

As was their typical phone conversation, Ryan answered, and his analyst dove straight in with her findings without any introduction.

"So, per the usual, you didn't give me a whole lot to go on, boss. I was able to find out a few tidbits of rudimentary information, which I am guessing you already know."

"I know the basics—where she grew up, lived, marital status, and so on."

Ryan was almost afraid to lift this specific rock to see what was hiding underneath. A vision of a venomous snake den entered his mind for a split second.

"Okay, I will bypass that information. It looks like she spent most of the last fifteen years moving around in the Middle East and Europe. She came back to the US twice a year and never stayed for more than a month."

"That is noteworthy," Ryan commented and scratched his head.

Ryan never asked his analyst how she was able to get her information to provide him and others like Hunter with complete deniability.

"On the surface, it looks as if she was on assignment with your previous employer. The stateside visits seem like debriefings and new assignments or meetings with her handler." The analyst paused before continuing. "Ryan, I can't give you anything

Wicked Nemesis of the Hunted   81

concrete. This is just a feeling I have based on the pattern I am starting to see emerge. Plus, some other similarities rising to the surface."

Ryan knew that the analyst's gut feelings were usually spot on. "Understood."

"I would like to see if I can find a connection between Sue and Greg. Again, I have absolutely nothing to back this up."

"I get it. It is just a feeling." Ryan shivered at this notion.

"We have always thought of Greg as a gun for hire, as you put it. What if he is some sort of operative or asset as your former employer calls them?"

The analyst leaned back in her chair contemplating what she unveiled and quickly second-guessed if she should have revealed this.

Ryan's eyes widened and he tried to hide the shock in his voice. "That scenario never crossed my mind."

"Or both could be working for the dark side. Your friend may only be pretending to still be working for your former employer." The analyst cringed slightly.

"All are valid points and avenues we need to investigate. Keep going on the research and let me know what you uncover—good or bad." Ryan now had a headache.

"You got it, boss." The analyst disconnected knowing the monumental task in front of her. For-

82   *Tracey L. Ryan*

tunately, she considered it a challenge and thrived on challenges.

Before Ryan could digest what he learned, the oven timer rang, signaling it was time to fill his body with nutrients. Ryan had a sinking feeling nothing would be the same once more information was uncovered in this ever-evolving plot.

CHAPTER 8

Ryan contemplated telling Hunter about his uninvited visitor over the weekend in addition to his analyst's theories. The secrets of Ryan's past, which he believed were successfully concealed long ago, now threatened his future.

When Hunter arrived at his office unannounced, Ryan was beginning to wear a pattern on the carpet. Leaning against the door jam, Hunter observed his best friend in curious silence. Hunter knew too well this was what Ryan did when he was trying to solve a challenging problem. The big question for Hunter was which specific problem had Ryan riled up.

Ryan sensed a pair of eyes staring at him and looked over at Hunter. The expression on Hunter's face was a combination of uneasiness and inquisitiveness, Ryan noticed. Ryan was still torn about whether to share the latest developments with Hunter.

"You know wearing out the carpet in your office won't get you a new one," Hunter commented mockingly.

"Damn. There goes that plan." Ryan stopped and plopped himself in his chair.

"Emma said to say thank-you again for the beautiful bowl. Please text her and tell her I said those exact words."

Ryan managed a small smile. "I will let her know you fulfilled your husbandly duties."

Staring at the untouched blueberry muffin sitting in front of Ryan, Hunter knew something heavy was weighing on him. "Do not take this the wrong way, but I don't think I have ever seen you just leave a muffin on your desk without consuming it. Usually, the only evidence left behind is the slightest hint of crumbs."

A heavy sigh escaped from Ryan's chest. "I don't think I ever told you about my last assignment with my former employer, did I?"

Hunter shook his head and took a seat in his usual spot.

"I can't tell you all the details since they are still classified. What I can tell you is I was part of a highly specialized team of operatives. We did a great deal of recovery work—whether it was people or information."

Hunter nodded for Ryan to continue.

"We were a team of three including Frank and a female agent. We thought we had made it in and out without any difficulty, then the world around us exploded...literally. Frank and I made it to the rescue helicopter, but the female agent dropped the package we were sent to retrieve. She insisted on running back to get it." Ryan slowly inhaled. "I tried to stop her and got shot for my troubles."

Hunter's mouth fell open. "Wait, you got *shot*? By whom?"

"I was shot by the female agent. It was not life-threatening. She shot me in my right forearm, but it was enough to neutralize me at that moment." Ryan subconsciously rubbed the faint scar, which was a permanent reminder of that day.

"You never told me you had been injured," Hunter commented, trying to understand why Ryan decided to divulge this information now.

"It isn't something I particularly like to discuss…especially since I was shot by one of my teammates." Ryan paused to take a sip of the now cold dark roast coffee he was holding before continuing with the abbreviated walk down memory lane. "Frank nor I ever saw our teammate again. The last glimpse we had of her was from the helicopter as it lifted us out of there—she was running back into enemy territory."

Hunter stared closely at Ryan for a few seconds, gathering his thoughts. "So, what you seem to be indicating is this woman was either insane or may have been working for our enemies at the same time she was working for the agency?"

Ryan silently stared into his paper coffee cup

as he fought the flood of memories from overtaking his mind.

"It sounds like she did not want whatever information you found to get back to your employer," Hunter added even-toned.

"More than likely. Frank and I never knew exactly what the information was. We were only told there was a potential threat to national security." Ryan played with the paper cup.

"It sounds like this woman may have been a little torn. I am guessing she was an expert shot, given where all of you worked. She could have killed you and Frank but instead chose to only give you a minor wound in the big scheme of things," Hunter said, trying to sound empathetic.

"I guess you are right. I never really thought of it that way. This all happened fifteen years ago and, to be honest, I haven't thought of it since then," Ryan responded.

"So, I must ask, why is this coming to the surface now? I know you, Ryan, and you are grappling with something. I won't pressure you to tell me anything you don't want to or can't." Hunter tried to be empathetic, although he knew little about Ryan's time back then.

With a deep breath, Ryan explained, "After I got home from your dinner party on Saturday night, which was lovely by the way, I walked into my apartment to find my former female teammate sitting on my couch."

Hunter could not hide the dumbfounded look on his normally indifferent face. "What do you mean? How did she get in? That place is like a fortress."

Ryan managed to chortle. "She has the same training as I do, Hunter. And is one of the best I have ever seen with getting around any alarm system or locks. It's a gift." Ryan silently admonished himself for not being able to hide his admiration for Sue's skills.

Hunter rubbed his temples. "Okay, so the woman who shot you fifteen years ago was suddenly sitting on your couch. That is a bit creepy if you ask me."

"Creepy doesn't really cover it. I was flabbergasted, to say the least. Frankly, I never expected to ever see her again. I wasn't even sure she was still alive. I guess part of that was wishful thinking." Ryan's voice drifted off while he blankly stared at a slightly discolored ceiling tile above Hunter's left shoulder.

"Did she tell you why she was there?" Hunter feverishly tried to connect the bits and pieces of information together without pressuring Ryan to divulge more than he was ready to.

"Well, in a way." Ryan sprang out of his chair and paced around the office all over again. "She told me she was here to help me and dropped Greg Smythe's name."

"Help you?" Hunter was perplexed. "With what exactly? And how does Greg Smythe fit into this?"

"Those are the million-dollar questions! She would not elaborate and acted as if we had just lost touch over the last fifteen years. It was like she was here to rekindle an old friendship." Ryan replayed the conversation in his head again.

"What do *you* think she wants?" Hunter cautiously inquired.

"I seriously have no clue. She alluded to the fact the agency always keeps track of its former employees. I couldn't tell if she was still working for them or freelancing. Before she left, she told me that we would see each other again soon." Ryan stopped pacing and met Hunter's steel blue eyes.

"Very cryptic. But then again, isn't that part of the qualifications for being a spy?"

Ryan shook his head. "That is an understatement." He sat back at his desk and fidgeted with a pencil. "I don't want to see things that aren't there."

Hunter nodded nudging Ryan to continue.

"You can guess where my head is going. I wonder if this ties into our own mystery somehow. You know how I loathe coincidences. Especially with casual references to Greg."

Hunter pushed himself up from the chair and walked around the office like someone admiring great works of art in a museum.

"It is definitely an interesting theory." It was all Hunter could manage as a response.

"Hear me out. I find it ironic how she shows up after the debacle in Hardwicke and exactly when we found out how Greg escaped. Also, at the same time, we are starting to delve into the few leads we have."

Hunter turned to face Ryan. "On the surface, I do agree the timing is a tad suspect. But, Ryan, I worry we are trying so hard to fit all these pieces neatly into a rational puzzle that we might be inadvertently creating connections where none exist," Hunter replied warily.

Ryan ran his hands through his disheveled hair. "I know. I have my analyst trying to track down more information on those lost years, but it will be tough to find out anything."

"What does your buddy, Frank, think?"

Hunter assumed Ryan would have already confided in someone who lived through these experiences with him. Even though Hunter was grateful to Ryan for sharing this information, he would never understand the depths Ryan's experiences ran in his past line of work.

"He is having the same reaction I am—why did she show up now?"

"Is Frank going to check with his contacts as well?"

"Yes. Not sure he will get any further than I will. The agency tends to bury secrets as deep as the Titanic when it comes to things like this."

"My opinion, not that you asked, keep chasing all angles. We would hate for these things to *be* connected and *not* follow through on them. The best case is your female friend regrets what happened and is done with that part of her life. The worst case is she is up to her eyeballs in this whole mess," Hunter responded trying to be the voice of reason.

"I agree. We will see where the clues lead us and not jump to unwarranted conclusions."

Hunter assumed there was more to their storied past than Ryan was telling him and mentally noted how Ryan never once mentioned this woman's name during the conversation.

"Is there anything else I should be aware of regarding this?"

Ryan hesitated. "No, not right now. If it becomes necessary at some point in the future, I will give you the unabridged version."

"Okay. Robert and I are looking at a few more potential acquisitions, so I need to get back upstairs to plow through the endless reports." Hunter headed in the direction of the elevator without any further discussion.

After Hunter left, Ryan gazed at the ceiling hoping for divine inspiration. When no celestial prophecy materialized, Ryan decided it was time to get back to his day job.

CHAPTER 9

The rest of the day was filled with the routine but necessary security tasks that were a necessary part of Ryan's work. Ryan always laughed when he saw people's eyes light up after telling them what he did for a living. Most people thought corporate security was full of espionage and escapades like they saw on TV and not the mountains of incident reports and mundane duties.

As the day concluded, Ryan still had lingering doubts about his once-keen intuition since coming back from vacation. The Bahamas, Ryan thought, would be the perfect place for his mind to recharge enough for an epiphany to happen. But it had not, which caused him trepidation.

The thought of going back to his empty apartment, or maybe not-so-empty apartment, did not help calm Ryan's restlessness. Without much contemplation, he changed into the T-shirt, shorts, and running shoes he kept in the office.

Dusk was starting to transform the sky above when Ryan stepped outside. He noticed the faint hint of saltwater scent in the air permeating around him and felt a crisp autumn breeze against his skin. He had already completed his warm-up in his office so Ryan hit the ground running.

Dodging commuters on their way to catch their trains at South Station, Ryan headed toward Chinatown. Cutting through the compact streets, catching whiffs of various Chinese delicacies, the Boston Common and public garden came into view ahead of him.

While Ryan got into his stride, he recalled the history of the Boston Common. It had been designed by Frederick Law Olmsted and was considered the oldest public park in the United States. The Common had hosted everything from British Troops in the Revolutionary War to cattle grazing in the 1800s. Now it was used by locals to walk their dogs, have a picnic, or go ice skating in the winter.

Ryan decided to head up Tremont Street, then Beacon, and finally Charles Street before entering the Common. The multitude of sidewalks within the park made it a runner's dream. Ryan crisscrossed the entire area, admiring the historical value with each stride.

Believing he had expelled as much energy as he could, Ryan exited the Common on Boylston Street and headed back toward the massive glass prism where his office was located. Once safely back in his basement kingdom, Ryan grabbed his backpack and headed to his car parked in its designated space in the underground garage.

When Ryan approached his parking spot, he noticed a white envelope tucked under the driver's side windshield wiper of the Mercedes. Immediately, Ryan scanned the garage for anything out of place and listened for any peculiar noises. The only footsteps he heard were his own along with his increased heart rate.

Cautiously, Ryan visually examined the envelope as best he could without touching it. There did not seem to be any hidden wires indicating some type of explosive device. Carefully, Ryan grabbed the envelope by the top right corner, not wanting to destroy any potential evidence.

Holding the envelope in the direction of the overhead lights in the garage, Ryan surmised it contained a photograph. Again, carefully opening the unsealed envelope and peaking inside, Ryan saw a single picture of himself running in Boston Common a brief time ago.

The picture was an image of Ryan entering the park in full stride. Automatically, Ryan did a 360-degree turn to see if anyone had joined him on this level of the garage. Once again, the only sound he could hear was his pounding heartbeat.

Still holding the envelope, Ryan looked it over

again, this time more closely. There were no identifying marks or writing. The picture looked like something taken from a cell phone and printed from a portable printer. When Ryan tipped the envelope to view the backside of the photograph, it was blank from what he could see.

Someone was clearly sending Ryan a message—the question was whether it was friend or foe. Ryan's run had been an impulsive decision and not something he had planned. No one at the office knew Ryan would be heading to the Common to burn off some energy.

The photographer could have easily seen Ryan leaving in his running clothes and theorized what he was about to do. The challenge, Ryan thought, was the photographer would not know the exact route he was planning to take. As Ryan played the scenario in his head, he became unnerved. Ryan admitted this meant at least one unknown person was watching and following him. Suddenly, Sue's parting words screamed through his brain like a freight train.

Taking another look around the garage and satisfied he was the only person within viewing distance, Ryan retreated to his office with the envelope in hand. Once safely behind closed doors, Ryan called his analyst while trying to calm his nerves.

"Hi, boss," she answered with a twinkle in her eye.

"Need you to do me a favor," Ryan replied without any preamble.

"That is usually why you call."

"Pull the video footage from the second level of the parking garage here. Say from just before five p.m. to now." Adrenaline still pulsated through Ryan's body.

"Alright. Am I looking for anything in particular?" The analyst's curiosity was aroused since she knew the Logan headquarters was virtually Fort Knox from a security standpoint.

"Not exactly sure. Just send it to me when you have it." Ryan didn't have time to explain the events from a few minutes ago or speculate what they might mean.

"You got it, boss. Will only take a few minutes."

The analyst disconnected and had a feeling something wasn't right. Bizarre requests from her employer were not anything new. Ryan's anxiety protruded through the phone, which gave her pause—something had just happened at one of the most secure buildings in the city.

As promised, three minutes later Ryan's cell phone chimed, signaling a new email had arrived. Instead of viewing it on his phone, Ryan opted to power up his laptop to provide a larger viewing area of the video to ensure no detail was missed.

Deeply inhaling to brace himself for what he might see, Ryan opened the designated email and then played the video. He half expected a drum roll before the video began. The garage was quiet

96　　　　*Tracey L. Ryan*

until 5:13 p.m. when a figure dressed all in black entered the top right frame of the video. The white envelope could clearly be seen in the person's left hand as it was placed where Ryan had found it on his car windshield. After delivering the envelope, the figure quickly departed in the same direction they entered from and was no longer within sight on the video.

Leaning back in his chair, Ryan replayed the video. By the third time watching it, Ryan decided there was nothing left to learn. And the little bit of evidence he gleaned from the video and still frame picture only led to more questions, which was par for the course lately, Ryan confessed.

Questions that always seemed to lead back to where this quest had started.

Questions that now brought Ryan face to face with his past.

In Ryan's psyche, the two potential suspects were the sultry Sue and the elusive Greg. Either one of them could, theoretically, be tied to the cancer-prevention drug. An uneasy feeling started to overtake Ryan. He was being led down an unknown and possibly sinister path. Ryan assumed this must be how Hansel and Gretel felt.

When Ryan was packing up his things for the second time, the plain envelope sitting next to his laptop caught his eye. He abruptly sat back down in his chair and hit speed dial on his cell phone.

"O'Reilly."

"Evening, detective."

"Ryan. To what do I owe this pleasure just as I was about to go home?" Detective O'Reilly asked warily.

"Gee, I can't call just to check on my favorite police detective?" Ryan tried to sound jovial.

"Sure, but with you, it is never that simple, Ryan."

Ryan snorted. "Okay. You got me. I need a favor."

"Will this be a 'put my pension at risk' favor or just a 'being chewed out from my boss' favor?"

"I promise you won't lose your job or even get reprimanded. I need some analysis done on an envelope and picture. Nothing more than that."

"Then why is my indigestion suddenly coming back?" the detective questioned while rubbing his stomach.

"I dunno. Something you ate for lunch?" Ryan joked.

"Alright, give me the lowdown, Ryan. And don't leave out any details if you want me to help you."

Ryan exhaled. "A little after five p.m. tonight, I decided to let off some steam and go for a run through the Boston Common. After I went back to my office, gathered my things, and went to my car in the *secure* underground garage, someone left a surprise on my car windshield."

"Go on." The detective waited patiently, unsure what Ryan would reveal next.

"There was a plain white envelope with a picture inside of me running through the park only moments before. No note was left—just the picture," Ryan stated, still feeling unnerved.

"Okay. And what is your theory, Ryan? Because I know you have one. You always do," Detective O'Reilly inquired.

"Best case scenario is I have a secret admirer. Worst case, I think it was some sort of warning. My gut says someone is putting me on notice they are watching me."

"I don't like the sound of this."

"Neither do I. I never considered myself prey," Ryan admitted.

"Bring me the envelope and picture. You know it is a long shot we would be able to get anything off either item." The detective paused. "Ryan, your building is like the White House with security. How could someone off the street sneak into the garage and then sneak out without being detected?"

"I know. It seems improbable. But it happened. I can email you the surveillance footage and you can see it for yourself. The person—I can't tell if it is male or female—avoids the cameras and is dressed in all-black."

"Is there anything that could help identify this person? Skin tone? Height? Weight?"

"When I say 'all-black' I mean covered from head to toe. It looked like they were wearing a black hazmat suit, so not a speck of skin is showing. As far as height and weight, I'd venture approximately six feet tall and at least two hundred pounds. Medium build. But the hazmat suit distorted everything. I'm going to have one of my analysts try to see what they can do with the video but am doubtful she will be able to retrieve anything useful." Ryan leaned forward on his desk, resting his head in his hands.

Detective O'Reilly shook his head in disbelief. "Send me the video. I can have my tech folks look at it as well. Based on my experience and yours, this sounds like a professional. No amateur would be able to get into the building and pull this off undetected. Unless—"

"Unless it was an inside job." Ryan finished Detective O'Reilly's statement.

"Exactly. Ryan, I know I don't need to remind you of this but, as your friend, I am going to anyway. Watch your back. If these are the same people responsible for the incident in Hardwicke, they play for keeps. I will do what I can from my end, but you know my resources are limited. Off the record, you may want to call in some backup from your side."

"Thanks for your concern. I am on red alert more now than ever. I have a friend who may be able to help. I trust him with my life. God knows he has saved it on more than one occasion," Ryan stated truthfully.

"Good. I will let you know if I find anything. Another thing, hand deliver the evidence directly to me. Do *not* hand it to anyone else. I am almost certainly being paranoid, but that's who I am."

"Will do. I will bring it by first thing in the morning."

"Stay safe, Ryan."

"You as well. And thank you." Ryan disconnected, not feeling any better than he did prior to the call.

Before leaving and after snapping a picture from his phone of the envelope and photograph, Ryan secured the originals in his private safe—a safe no one in the office knew about except him, not even Hunter. The well-hidden safe had been something Ryan installed shortly after starting his job at Ares Logan. His experience offered him the skills necessary to create a perfectly secure hiding spot in the event there was a security breach.

On the short drive home, Ryan almost gave himself whiplash from continuously looking in all directions to confirm he was not being followed. With his mind racing and calculating the probabilities of the various potential scenarios, Ryan entered his apartment without noticing the alarm had once again been disarmed.

This time sitting in front of him on the couch was Frank, flipping through the channels trying to find highlights from last night's football game. Ryan almost had a heart attack when he saw his former colleague relaxing with his feet on the coffee table.

"Geez, dude, are you trying to put me in an early grave?" Ryan questioned as he dropped his bag on the floor next to the couch and sank into the opposite side of Frank.

"You seriously need to get a better alarm system. It only took me two minutes to disarm the thing." Frank took a long swallow of the Guinness in his hand.

"My apartment used to be my sanctuary. Now it is a revolving door for former agents. Did you take the last beer?" Ryan pushed himself off the couch and headed toward the kitchen.

"Don't worry. I brought more." Frank seemed unfazed by Ryan's agitation.

After popping the top off his own Guinness, Ryan headed to the living room, walking back and forth in front of the TV.

"Do you mind? I am trying to find the scores from last night." Frank tried to peer around Ryan.

"Please, by all means. Make yourself at home," Ryan commented sarcastically as he motioned his hands across the room.

"Thanks. I already did," Frank answered.

"What are you doing here, Frank?" Ryan questioned.

"Well, I had a strange feeling something was amiss." Frank took a long swig of his beer.

"Amiss? What are you, Sherlock *Freaking* Holmes?" Ryan drank half of his beer in one long swallow.

"And it seems my intuition was right. You are pacing around like a caged animal at the zoo."

Frank never took his eyes off the TV for fear of missing the scores.

"You do know you can get any score you want on your phone. It's called the internet. Most people use it to find out whatever they want to know these days." Ryan's sarcasm consumed the small space.

"Ha. Ha. There is something appealing about waiting for the score to appear on the TV. Stop stalling and tell me what is going on."

Ryan gave Frank the highlights of the picture and the way it was left for him. He left out the part about where he had hidden the picture and accompanying envelope, plus his request for further analysis of them. Ryan wasn't sure why he decided not to tell Frank. He trusted Frank with his life. The entire situation caused Ryan to second-guess his instincts at every turn.

"Sounds like you have a secret admirer. This whole mess of yours is heating up a few notches, wouldn't you agree? Getting into your company's garage is no easy task," Frank reminded Ryan.

"I don't want or need a secret admirer. Every time we think we have figured out a lead, more questions surface. One step forward...ten steps back." Ryan consumed the rest of his Guinness and settled in on the couch, staring at the beige wall behind the TV.

"Ryan, I am not here as a DEA agent. I am here as your friend and former colleague," Frank replied while his eyes remained glued to the TV.

Ryan did not respond. Instead, he stared at the empty Guinness bottle in his hand.

"Alright. Now that we have that established, I might be able to help. But first things first. I am concerned you have gotten yourself into something much bigger than you understand." Frank let his words hang in the air.

After a few seconds, Ryan responded. "I started to have that same thought. We know someone is going to great lengths to get the cancer-prevention formula and 'magic' seeds."

"Agreed. It seems probable that is still the primary objective," Frank said flatly.

"We also know Greg Smythe is up to his eyeballs in this plot, *and* he is a sociopath," Ryan added.

"Can't argue with you there, buddy." Frank's eyes still had not left the sixty-inch screen in front of him.

"And we know whoever Greg's employer is that they have what seems to be unlimited resources. Just the yacht conducting surveillance in Chatham and the daredevil helicopter escape are proof of that. Plus, they were able to locate Hunter's half-sister even he didn't know about."

Suddenly Frank shouted, "Yes! Finally!"

Ryan almost jumped out of his skin when Frank found the scores he had patiently been waiting for.

"Now, if we could move past the scores and concentrate on my life-and-death situation, that would be swell." Ryan rolled his eyes in annoyance.

"Swell?" Frank raised an eyebrow toward Ryan.

"Just trying to match your 'amiss' comment earlier."

Frank shook his head. "Please continue with your assessment. You now have my undivided attention."

"Thank you. Now, where was I? Oh yes, Greg's elusive employer."

"I am going to go out on a limb and assume nothing has popped from the money perspective."

"You are correct, my friend. I have some folks working on an in-depth review of Ashley's financials, but nothing has floated to the surface yet. And not knowing Greg's identity, or what his next identity is, has stalled our efforts to trace any money connections."

"And that brings us to the next piece of your growing puzzle…Sue."

Ryan flinched. "This was a wildcard I never anticipated."

"Put aside your personal feelings about Sue for a minute. We know she doesn't do anything unless it benefits her in some way. I think if we can figure out what that might be, it may lead us down the path to finding answers to some of your other questions."

"For the record, I have *no* personal feelings about Sue." Ryan could feel his blood pressure rising.

"Ryan, whether you like it or not, you can't rewrite history. You two were intimately involved, against better judgment. She betrayed both of us from a professional standpoint, but her betrayal toward you went deeper. It was a double-edged sword. I think you need to deal with that first or else it will be a ghost haunting you forever."

"Look, Frank, I know you never approved of my relationship with Sue. You made it abundantly clear back then. There is no reason to bring it up again. I got over it a long time ago," Ryan declared with an edge to his voice.

Ryan knew he just lied to Frank. He also knew Frank would more than likely see right through it like a piece of plastic wrap.

"Ryan, I need you to think about something. Have you had any real relationships since Sue? One-night stands do not count. Have you ever been in love with another woman?"

"I don't see how this is relevant to the current situation. My personal life is just that, *personal.*"

The agitation in Ryan's voice elevated.

"Your defensiveness tells me I am right."

Ryan started to protest.

"You can protest all you want but facts are facts. You fell in love with one of your teammates. It happens to the best of us. We cannot always control our hearts no matter how well-trained we are. She was like a great white shark silently stalking its prey from the depths, then ripping you to shreds when you least expected it. And Sue was an expert in manipulation. When push came to shove, she chose her extracurricular activities over you. My God, she shot you!"

Ryan hung his head and tried to block out the hard reality Frank was conveying.

"Buddy, I'm not trying to dredge up painful memories. I am trying to help you move forward because this twisted game you're entangled in could cost you your life and the lives of those around you. You need to compartmentalize those memories of Sue and focus on what is happening in the here and now." Frank finished his beer and waited for Ryan to process his words.

Ryan closed his eyes and tried to quell the demons inside him before responding to Frank.

"Logically I know you are one-hundred-percent right. I won't lie—when I saw her here the other night, the memories came rushing back like a flash flood. In those few minutes, I thought I was going to be swept out to sea and drown."

Frank did not interrupt and patiently watched Ryan process the conversation.

"There are no second chances with me. You know that, Frank. So, rest assured I will not be falling helplessly into her bed again. The blinders are off when it comes to that minx." Ryan looked Frank square in the eyes.

"I believe you. Now that we have that out of the way, what is your gut telling you about her current status with our former employer?"

"I am fifty-fifty. On one hand, we know how devious the agency is. On the other hand, they don't generally get involved in state-side operations like this. What do they care about a cancer drug?" Ryan questioned.

Frank leaned back and closed his eyes for a minute, contemplating what Ryan had said. "I have to agree with you. This does not smell like an agency-sanctioned operation. Unless…"

"Unless what?"

"What if, and this is a big *if*, the cancer drug could be weaponized?" Frank inquired.

Frank, unfortunately, saw firsthand what drugs did to people being part of the DEA. Kids using aerosol cans or cough syrup to get high. The unimaginable means addicts went to buy drugs. And the countless lives wasted. In Frank's mind, this had the potential of being worse. A bioweapon could kill thousands or millions of innocent people in the blink of an eye.

Ryan ran his hands through his hair, then clasped his hands behind his head. "That is an interesting question. I guess, theoretically, any drug could be made into some sort of weapon. You of all people know the toll illegal drugs take on humanity. I am not a chemist, so I would need to get some expert opinions to even wrap my head around something like you suggested."

"It's just a thought given the current and potentially fresh players involved. I doubt any of their motives are altruistic." Frank sprang off the couch cat-like to put his empty beer bottles in the recycle container.

"I don't think we ever considered the weapon aspect of the drug…only the money side of the equation when it came to Greg and Ashley. We know whoever is first to market with this type of drug will be billionaires overnight." Ryan perched himself on the edge of the couch.

"Well, my work here is done for tonight. You might want to talk to Hunter's experts to see if this is even a possibility. If it isn't, then no harm, no foul. If it is, I think you need to explore that angle more deeply."

"Thanks, Frank. I mean it. I will let you know what I find out." Ryan walked Frank to the door and locked it behind him.

Ryan settled in for another restless night fighting dragons he thought had been slayed long ago.

CHAPTER 10

The next morning, Ryan made a quick stop by his office to retrieve the photograph and envelope on his way to drop them off with Detective O'Reilly. The handful of people who happened to be in at this early hour did not even blink when they saw Ryan.

Digging out his cell phone when he exited the building for the short walk to the precinct, Ryan hit a number—all too familiar lately—on his speed dial.

"Top of the morning to you, detective," Ryan said when the call was answered.

"You seem awfully chipper for a guy with a mysterious admirer, Ryan," Detective O'Reilly responded in his gruff morning voice.

"Well, I figure the sun is shining and I woke up this morning, so it can't be all bad." Ryan forced a laugh.

"Are you on your way with your special package for me?"

"I am about five minutes from your front steps."

"Alright. I will meet you in front of the building. Trying to get you through security at this early hour would be a nightmare."

"Sounds like a plan."

Both men disconnected while Ryan continued his quick stride toward the large cinder block building in front of him. When he was approximately one hundred feet away, Ryan could see the distinct features of Detective O'Reilly trying to shield his eyes from the bright sunshine sneaking through the buildings.

Ryan held out his hand to the detective. "Good to see you, detective."

Detective O'Reilly reciprocated. "Same here. I take it no one tried to abduct or shoot you on the way over."

"Nope! See, it's going to be a fine day for me." Ryan snickered.

The detective smirked while Ryan dug the evidence from his inside jacket pocket.

"Glad to see you remember some of what they taught you back in the day," Detective O'Reilly commented when he saw the envelope and picture sealed in their own plastic bags.

"It was the least I could do. And I was careful to only touch the top right corner of each piece in the off chance there were any fingerprints."

"Wow! I am impressed with your crime scene investigative skills, Ryan. Who would have thought?"

Wicked Nemesis of the Hunted   111

The detective let out a belly laugh, catching the attention of a random passerby.

"I know the odds are slim at finding anything, but I guess it is worth a shot."

"I will see what my lab folks can come up with. This will be done on the side—no records will be filed—so I can be sure we don't have any prying eyes in the department. Honestly, I don't think there would be a problem, but I just want to be extra cautious for now. With that said, it may take a little longer to get anything back since this is off the books."

"Fine by me. Take all the time you need. I really do appreciate the help," Ryan responded sincerely.

"Alright, let me hand this off to one of my people who just happens to be in early this morning. I will call you as soon as I learn anything. Stay safe, Ryan."

"You too!"

The men shook hands once more and went their respective ways to start the day.

After Ryan completed his errand at the police precinct, he went straight to Hunter's office when he entered the building, bypassing his usual stop in the cafeteria. Ryan had not bothered to let Hunter know ahead of time he would be popping in but had consulted his online schedule to confirm Hunter would be free until nine a.m.

Ryan knocked twice before he opened the door. "Morning, Hunter."

Hunter was startled by the intrusion and perceived this was not a social visit. "Morning, Ryan. To what do I owe this unexpected appearance so early in the morning? And I don't see your usual muffin in hand, so this must be important."

Before answering, Ryan strode to the expansive windows highlighting Boston Harbor and the deep blue Atlantic Ocean beyond.

"Just came up to check out the view since my office only has a view of cement walls."

Hunter scoffed. "How quickly you forget. I offered to put you up here in the clouds with me, but you said the basement was more your style."

"I am not sure those were my exact words." Ryan continued to gaze at the cobalt-blue water before him.

"I may have paraphrased."

Hunter leaned back in his executive-style, espresso-colored leather chair, waiting for Ryan to tell him the actual reason for the unplanned visit.

Ryan turned to face Hunter. "Do you think you could ask your team of pharmaceutical geniuses something for me?"

"Sure. Guessing this has something to do with your investigation," Hunter commented through pursed lips.

"A theory has surfaced, and I need to either disprove or prove it could be a possibility. If it turns out it could be a possibility, then this is a whole new ball game," Ryan asserted not hiding his angst.

Wicked Nemesis of the Hunted   113

"Great—*another* theory. We need more than theories, Ryan. We need answers." Hunter unconsciously flexed his fingers.

"Don't you think I understand that, Hunter? *But* we cannot get answers if we are heading in the wrong direction. It is like if you are sick, and the doctors don't know what is wrong with you. It is just as important for them to understand what is *not* wrong with you to narrow down the options of what could be wrong," Ryan explained.

Hunter narrowed his eyes. He could not believe they were having this conversation at this early hour in the workday. "What is it you need the team to either confirm or deny so you can get back to the job I pay you for?"

"Can you ask them if there is a chance, no matter how remote, someone could turn the cancer-prevention drug into a biological weapon?" Ryan requested knowing this would grab Hunter's full attention.

Hunter's mouth dropped open and countered, "You think this could be weaponized?"

"I honestly don't know. That is what I need the scientists to tell us."

"Where did this suddenly come from, Ryan?"

In an instant, Hunter's mind was spinning. He did not want to imagine that the deadly plot they had been forced into could revolve around a bioweapon.

"I can't take credit for the idea. Frank came over last night and planted the seed…no pun intended."

Ryan moved from the windows to one of the chairs opposite Hunter's enormous desk.

"I guess that makes sense, given Frank's job. Does he think it is a real possibility?"

"Neither of us is sure, but he sees some crazy shit with the DEA, so I guess anything is feasible."

Hunter sighed. "Ryan, this is not good if it turns out to be a viable option. I honestly never even considered this groundbreaking drug could be used for anything nefarious. Or I was seeing the world through rose-colored glasses."

"I know what you mean. This drug has the potential to help so many people but not if it falls into the wrong hands." Ryan slouched in the chair.

"I will ask the team and see what they think. They are still having issues replicating the seeds, so this may all turn out to be a moot point," Hunter said.

Ryan rose and headed toward the door. Before leaving, he turned to Hunter. "Let me know as soon as you hear back. It could significantly up the ante."

Without waiting for Hunter's response, Ryan hopped in the express elevator to be delivered to the depths of the basement.

Back in his private haven, Ryan tried to occupy his morning with menial tasks to escape the nasty thoughts threatening to pull him into a black hole.

Wicked Nemesis of the Hunted   115

A pit formed in the bottom of his stomach as the hours passed waiting for Hunter to obtain the requested information. As each minute passed by, Ryan knew the probability of a biological weapon became more of a reality.

By mid-afternoon, Ryan had the answers he was waiting for. The game had changed drastically. Within the ten minutes it took for Hunter to relay the information, their world descended into what felt like a bottomless chasm.

Everything Ryan and Hunter had presumed was turned upside down. There was now a new playing piece added to the game—one that need to be eliminated before a catastrophe of epic proportions occurred.

The team of scientists confirmed, with some manipulation of the formula, the drug could be converted into a biological weapon. Without additional analysis, the team did not know how dangerous of a weapon it could be or how easy it would be to accomplish.

Ryan prayed the scientists would be wrong, but deep down he knew this would be the outcome. Part of him wished Frank never mentioned the possibility and another part of him was grateful Frank did.

Given this new twist, Hunter reassigned a small group of scientists to identify a way to prevent the drug from undergoing a metamorphosis from good to evil. Ryan and Hunter did not know the probability of accomplishing this task but knew it needed to be explored—and fast. Both men understood the importance of creating a safeguard before the drug was mass-produced.

Ryan leaned back in his office chair, closing his eyes, hoping to discover veiled answers, which weren't there to be found. An image of the seductive Sue crept into his mind, a siren singing her tempting song. Different scenarios were churning through his brain and none of them were pleasant. Once again, coincidences were amassing that naturally troubled him.

Hunter was standing before Ryan when he opened his eyes.

"Did I interfere with your little nap?" Hunter questioned with a grin.

Ryan yawned for effect. "I find at least one catnap a day keeps the doctor away. You should try it sometime."

Hunter took his usual seat across from Ryan's modest-sized desk.

"I put four scientists from the team on this side project of ours," Hunter affirmed.

Ryan let out a long, low moan. "I am not sure why I am so surprised by this possibility. It probably happens more than we think."

Hunter could tell Ryan was hesitating.

"Ryan, spit it out. What is going through your head that you aren't saying?" Hunter clenched his jaw.

Wicked Nemesis of the Hunted   117

"Okay. A couple things are rattling around. The first is about your father."

Hunter nodded in consent. He had been wrestling with this exact potential connection.

"I know we have been assuming Philip, for once in his life, was being altruistic and trying to create something for the greater good. Obviously, if Philip held the patent, he would have made billions. But what if he was double-dipping, in a manner of speaking?"

A puzzled look swept across Hunter's face. "Double-dipping?"

"What I mean is—what if Philip somehow realized both the good and bad of this potential drug? Would he be callous enough to create one version to prevent cancer and another version that could be used as a bioweapon to sell to the highest bidder?" Ryan watched Hunter closely.

Hunter sprang from the chair and started to pace like an African lion in captivity.

"I have been told by management if you wear out the carpet it won't be replaced," Ryan mockingly remarked.

Hunter stopped and retreated to the chair he had occupied minutes before.

"Ryan, I just don't know the answers to your questions or even how to respond. They are absolutely legitimate questions. Obviously, my father could be that 'callous,' to use your word. He had

Craig Sharpeton murdered, for God's sake, and I doubt he lost any sleep over it."

"Before we dive too deep into Philip's psyche, here is the other thing. It is very convenient how my former unscrupulous colleague showed up at this specific point in time. Back in the day, there was more than a good chance she was a double agent when I worked with her. It would *not* be a stretch to believe her current employer is also from the dark side or she's contracting for the highest bidder."

"You obviously know her, and I don't, so I will trust your assessment. I know I am not a former spy but try this on for size. What if my father had employed your former friend at some point? Have we—and by 'we' I mean you—ever looked to see if there is a connection?" Hunter began fidgeting with his hands.

Ryan pondered Hunter's questions for a minute before responding. "Honestly, I didn't think of that until now. With those two, anything is possible, I guess. Neither one would win the Nobel Peace Prize for their humanitarian efforts. Plus, both are driven by greed and power."

"And I hate to sound like a broken record but how does this tie into the Hardwicke debacle?" Hunter added.

Ryan ran his hands over his face. "It all must be connected somehow. With each passing day, I am more inclined to think none of this is a coincidence. There is a reason why all of this is happening. I just don't know what it is or how the pieces fit together…*yet*."

Hunter casually glanced at his watch and noticed it was already past five o'clock.

"Look, we aren't going to solve this today. Let's get out of here and start fresh tomorrow. If I am not home by six tonight, my beautiful bride is going to divorce me."

"It is best not to keep Emma waiting. I have witnessed firsthand her wrath and it is a bit terrifying." Ryan chuckled while Hunter made his way to the door.

"I have a meeting at eight a.m. with the science team. Why don't you join me so we both can hear what they have to say?"

"Sounds like a plan. I will meet you at the lab in the morning."

Hunter strode to the elevator leaving Ryan alone once more with his grimmest thoughts.

CHAPTER 11

Ryan was finishing his dark roast coffee and a chocolate chip scone when Hunter parked next to him outside the oatmeal-colored concrete building. Wiping the remnants of the devoured scone from his pants, Ryan exited his vehicle and waited for Hunter.

"Nice morning for a trip to the most boring-looking building on the block," Ryan remarked, trying to sound chipper and not as defeated as he felt.

"If you say so. I have this foreboding feeling. Hardly slept a wink last night."

"Why? Just because there is a good chance our lives will never be the same after we walk through those very secure doors over there?" Ryan looked in the direction of the main entrance.

"Yes, something like that. Let's go. Procrastinating won't change the outcome."

Hunter swiftly headed toward the front entrance doors. Once inside, both men were asked for multiple forms of identification including retinal and fingerprint scans. After passing through the full-body scanner and placing their personal items on the conveyor belt to be x-rayed, they collected their belongings and moaned simultaneously.

"Well, I think a colonoscopy would have been less invasive," Ryan commented, smiling in Hunter's direction.

"You're the security guru. I blame you," Hunter countered.

Without allowing Ryan to add his commentary, Hunter quickly headed in the direction of an unmarked door directly in front of them, with Ryan following a few steps behind.

After entering the designated key code and verifying with another retinal scan, Hunter and Ryan entered a world vastly different from their typical daily lives. Although Ryan had reviewed blueprints of the building when the extra security measures were being implemented, this was the first time he saw it in person.

What Hunter called a lab, Ryan called a city. No one passing by the building on the outside would guess there was an entire self-contained ecosystem within the concrete walls. The building contained multiple levels, with most underground. There was only one floor above ground. And although the building was made of concrete, Hunter had it reinforced with steel plates to ensure the building was nearly impenetrable by outside forces.

Each floor of the complex was designated for different pharmaceutical research and testing. Plus, each individual lab had its own security measures, depending on what was being created. Some of the labs also contained clean rooms designed to maintain low levels of particles like dust. The entire facility had its own power supply to maintain several types of equipment and a self-contained air filtration system. All these measures were designed to help thwart any attempts to infiltrate the complex.

Hunter and Ryan walked down a lengthy sterile-looking hallway, which led them to one of the multiple elevator banks. This reminded Ryan of a cornfield maze. There were endless amounts of hallways, some not leading anywhere. Again, this was all purposefully designed so that, in the unlikely event anyone was able to gain unauthorized access, they would get lost in the labyrinth.

Inside the elevator, Hunter slid his personal key card into the specified slot. This was another security measure Ryan had insisted on. Without notice, the elevator brought them to the chosen floor with speed and efficiency. The doors slid open to reveal long rows of stainless-steel tables and workstations with a variety of different equipment.

Ryan looked around in awe. There was everything from high-tech microscopes to large machines resembling ovens. From what he could deduce, two specific groups of people worked here—ones with the typical generic white lab coats and gloves and the ones who looked like they were encapsulated in space suits, with air tubes inserted into jet packs in the backs of the suits.

"Ryan, are you coming?" Hunter snapped.

Startled, Ryan followed Hunter and someone he presumed was the lead scientist who had magically appeared on their stroll down the hallway. The men were led into a small conference room containing a faux wood table and four rigid plastic beige chairs.

Once the three men were seated, Hunter began. "Thank you for seeing us on such short notice, Dr. McGrady."

Dr. McGrady removed his glasses before responding. "Anything for you, Mr. Logan. How can I help you today? I am guessing you would like an update on our progress." The doctor tried his best to quell his nervousness.

"Yes, an update would be great. I am also wondering if you were able to uncover any additional insights regarding our discussion yesterday."

Dr. McGrady's eyes briefly shifted in Ryan's direction, then at Hunter. "Before I begin, I don't believe I have previously met your associate."

Ryan stood and leaned across the table with an outstretched hand. "Forgive me for not introducing myself. I was honestly taken aback with amazement when we entered the laboratory. I wasn't sure what to expect and it looks remarkable. I am Ryan Donovan, head of security."

Dr. McGrady visibly relaxed and grasped Ryan's hand. "Forgive me, Mr. Donovan. I did not recognize you. It is a pleasure to meet you. And thank you for your kind words about the laboratory. Thanks to Mr. Logan, it is state-of-the-art in every way. I am guessing I have you to thank for the elaborate security."

Ryan chuckled. "Yes, all the added security was my idea. I hope it is not too cumbersome for your team."

"I really appreciate knowing we are completely safe, which allows the team to concentrate on doing what we are paid to do. You would be surprised by the lack of security at some of the pharmaceutical facilities I have worked at in the past." Dr. McGrady absently shook his head in disgust.

"Dr. McGrady, have you made any progress?" Hunter tried to get back on track.

"Sorry, Mr. Logan. Yes, we have made some headway. Which would you like to cover first—the seed replication or the idea of a bioweapon?"

"I will leave it up to you where to start," Hunter replied brusquely.

"Well, the bad news is we are still unable to replicate the seeds to the degree we need to. What I mean is we have replicated a small batch of seeds, but they are not at the efficacy needed for the drug to work properly. Think of it like this—buying a store brand versus a name brand. Sometimes they work just as well and other times they do not.

"This is not a risk we want with a cancer-prevention drug. We want to make sure it is the most potent strength feasible, and it can work on a multitude of distinct types of cancer, not just one or two. If we could get living plant samples, then we will have a better chance of reproducing the plants and, subsequently, the seeds."

Hunter rubbed his forehead. "Is there no other way?" he asked, knowing he did not want to hear the answer.

"Unfortunately, we believe it's the only option. I wish I had better news."

The doctor had been apprehensive to deliver this information to his employer, given the whispers of the ruthlessness of Hunter's father amongst the veteran staff.

"Alright. Let's table that one for now. How difficult would it be for someone to turn this into some type of bioweapon? Especially if they do not have access to the plants or seeds."

"The good news is that you cannot create a bioweapon from the formula unless you have the plants or seeds. Without them, it eliminates the threat of a bioweapon being created...but it also eliminates the opportunity to prevent cancer."

"Let's pretend we had the plants and seeds and were able to create the drug. Is there a way to prevent it from becoming some form of a bioweapon during the development or production process?"

"Scientifically speaking, yes, there is a way to prevent the drug from being weaponized without negatively impacting its effectiveness."

"I feel like there is a 'but' coming." Hunter narrowed his eyes.

"You know by now that things sometimes look promising on paper, but the reality can be vastly different. I cannot say definitively until we begin running simulated tests. And again, I caution you, these tests will bring us to the next level by providing more data. But that doesn't necessarily mean it will work with real-world scenarios." The doctor trod lightly.

Ryan chimed in. "Next level?"

"Yes, think of it as moving from pen and paper to a computer algorithm or artificial intelligence."

"So, we are basically bloody screwed unless we find the live plants, Dr. McGrady." Hunter did not hide his frustration.

The doctor cringed. "That is one way to look at it. My team will continue looking into both options and do the best we can with the tools we currently have. I cannot stress enough the importance of finding more of the plant itself. This would be a tipping point in the truest sense."

"Okay. It looks like we need to find the plants, which will be like finding the proverbial needle in a haystack."

Hunter rose from his chair and outstretched his hand in the direction of the doctor.

"Thank you for your time today, Dr. McGrady. Please keep me apprised of any additional updates or roadblocks you encounter," Hunter said earnestly.

"Certainly, Mr. Logan." Dr. McGrady turned in Ryan's direction. "It was a pleasure to meet you as well, Mr. Donovan."

Ryan smiled as he stood up and followed Hunter out of the conference room. The two pairs of eyes momentarily stopped and admired what was in front of them. It wasn't lost on either of them that the brightest minds in the world just told them they were dead in the water without the live plants. The question now was whether to continue to pursue the endeavor or lock the discovery in the vault to prevent an unintended catastrophe.

The two men maneuvered through the labyrinth following their original path. Any employees Ryan saw were completely absorbed in their assigned duties. He felt invisible and wasn't sure anyone noticed the two strangers walking amongst them.

Outside, the sun was filtered by hazy altostratus clouds, a sign of an impending cold front moving in to moderate the abnormally warm autumn weather. Ryan leaned against Hunter's luxury car and visibly exhaled.

"Well, that sure dampened my mood," Ryan declared.

Hunter leaned next to Ryan against the car. "We are damned if we do and damned if we don't."

Even though the sun was obscured, its radiant heat still managed to cascade down to where Hunter and Ryan were standing. Both men tilted their heads upward to absorb the invisible rays of the sun.

"At least we know the bioweapon is a possibility but only with the plants and seeds. And based on what Dr. McGrady said, there is a chance that scenario could be prevented," Ryan commented, desperately searching for a silver lining.

"I suppose you are technically correct," Hunter replied flatly.

"Listen, all is not lost. We just need to find the plants and—presto! We have a drug that will help millions of people. Easy peasy." Ryan cocked his head in Hunter's direction, trying to exhibit some semblance of confidence.

"Look, Ryan, I appreciate what you are saying. The fact of the matter is we have no way of finding the live plants. The only person who knew remotely where they were in the damn rain forest is my father. And in case you have forgotten, my father cannot reach out from beyond the grave to provide directions for us."

Ryan ran his hand over the stubble on his chin as Hunter's last words rattled through his brain. "That might not be quite true."

Hunter looked at Ryan, shook his head, and rolled his eyes before responding. "Say what? What are we going to do? Hold a séance?"

Ryan chuckled. "No, nothing that drastic. What I mean is we found the formula to begin with hidden in Craig Sharpeton's office at his house in Hardwicke. Would your father have done something similar and hid the information somewhere at your family's Hardwicke estate?"

Hunter pushed himself off the car and looked up at the clouds above. A single black crow cawed in the nearby oak tree, sending a chill down Hunter's spine. Crows and ravens had a long history of being a bad omen, Hunter remembered looking up at the bird.

Ryan saw where Hunter's mind had drifted to. "Don't mind that damn crow. The world will not end because one crow decided to make his presence known."

"Sorry. It was just a little too strange the crow showed up right when we were talking about my father."

Ryan sneered and stared at the crow that was eyeing them.

"I highly doubt Philip would reincarnate himself as a crow. My guess is it would be more like an anaconda or a hyena."

Ryan stuck his tongue out at the winged demon that continued to glare in their direction.

"After my father was legally declared dead, we went through all the files we could find. My mother had put into storage anything we weren't sure of its importance—if I remember correctly."

Hunter scratched his head trying to recall the weeks after he and his mother were officially notified. It had taken ten years before his mother could even file the petition to declare Philip dead with the government. Hunter remembered how time passed slowly for his mother and himself. Every phone call or knock on the door caused them to hold their breaths, wondering if that would be the day they would finally find out his father's fate.

"How about we find out where Philip's things are being stored and then see if there is anything of value? It's a long shot but can't hurt at this point."

Ryan did not want to tell Hunter the key to solving part of this mystery could be hidden under dust in some storage facility.

"I may know where they are." Hunter's chest heaved heavily.

Ryan was hesitant to ask. "Why do I get the feeling I am not going to like your answer?"

"It means a road trip to the rolling country hills of Hardwicke."

Ryan was not keen on heading back to the sleepy Norman Rockwell town, considering the last time he was there he was being shot at.

"I somehow knew you were going to say that," Ryan replied.

Hunter opened the driver's side door of the Mercedes. "I'll meet you back at the office. I have a few meetings today and then we can figure out the plan."

"Are you going to tell Emma any of this?" Ryan questioned.

"Not right now. I do not want to put her in more danger. And before you say anything, I know that she is still potentially in danger whether I tell her or not. Let me work this out in my head. I'll come to your office later this afternoon."

Hunter slid into the Mercedes and sped out of the parking lot, leaving Ryan standing by himself to contemplate the possibilities with the crow perched on the branch above him.

CHAPTER 12

Back at the office, Ryan checked in with his expert analyst. She was still attempting to track down more information on Sue and any connections to the current situation Sue may have had over the last few years. The search was going slower than normal. The analyst appreciated the specifics of Sue's life were buried deep, given her previous and conceivably current line of work.

Ryan leaned back in his chair as he had done on so many occasions since this lethal chain of events began. He was not sure what enlightenment would come out of staring at the ceiling or why he kept expecting a different outcome with this ritual.

"What is the definition of insanity?" Ryan asked aloud to an empty office.

Instead of driving himself crazier than he already was, Ryan decided to call a former colleague with a higher security clearance than he currently had. He pulled out the bottom drawer of his desk and lifted the fake bottom to expose a small keypad. He entered a code, and a lid opened revealing passports, various monetary denominations from different countries, a Glock 9mm, plus a simple-looking, flip-style cell phone.

Ryan pressed the power button on the cell phone. Once activated, he entered another code and closed the phone. To the common person, the phone would look like something advertised on TV for elderly people. In reality, it was a sophisticated encrypted phone from his former employer. The phone could be used anywhere in the world and was virtually untraceable.

Within ten minutes, Ryan's special phone vibrated, signaling his message had been received. Ryan closed and locked his office door so he would not be disturbed. Once accomplished, he opened the phone and responded to the message, letting the receiver know he was able to talk.

The phone once again vibrated and Ryan answered, "Encrypted."

On the other end, a middle-aged woman responded, "Encrypted."

"Ryan, it has been a long time. I read the report on your exploits across Massachusetts. Glad you came out of it without a scratch," the caller remarked with a hint of sincerity.

A sly smile formed on the caller's face. She had been expecting this call, given the details she was receiving at regular intervals from her team.

134   *Tracey L. Ryan*

"Thanks, Carolyn. Unfortunately, the situation isn't completely resolved. There have been some recent developments, and I think our mutual interests have collided."

"That sounds a bit ominous but intriguing," Carolyn stated, even-toned.

"I was paid a visit by an old friend of ours. She decided to drop in unannounced to my apartment. Plus, I believe she surveilled me taking an evening run around the Boston Common."

"Hmmm. That *is* intriguing, indeed. Although I am sure that you have many old friends who would want to stop by," Carolyn commented, noncommittal.

An image of Ryan's former handler popped into his mind, forcing him to raise his defensive walls. Ryan knew his former line of work would be tough on anyone, let alone a female agent. Being able to climb the ranks of a typically male-dominated organization was admirable in his eyes, although he also knew women like his former handler had to be stone-cold to be effective.

"Not many of my old friends have been raised from the dead, or so we thought. And for a dead person, she looked good."

"I am guessing you have some questions you would like answered, Ryan, which is the purpose of your call."

"You would be correct. Obviously, she is alive and wasn't killed by the enemy as suspected."

Carolyn paused. "Before I divulge any information, I need to make sure that you understand the terms."

Ryan had been afraid of this, but he knew his analyst would not be able to find out everything he needed to know. "Yes. I understand," Ryan answered still conflicted by his decision.

"And to confirm, you are agreeing to our previous terms that you, at the time, wanted no part of." The woman Ryan knew as Carolyn recognized that Ryan couldn't refuse.

It was Ryan's turn to pause. *Was this worth it?* he silently pondered. This was not a decision to take lightly—like deciding what to order for dinner.

"Ryan, if you are not absolutely certain, then we need to terminate this call."

"Yes. I am agreeing to the terms previously discussed," Ryan said through gritted teeth. He knew he had just made a deal with the devil but, after weighing all options, did not see an alternative.

"Very well. All the information you are seeking will be delivered to you in an encrypted file. I believe you still remember how to access our files," Carolyn stated with a devious smile.

"Yes."

Before disconnecting, the woman said, "And Ryan, please tell your analyst she can stop poking around in our systems." The phone went dead.

136   *Tracey L. Ryan*

Ryan stared at the phone in his hand in disbelief. This confirmed Ryan's former handler had been tracking not only him but those around him. And Ryan wasn't sure if this was advantageous or dangerous.

There was nothing else that could be done for the time being. The deal was made, and Ryan would need to live with his choice. He only hoped it was worth it. Right now, getting lost in the Amazon did not seem like such a bad idea to Ryan.

CHAPTER 13

Around three o'clock, Hunter headed down to the bowels of the Ares Logan headquarters to meet with Ryan. During the expedited elevator ride, Hunter reflected on the conversation earlier with his science team. The odds of finding something useful at the Hardwicke estate were slim, knowing the lengths Philip went to in order to keep his secrets securely hidden—something Emma and her mother knew firsthand with the murder of Craig Sharpeton.

Without knocking, Hunter turned the door handle, expecting the door to swing open. Instead, he almost went headfirst into the door.

"What the bloody hell?" Hunter blurted out.

Within a few seconds, Hunter heard the undeniable sounds of the door being unlocked.

"Sorry, buddy. I forgot I locked it earlier. Which would explain why I have had an uninterrupted afternoon until now."

"Do I even want to know what you were doing behind a locked door?" Hunter quickly scanned the room thinking he may have interrupted something he did not want to see.

Ryan snorted. "For your information, there isn't anyone here if that is what you were implying. You can check the coat closet if it would put your mind at ease." Ryan motioned with his left hand toward the small utility closet in the corner.

"I will take your word for it." Hunter sat in his usual chair opposite Ryan's desk.

"Have you given any more thought to telling Emma about the latest madness?" Ryan tried to deflect the conversation so he wouldn't be forced to lie to his best friend as to the real reason the door had been locked.

"As I said previously, we cannot tell Emma until we know more. My stance on this is unaltered. I have added extra security as a precaution. She, hopefully, won't notice," Hunter responded tersely.

"Fine. Just wanted us to be on the same page in case she gets curious. Like she tends to do." Ryan shrugged.

"I think we should take a drive out to the country tomorrow morning," Hunter announced.

"We can do that," Ryan confirmed and made a mental note to bring his weapon.

"Let's meet here so Emma doesn't get suspicious. Plus, I know you need your morning coffee and muffin otherwise you are a bear for the rest of the day." Hunter joked.

"Very funny. I can meet you here at eight a.m. if that works. How about I drive to Hardwicke in case Emma decides to surprise you at work and parks in the garage? If she doesn't see your car, you know there will be an inquisition headed your way. Not seeing my car will be easier to explain," Ryan said, feeling like he was preparing for an undercover mission.

"I guess that is a very sensible line of thinking. You would almost think you used to be a spy."

Ryan flinched and flashbacked to his recent conversation. "Glad we settled that. Do you have any ideas on where Philip's files could be? It's a large estate, and he could have buried them in the backyard for all we know."

Hunter knew this could be like trying to find the lost city of Atlantis and surreptitiously prayed Ryan's past skills would prove useful.

"The obvious place to start would be his home office," Hunter answered.

"But we know Philip was not a logical man. He was paranoid...so paranoid that he killed Emma's father after he found out the plants and seeds had significant value. Just to protect his secret and guarantee Craig Sharpeton would never divulge anything he found to another living soul."

"I know." Hunter rubbed his temples. "I say we start with the office to cross it off the list. I will think about other potential hiding spots as well."

"Sounds like a plan. I am going to wrap up a few things here and then head out," Ryan concluded.

Hunter strode to the open doorway and paused. Looking back at Ryan, he asked, "Is there anything else I should know?"

Without hesitation, Ryan answered, "No."

Silently, Hunter turned and made his way to the elevator to be taken to the top of the Boston skyline.

A heavy sigh escaped Ryan and he slumped back in his chair once he was alone. He knew this was going to be a challenging balancing act. But if his controversial choices kept everyone he cared about safe, Ryan was willing to take the risk. He would find a way to atone for his future sins after this game was finally finished to his satisfaction.

CHAPTER 14

Ryan pulled into the Ares Logan parking garage at seven thirty a.m. to provide enough time to pick up his daily muffin. He left two cups of dark-brewed coffee from Kern's in the car while he made the quick jaunt to the cafeteria.

By the time Ryan made it back to the car, Hunter was wandering around the garage like a lost child.

For both men, the thought of heading back to the place where their lives had been changed forever was unnerving. For a moment, Hunter's thoughts drifted to his mother, who was now a permanent resident of a psychiatric hospital—all because a lifetime's worth of secrets came crashing down on top of them like a cave-in.

Ryan approached Hunter, noticing he was completely absorbed in his thoughts.

"Earth to Hunter."

"Sorry. Just thinking about my mother."

"Hey, I get it. A lot of bad voodoo happened in Hardwicke."

"Voodoo?" Hunter questioned with a raised eyebrow.

"Sorry, it was the only word I could come up with given I haven't had my muffin and coffee yet. There is a coffee in the car for you as well." Ryan opened the driver's side door.

"Thanks. I appreciate it. Ryan?"

"Yes?" Ryan looked at Hunter across the roof of the Mercedes.

Before Hunter opened the passenger side door, he stated, "We really need to find my father's notes. Otherwise, we are at a dead end. No pun intended."

"I get it. Hopefully, there are at least some clues at the house. Let's hit the road. There won't be much traffic since we are heading in the opposite commuter direction on the Mass Pike."

Ryan put on his black aviator Ray-Ban polarized sunglasses and slid behind the wheel while Hunter buckled himself into the passenger seat. Within a few minutes, the Mercedes was heading west on the Massachusetts Turnpike. Hunter gazed out of the windshield, watching the traffic on the eastbound side moving at a crawl for as far as his eyes could see.

With one hand on the steering wheel, Ryan maneuvered his way around the few cars on the westbound side of the highway while demolishing the blueberry muffin he held in his opposite hand. Crumbs sprayed the driver's side like a sprinkler watering the lawn. Out of the corner of Ryan's eye, he could see Hunter was deep in thought.

The pair rode in virtual silence the hour-and-a-half drive to Hardwicke, with only the faint sound of a classic rock satellite station floating through the car. Ryan still contemplated his decision to make an allegiance with his former employer while Hunter wondered if his family would ever be truly safe.

After the picturesque final few miles through an explosion of autumn colors, Ryan came upon the front gate leading to the Logan estate. Ryan noted the estate did not look as ominous in the morning light as it had that dark, rainy night when all hell broke loose. The setting looked picturesque, with the fall colors painted in the background of the mansion. A gentle breeze rustled the leaves on the hickory trees lining the long driveway while the sun's autumn rays danced above them.

Ryan pushed the button to lower the window and leaned out of the car to type in the security code. After the deadly events that had taken place here, Ryan brought in his team to redo all the security systems. He was afraid, given the level of national news, this would become some type of morbid tourist attraction.

The light on the keypad turned green, signaling the next step in the process—for Ryan to look straight into the camera on the keypad for a retinal scan. The light on the camera turned green and the large gates slowly opened.

Another enhancement Ryan added was sensors built under the driveway to detect when the car had cleared the gate. Then magically, the gate swung closed at a high speed. Anyone who was caught in the gate when it closed would lose a limb or worse.

Driving slowly down the long driveway toward the main house, Ryan left his window open to inhale the fresh country air. The smell of autumn was not something he experienced in the city. Birds sang a welcome tune, inviting the visitors to enjoy a little piece of serenity. Ryan almost forgot all that had happened here.

"We have arrived," Ryan declared.

"Thank you for that astute observation," Hunter replied with a hint of apprehension.

Ryan parked the car in front of the entrance to the main house. Once out of the car, he stretched his muscles. He wasn't used to being in the car for this length of time and his body shrieked at him. Silently, he watched Hunter soak up the surroundings. Pain washed over Hunter's usually indifferent face.

"How about we head inside to Philip's office? At least we can cross that off the list first before we focus on this treasure hunt."

Hunter agreed and began to solemnly lead the way.

"I feel like we should be on the *Discovery Channel*," Ryan remarked, flashing a bright smile in Hunter's direction but receiving no response.

Taking the lead, Ryan proceeded to what used to be Philip Logan's home office. Ryan noticed the furniture had been covered in giant white sheets when they passed by the myriad of rooms leading to the office that overlooked the backyard.

Flashbacks of that deadly night replayed in Ryan's head.

The pounding rains.

The terrorized hostages.

The devastating aftermath.

"Here we are. Looks like it hasn't been touched in years," Hunter commented sullenly, peering into the open doorway.

The sun beamed through the French doors showcasing the patio and the magnificent scenery beyond. Hunter entered the office first and flipped the wall switch to help illuminate the room for the task at hand.

Ryan stood in the doorway and surveyed the room. The walls, floor, and ceiling were crafted in hand-carved dark wood. This was not the standard paneling of the 1970s, Ryan assessed. It was mahogany with intricate custom designs. An elaborate fireplace was located on one wall with the opposite wall hosting built-in shelves lined with first editions. The coffered ceiling provided more depth and recessed lighting. Ryan was awestruck.

"Earth to Ryan," Hunter repeated Ryan's words from earlier in the garage.

"Sorry. This room is exquisite," Ryan replied and gently ran his hand across the mantle of the fireplace.

"I think you have been watching too much HGTV, my friend." Hunter grinned.

"You seriously don't think this is amazing? This looks like it was all hand done. The craftsmanship is better than the Newport mansions!"

Hunter gazed around and, for the first time, appreciated what Ryan was describing.

"I can see what you mean. This room was completely off-limits growing up, so I always associated it with my father just being a bastard. It was his and *only* his space. I guess I must learn to push through the bad memories to uncover the good."

"That was very profound, Hunter."

Before things got uncomfortably emotional, Ryan decided to test a theory he had been keeping to himself. Systematically, he began gently knocking on each panel of the walls.

"I don't think there are termites if that is what you are looking for," Hunter asserted.

"Funny. I am testing out a theory."

Listening carefully, each knock of the wood produced a hard thump sound, indicating the wall was solid. On the last panel before the fireplace, the sound of Ryan's knock was slightly different. For the next five minutes, Ryan examined the wall in detail by gently tapping on different sections.

Feeling Hunter's eyes burrowing a hole into the back of his head, Ryan explained, "I think this is hollow. Did you notice the slight difference in sound?"

Hunter concurred, although he wasn't exactly sure what Ryan was talking about.

"It sounds like there's an empty space behind the wall approximately three feet wide and six feet tall."

Ryan gawked at the wall, contemplating options to get behind it without damaging the exquisite woodwork. Glancing down at the floor, he could see faint scrapes on the hardwood in front of the exact location he was analyzing. His eyes were drawn to a slightly askew marble tile in front of the fireplace. Ryan noticed everything else in the room was impeccable except for that one tile.

"Here goes nothing," he said with a shrug.

Ryan stepped on the tile and was rewarded with a soft pop, followed by a small cloud of dust when the concealed door slightly opened.

"Well, I'll be damned." Hunter could not believe what he had just witnessed.

Ryan took a bow and applauded himself, although even he had not been convinced his impromptu theory would work.

"Now I feel like we are heading into an Indiana Jones movie," Ryan commented, only half-joking.

"Which is why, since you made this discovery, you are going first," Hunter pronounced.

"It is your house; therefore, you should have the honor of going first," Ryan countered.

Hunter did not budge from where he was standing.

"Do you have any flashlights?" Ryan asked. "I don't think the ones on our phones will cut through the blackness."

"In the kitchen. Give me a minute."

Before heading to the kitchen, Hunter grabbed a fireplace poker and handed it to Ryan, which was met with a quizzical look.

"In case anything in there decided to come out."

Hunter quickly left to get the flashlights before Ryan could hit him with the poker.

CHAPTER 15

R yan peered into the darkness and listened carefully. His unspoken prayer was answered when all he heard was silence. He may have been in some of the most dangerous places on earth in his lifetime, but creepy crawlies freaked him out.

Before long, Ryan's right hand started to throb. Looking down, he noticed his knuckles had turned white from holding the fire poker in a death grip.

Five minutes later, Hunter rejoined Ryan with two LED flashlights. Ryan took one of the flashlights and decided to keep the poker with him on the quest before them. He chided himself for not taking the Glock, which was secured in the glove compartment of the car. Quickly weighing the probability of significant danger, Ryan decided not to retrieve the gun from the car.

Using his shoulder as leverage, Ryan pushed the door open wider and shone the powerful flashlight into the pitch-dark abyss looming in front of him. The light barely cut through the blackness. which unsettled Ryan. Ryan admitted that night vision goggles would have been helpful at this moment. He still was not convinced there weren't any creatures lying in wait to attack as soon as he stepped inside.

"If this was used as some type of storage area, there must be a light source. I doubt Philip would be fumbling around in the dark," Ryan postulated while Hunter remained silent using Ryan as a human shield.

Trying not to think about what he might touch, Ryan gently leaned the poker against the fireplace and focused the flashlight beam on the right-hand wall while running his hand across it looking for a light switch. Approximately five feet into the doorway, Ryan found what felt like a light switch. Flipping the switch on, the space became dimly illuminated when the overhead fluorescent lights flickered to life.

"Holy crap!" Ryan yelled, startling Hunter.

Hunter poked his head around Ryan and was astonished at what he saw.

A spiral granite staircase descending to the depths below presented itself to the two men. The secret passage was about seven feet tall, six feet wide, and fifteen feet deep, by Ryan's brief assessment. The space was just large enough to fit the staircase. The air was stale, musty, and damp, causing Ryan to instinctively wrinkle his nose. It was clear no one had ventured down these stairs in many years based on the dust and cobwebs.

"Ready, partner?" Ryan looked back at Hunter.

"As ready as I will ever be," Hunter responded with a knot in his stomach.

"This may just be another entrance to the basement."

"A secret entrance to the basement? Even you cannot believe that one, Ryan. More likely it is leading to the depths of hell, knowing my father," Hunter refuted.

Ryan rolled his eyes and took the first step into the crypt.

Cautiously, the men moved down the gray granite stairs, paying close attention to every detail along the way. The circular wall outlining the staircase was also made of the same salt and pepper-colored blocks. The end of the staircase opened to a large room, and based on the temperature and dampness, Ryan knew they were officially underground. The room was about half the size of the house above, without any other discernable doors.

Standing at the bottom of the stairs, Ryan scrutinized Hunter's expression. Hunter's eyes darted wildly around the room from top to bottom and in every corner. This basement was different from the one at Emma's family's house located in the center of Hardwicke. Emma's basement was a necessary part of the foundation for the colonial-style house while this was purposefully designed.

File cabinets were positioned against the smooth granite wall on the left side of the chamber. Some type of greenhouse with funky purplish lights and a row of wooden gardening benches approximately four feet high and five feet long was positioned against the opposite wall.

"What do you make of this, Hunter?" Ryan asked as he continued to inspect his surroundings.

"I have absolutely no bloody clue. I never knew this even existed." Hunter was visibly baffled.

Ryan headed toward the gardening tables and found remnants of long-ago dead plants, which reminded him of their similar discovery in Emma's basement.

"Hunter, you need to see this. This might be where your father kept the plants he smuggled out of the Amazon."

Hunter made his way to where Ryan stood and stared at the hundreds of green plastic plant containers sitting on the potting benches in front of him. His mind was swirling, trying to absorb what he was looking at. Hunter contemplated this was another secret his father almost took to the grave.

Ryan watched Hunter softly brush his fingers along the length of the gardening tables like he was in a trance. Hunter could feel Ryan staring at him, waiting for some sort of response to their latest discovery.

Without looking in Ryan's direction, Hunter said, "Ryan, I know you want me to somehow provide an explanation for all of this, but I just can't. We keep peeling back the onion, as they say, without getting any closer to the core. On the drive here, part of me was praying we wouldn't find anything. The man who was my father is an enigma to me."

Slapping his hand on Hunter's shoulder, Ryan responded, "I know, buddy. Forgive me for saying this, but it keeps getting more bizarre where your father is concerned."

Hunter barely acknowledged Ryan's comments and began to survey what he now considered Philip's lair. Suddenly, all his father's past deceptions and murderous actions hit him like a giant rogue wave. It felt like the oxygen had been sucked out of the room for him.

Ryan witnessed what looked like Hunter having a panic attack and rushed to his side when he started to teeter. Not wanting Hunter to crumble to the cold cement floor, Ryan grabbed him by the arms.

"Hunter, are you alright?" Ryan asked concerned.

Without waiting for an answer, Ryan maneuvered Hunter to the stairs and motioned for him to sit down.

"Thanks, Ryan. I am not sure what came over me. It felt like an out-of-body experience of some sort. I can't explain it. A tsunami filled with my father's past sins threatened to drag me under in those few moments."

"Look, Hunter, we can do this another day. Now that we know this place exists, we can come back at any time to snoop around."

The color gradually started to return to Hunter's face and his breathing began to steady.

"I appreciate the offer, Ryan. But I think we need to start rummaging through all this stuff sooner versus later. Plus, we are already here. Let's just do what we came here to do. I will be fine. It just caught me off guard, that's all," Hunter replied, trying to regain his composure.

"If you think you feel up to it," Ryan responded with a slight hesitation in his voice.

"I will be fine. Let's pray there is something here to find." Hunter slowly rose to his feet and headed toward the row of filing cabinets located on the opposite wall from the dead plants.

"Hunter, I think we should take some of these dead plants back to the lab for analysis. Maybe we'll get lucky. Who knows, they may provide another clue."

"Makes sense," Hunter replied without much conviction.

"Will you be alright for a few minutes? I am going to run up to the kitchen to see if there are any garbage bags we can use to put the plant trays into."

"We used to keep the extra bags in the utility closet next to the refrigerator," Hunter offered.

Wicked Nemesis of the Hunted   155

Without wasting any time, Ryan sprinted up the stone staircase and into the kitchen. He quickly found the closet Hunter referenced and found an unopened box of tall kitchen bags. Ryan noticed on the same shelf as the bags was a box of latex gloves. Grabbing both boxes, Ryan headed back toward the underground hideaway.

On the way to the office, Ryan briefly paused at the entrance to the living room where the tragedy had unfolded. Although the cleaning company did a phenomenal job removing any hint of what had occurred, Ryan knew from experience memories were much harder to erase.

Not wanting to leave Hunter alone with his demons any longer than necessary, Ryan continued his trek and carefully maneuvered down the steep steps, trying not to tumble down the stairs. When Ryan reached the bottom step, he noticed Hunter knee-deep in file folders and dust.

Without looking up from the mountain of paper in front of him, Hunter casually inquired, "Did you find the garbage bags?"

"They were right where you said they would be. Plus, I found a box of latex gloves," Ryan responded proudly.

"Are your hands so delicate you need to wear gloves, Ryan?" Hunter's typical sarcasm filled the stale air which brought a smile to Ryan's face.

"Very funny. No, dumbass, it is to preserve any

evidence potentially on all this crap down here. That's how us spy guys roll." Ryan mockingly rolled his eyes and placed the boxes on an empty table.

Ryan opened the box of black latex gloves and slid a pair on his hands. Thankfully, the gloves were a size large; otherwise, Ryan's hands would have broken through them. Then he opened the box of garbage bags, took a few out, and headed to the first table of plants he assumed were once a vibrant pink color.

Moving slowly so he wouldn't damage the containers or drop any of the dehydrated soil, Ryan gently placed one tray into a garbage bag. Each tray could hold twelve plants, and there were four trays per table. Through some quick math, Ryan guessed there could have been over two hundred plants at one time if all the trays were filled to capacity.

Ryan noticed the containers on the far end of the room still had remnants of the actual plant contained in their compartments, which puzzled Ryan given their estimated age. Scratching his head, Ryan walked to the tables closest to the staircase and purposely retraced his steps down the length of the room.

"Find something, Ryan?" Hunter asked while his eyes followed his movements.

"Umm, I'm not sure. Come here and look at this," Ryan responded, pointing to the tables.

Hunter sauntered over to where Ryan stood.

"What am I looking at besides dead plants and lots of dried-out dirt?" Hunter asked bemused.

"The containers on the tables closest to the stairs are basically dusty soil and have no signs life ever existed within them."

"And the point would be?" Hunter nudged.

"Look at the containers on this table," Ryan said, gesturing to the last table in the row.

Hunter looked more closely before reacting with wide eyes.

"Wait! These have actual dead plants in them whereas the others only have the soil we assumed once held plants," Hunter announced.

"Exactly!" Ryan roared. "So, what would make this table different than the others?"

Hunter shook his head. "I'm not a botanist, so I have no clue, Ryan."

"I wonder if the plant trays are in chronological order." Ryan held up his hand to stop Hunter when he opened his mouth to speak. "Hear me out. The ones on the first table have obviously been gone a long time. If you look at each bench, there are more and more of the plants remaining until you get to this last one. I can still see a hint of the bright pink color the plant used to be. Come here, look closely," Ryan expressed excitedly.

Hunter leaned over the table to where Ryan was pointing and couldn't believe what was in front of him. Pink hues were electrified under the purple,

158   *Tracey L. Ryan*

fluorescent lights over the tables. These plants, if Ryan's theory was correct, were the last ones collected by Philip before his demise in the Amazon.

"Holy shit! These look almost preserved. Are you thinking what I am, Ryan?"

"That your team of top-notch scientists may be able to glean something from these?" Ryan was unable to contain his exhilaration.

"Yes!" Hunter exclaimed.

"Let me pack these more recent trays with the plants and then just take a few samples of the other ones, in case there could be something of use. Grab me some more bags from the box, would you?"

Hunter brought the box as instructed and held the bags open while Ryan carefully placed each tray in a separate bag. When they were finished, it looked like someone had a tremendous clear-out of unwanted junk.

"Hunter, I wonder if the conditions down here had something to do with the preservation of the plants as well. Would be good for your team to research that avenue too."

"I will make sure they research any and all avenues. This may be the breakthrough we needed. If, and I know this is a *big* if, these plants are viable, we may be able to reproduce them and, ultimately, the seeds."

"Fingers crossed. Hey, did you find anything in those files?" Ryan probed.

Wicked Nemesis of the Hunted   159

Hunter walked back to the small mountains of paper and colorful files on the metal table next to the filing cabinets, with Ryan following behind.

"Well, it kind of reminded me of when Emma and I were going through her father's office in Hardwicke."

Hunter flashed back to the multiple piles of folders at Emma's house. When he and Emma had, on a whim, decided to search her father's home office, they hit the proverbial jackpot of information. At the time, neither could make heads or tails of the true value of the discovery. There were handwritten notes with formulas, pictures of different plants, and some typed notes. Emma had been the first to notice many of the folders were dated.

Once the duo organized them in sequential order, a story started to emerge. Craig Sharpeton had set up the folders as a research journal containing information on different experiments for the cancer-prevention drug results her father had been helping to develop for Philip Logan.

"Hello? Do these look like what you and Emma found?" Ryan asked, bringing Hunter back to the present.

"Yes and no. There are chemical formulas and rough drawings here that seem similar, but I honestly don't understand them. Another job for the team to decipher." Hunter stroked his chin.

"And…" Ryan prompted.

"Many of the handwritten notes seem to be in some sort of shorthand. It is my father's handwriting, but it looks like a foreign language to me. If I was to venture a guess, I would say he had his own little language only he understood out of fear of discovery. It still amazes me the depths this man went to in order to protect his secrets," Hunter replied in disgust.

Ryan surveyed the stacks of files in front of them, then looked in the direction of the plant tray tables. This back-and-forth motion continued for several seconds as if Ryan was watching an intense tennis match, with Hunter observing and cocking an eyebrow in Ryan's direction.

CHAPTER 16

Without a word, Ryan walked to the last file cabinet. He noticed it was perfectly aligned with the last gardening bench holding what they assumed were the most recent plants. Ryan tested his theory by opening the top drawer of the cabinet while Hunter continued to observe with immense curiosity and amusement.

Inside the drawer, Ryan found color-coded files like the ones Hunter had found in the first cabinet. Ryan pulled out several and began examining them.

"Ryan, what the hell are you doing?" Hunter asked abruptly as his curiosity quickly turned to impatience.

"Gimme a minute," Ryan replied with a bite, causing Hunter to unconsciously take a step back.

Ryan went to the next cabinet on the left and pulled a few folders out quickly, reading them before putting the folders on the floor. Repeating this process with all the filing cabinets, Ryan finally looked in Hunter's direction.

"Sorry. Didn't mean to snap at you. I just needed to check to see if I was right. And you will be happy to know that I am fairly certain I am." Ryan crossed his arms and smirked.

"Well, that clears things up," Hunter retorted.

"So, here is what I'm suggesting. We are fairly certain the rows of plants are in chronological order, correct?" Ryan waved his hand in the direction of the plants like a game show host.

"Yes. Go on." Hunter glanced at his watch, hoping to speed up Ryan's theatrical performance.

"Notice how these cabinets align precisely with the tables over there?" Ryan asked and pointed his finger in a straight line from one side of the room to the other.

"If you say so. I am not sure what this has to do with anything. My father was meticulous to the point of having obsessive-compulsive disorder, so this wouldn't be unusual."

"Exactly! Your father was unbelievably calculating about every aspect of his life," Ryan declared.

"I am still not following you, Ryan. What the bloody hell are you getting at?" Hunter snapped in frustration.

"Just like the plants, these files seem to be in chronological order. And I would guess each cabinet is affiliated to the corresponding table across from it," Ryan concluded arrogantly.

Ryan folded his arms with a self-satisfied look on his face and leaned against the third file cabinet. Silently counting to ten, Ryan waited for Hunter to draw the same connection.

"Holy shit!" Hunter shouted.

"Right! That was part one of my theory."

"There's more?" Hunter questioned in disbelief.

"I don't think the multiple colors of the folders are insignificant. As you just reminded me, your father had a purpose for everything he did. I believe each color represents something."

Hunter blinked at Ryan in surprise.

Ryan continued. "I think we need to be careful and keep the files in the exact order we found them. If I am right, these files will help us unravel the story of this enormously powerful discovery."

Hunter blinked again at Ryan speechless.

"I know much of this is written in some sort of code, Hunter, but I believe we will be able to decipher enough of it to piece together at least a historical timeline. And possibly uncover some other tidbits along the way. Think of this as a treasure hunt where 'x' marks the spot."

Ryan watched Hunter's reaction closely. This was both tantalizing and terrifying for both men. Each clearly understood what was at stake and the increased danger finding this secret hideaway could spark.

Hunter inhaled sharply before responding, "If

your theory holds water, and they usually do, we could have hit the jackpot."

"Yes. This could be like winning big on a progressive slot machine in Vegas." Ryan smiled brightly.

"Do you have any more revelations you would like to spring on me?" Hunter asked with a slight hesitation, knowing he couldn't handle much more at this moment.

"No. That should do it…for now," Ryan replied with a small grin.

"Alright. How do you want to handle getting the files and plants back to Boston?" Hunter inquired, knowing Ryan more than likely already had a plan forming in his head.

Ryan's watch revealed it was eleven thirty a.m.

"How quickly could we get a box truck here?"

"It would take a few hours at least to send one of the company's trucks."

"Okay. Is there a rental place nearby?"

"I think there used to be one in the next town over. Fifteen minutes away—if they are still in existence and have one available."

Ryan pulled his phone from his pocket and noticed there wasn't any cell service in the subterranean chamber.

"I am going to run upstairs to try to get some cell service. If I can, I will find the nearest rental company and see if they have a truck available for today and tomorrow."

Before Hunter could respond, Ryan raced up the stone staircase, leaving him alone in the slightly eerie basement. Hunter grabbed onto the few minutes of solitude and tried to come to terms with the events of the day. Even after his father's presumed demise, Hunter still struggled to understand Philip Logan. Philip's motives were almost always fueled by greed, which Hunter could never relate to. Flashbacks of his childhood popped into Hunter's mind.

The life lessons he was forced to endure.

The demand for perfection in school and sports.

The complete lack of emotion or unconditional love.

Ryan's footsteps jarred Hunter back to reality before he could delve deeper into the dismal days of growing up a Logan.

"Here's the deal. I was able to rent a small box truck for today and tomorrow. It comes with a hand truck, so we will be able to move the cabinets, once outside, more easily."

Hunter peered in the direction of the steep staircase looming in the background, then back at Ryan.

Reading Hunter's mind, Ryan responded, "I know it will be tough going up those stairs. There must be an alternative." Ryan slowly scrutinized the basement. "Would Philip have built an escape route?"

"Escape route? My father was many things, but a magician was not one of them, to my knowledge, Ryan."

"I know that. But since Philip planned every detail, I am wondering if he would have built a hidden exit to this place just in case he ever needed it."

Simultaneously, the pair surveyed the room. Ryan was the first to notice what looked like a straight-line crack under the staircase. Striding over to the perceived crack, Ryan examined it more closely. Next to the crack was a stone that was slightly different from the others used to build the staircase. Hunter watched in wonderment when Ryan pushed the stone and a door swung open.

"Well, I'll be damned. I guess you were right once again, Ryan," Hunter commented, and fake-clapped in Ryan's direction.

"That Philip was a crafty bastard," Ryan commented with a hint of admiration.

Unlike the passageway upstairs, this was automatically illuminated when the door sprang open. Ryan peered inside the small area, which looked to be about seven feet high and six feet long. He speculated the cabinets would just about fit through the opening.

Ryan entered the tight space and found the door leading to what he assumed was the backyard deadbolted from the inside. He had to apply some pressure to slide the deadbolt open and then gently pushed the door. Bright sunshine stung Ryan's eyes when he stepped outside.

CHAPTER 17

Getting his bearings, Ryan found himself standing adjacent to the patio in the area where the gardeners kept their tools and supplies. This area dipped down several feet from the patio as part of the natural landscape, which made it a perfect staging area for the landscapers.

Walking up the six steps to the patio, Ryan gazed at the vibrant autumn colors in the distance. Looking back toward the hidden door, Ryan noticed why no one would be the wiser it existed. The door was completely flush with the stonework of the foundation, and the hinges were made to look like part of the stones.

Hunter popped out of the tunnel with a heavy sigh.

Ryan turned to face Hunter. "Beautiful view, buddy."

"Yes, it is. It feels like I am noticing it for the first time." Another sigh escaped Hunter. "I lived here off and on for half my life and never fathomed the surprises this house held."

Ryan knew Hunter was not only referring to the concealed room they had just discovered. Unfortunately, Ryan believed the house contained even more surprises beyond what they already uncovered. Ryan silently prayed any additional secrets that surfaced wouldn't destroy Hunter and those around him.

"I cannot imagine what you are feeling, Hunter. And I wish I could tell you we found the last of the bombshells your parents were hiding. In my experience, that is rarely true."

Hunter needed to separate his feelings and changed the subject.

"What is the plan, Ryan?"

"I called a car service to pick me up at the front gate in a few minutes. They'll take me to grab the truck, and you can guard our hidden treasure."

It was not lost on Ryan how Hunter tried to deflect the conversation away from his family's hidden past.

Hunter froze. "Guard?"

Ryan chuckled. "Didn't mean to sound melodramatic. I just meant you can stay here. Let's go back inside and lock this door until we need it." Ryan's eyes drifted toward the wooded area to the right of the house. "You never know what kind of wild beast could be lurking in those woods over there."

"Ryan, this is Hardwicke and not the haunted forest in the *Wizard of Oz*. You seriously need to get out of the city more often."

Hunter hesitated slightly before moving back inside, trying to show a calm facade. Although he knew Ryan was mostly joking, Hunter had a strange feeling there was some truth in Ryan's warning. Since day one of this deadly adventure, Hunter and those around him had been watched and hunted.

After securing the door behind them, Ryan gave Hunter a brief list of tasks to do while he was bringing the truck back to the house.

"I need you to take pictures of all the cabinets in their current location and then the tables. Then I need images of the contents of each file drawer and corresponding plant table," Ryan instructed.

"Aye, aye, captain! Take a shitload of pictures." Hunter saluted in Ryan's direction.

"Fine. Be a smartass. I'm outta here. Be back in a jiffy, I hope."

Ryan disappeared upstairs leaving Hunter alone again in the depths of the basement with Ryan's parting words hanging in the air. Hunter swiftly started following his directions for the photos. Not wanting to be reprimanded by Ryan, Hunter went overboard with creating a photo extravaganza. Hunter methodically opened each drawer in what he hoped was chronological order, snapping pictures of the contents.

Trying to keep his mind busy and not face the monsters who occupied the house and his thoughts, Hunter sat on the bottom step with a few of the file folders he previously removed. Flipping through the files, Hunter desperately tried to recall any scrap of information from his high school biology and chemistry classes, which was a daunting task.

After perusing several red-colored folders, Hunter moved on to the green folders. This produced the same result—a potpourri of mumbo-jumbo notes. Hunter quickly moved through the other colored folders until he reached the final color—yellow. This color nagged at him, but he couldn't understand why.

Before Hunter could view its contents, footsteps could be heard directly above him. He froze with panic until Ryan yelled down at him. Hunter swiftly placed the folders back where he found them.

A few minutes later, Ryan bounded down the stairs carrying the hand truck.

"I hope I didn't startle you. I was trying to be careful with the hand truck. I didn't want to damage the woodwork," Ryan admitted.

Ryan unfolded the hand truck and walked over to the first cabinet. Hunter watched Ryan's muscular arms test the weight of the cabinet before attempting to move it. Satisfied the cabinet could be safely moved, Ryan motioned for Hunter to help him.

"I will do the heavy lifting since I know you are more fragile than I am," Ryan said mockingly.

Hunter rewarded Ryan with a fake punch in the arm.

Ryan's muscles protruded from his short-sleeved polo-style shirt when he moved the cabinet. Although Hunter was lean and in decent shape, he had always been a tad jealous of Ryan's solid muscular frame. Hunter moved passed his envy and did as was commanded. Ryan positioned the cabinet appropriately for removal on the hand truck and headed toward the hidden exit.

It took the two men an hour to move and load the cabinets into the rented truck parked on the edge of the driveway closest to the backyard patio. Once done, Hunter and Ryan sat on the back bumper to rest for a few minutes.

The warmer temperature coupled with the strenuous task caused the men to break out into a sweat. Ryan used his arm to wipe the perspiration from his forehead. Hunter stood to try and work the kinks from his back, deciding this passed as a workout so he could skip the gym for today.

Ryan hopped off the bumper and handed the keys to the Mercedes to Hunter.

"I will drive the truck back to the city so you can ride in the style you are accustomed to," Ryan teased.

"As it should be given you are my subordinate," Hunter joked.

Ryan ignored Hunter. "Let me do one more pass through the house to make sure it is secured. After we unload the truck, I'll need to drop it off at the satellite location down the street from our office."

Hunter started the car to cool the inside after sitting in the sun for the last several hours while Ryan sprinted inside the house. Putting on his Oakley sunglasses, Hunter gazed at the expansive estate sitting silently in front of him, trying to wash away the unwanted memories.

A gentle breeze ruffled Hunter's hair and rustled the leaves on the trees surrounding him. Hunter could hear a pair of blue jays holding an intense conversation in the distance. A chipmunk scurried through the grass, trying to evade any predators that might be lurking in the shadows.

"Enjoying nature?" Ryan asked when he reappeared next to Hunter.

"I always thought it was so tranquil here. Almost boring."

"And now?"

"Now the memories have been scarred."

"All your memories aren't bad ones. Don't forget Hardwicke is where you met your lovely bride," Ryan reminded Hunter.

"Very true. Emma has always been the silver lining to any storm clouds."

"We should hit the road so we can get back to the office before Emma notices you left the city limits."

Ryan and Hunter entered their respective vehicles and began driving up the long driveway to the main road, with Ryan taking the lead. Hunter afforded himself one last glance at the estate in the rearview mirror as the gates closed behind him.

CHAPTER 18

The setting sun caused the buildings on the horizon to glow like a wildfire as the two vehicles approached Boston. Ryan and Hunter pulled into the Ares Logan garage and their usual parking spots. Hunter noticed they had made it back to the city in decent time when he exited the car. Traffic had been unusually light, given it was the afternoon rush hour.

"That was an oddly quick drive back here," Ryan commented as he got out of the car and stretched his arms above his head.

"I know. Very unexpected but very welcome." Hunter eyed the box truck parked next to him. "Where would you suggest we put the files and plants for safekeeping?"

"How about we lock them in my office? I can start combing through them in the morning," Ryan answered with a yawn and glanced around the garage.

"What are you looking for?" Hunter allowed his eyes to wander.

"Sorry. Old habits," Ryan commented, still unsure about the building's secureness given the recent breach.

Hunter let a yawn escape. "Okay. Let's do as you suggested."

"Hunter, why don't you head home? I can get a couple guys from my team to help. Anyhow, what message would it send if the boss was seen doing manual labor?" Ryan laughed and gently clapped his hand on Hunter's shoulder.

"Good idea. But then again, that is why I pay you a handsome salary."

"I think I should renegotiate," Ryan said with a smirk.

"No one else would put up with your antics, Ryan."

"You never know. Anyway, get out of here and go home to your beautiful wife."

Hunter thanked Ryan and hopped into his car for the ten-minute drive home. During the short excursion, Hunter would need the time to convince himself it was the right decision to deceive Emma about his whereabouts today.

Ryan watched Hunter exit the garage. He then made a call to kick off the task of moving the contents of the rental truck he was leaning against. Ryan predicted the odds of the files holding the map to the pharmaceutical treasure were probably about fifty percent. Philip Logan's meticulousness came to mind, providing Ryan with the slightest glimmer of hope.

Before Ryan could contemplate the odds any further, two of his trusted security associates exited the elevator. Ryan knew he never had to explain anything to either of them. They would take orders, without asking any questions, and never divulge what they saw or heard.

Both men, standing six feet tall with rock-solid frames, strode over to Ryan and the truck.

"Hey, fellas. I hope I didn't take you away from anything important."

"Nothing that couldn't be put off for a little while, sir," replied the blond one on behalf of both men.

"Thank you both for helping me. I know it's not in your job description."

"Of course, sir. We are always happy to help," responded the brown-haired man. "Just let us know what you need done."

After hiring both men almost two years ago, Ryan tried to break them from calling him "sir" without any luck. Both men informed Ryan this was a sign of respect they had learned in the military. The blond man was a Navy SEAL, and the brown-haired man was an Army Ranger. Both had served in their respective branches for twenty years but were too young to completely retire. Ryan hired them for his special security team—essentially, ghosts to the rest of the company, always behind the scenes.

Ryan opened the back of the truck to reveal the contents to his two employees.

"I need to move these file cabinets to my office. We can use the hand truck, but they are a bit awkward, so it might help to have both of you bring one at a time."

The men nodded and went to work without ever asking what was in the file cabinets or where they came from. Ryan stood watch over the truck, so they did not have to lock and unlock it with each load. In a matter of thirty minutes, the file cabinets were unloaded from the truck and secured in Ryan's office. The only things remaining were the garbage bags containing the remnants of the plants, which Ryan could handle himself.

The men returned the empty hand truck to Ryan and headed back to the security office to finish their work for the day. Gently stacking each bag with the plant trays on top of one another, Ryan placed them on the ground next to the rental truck. He locked everything up for the night in preparation for returning the truck in the morning.

Unable to help himself, Ryan scoured the garage again for anything out of place. Sounds of cars leaving the garage echoed through the facility. The smell of exhaust permeated through Ryan's nostrils. And no one was in Ryan's sight line, allowing him to breathe a little easier.

Carefully carrying the dead plant remains, Ryan

opted to use the elevator to head down one floor to his office instead of using the stairs as he normally did. Ryan knew he would never live it down if he tripped down the stairs and ended up covered in dirt from the plant trays.

Staring at the closed office door in front of him, Ryan strategically balanced the trays in one arm and opened the office door with his free hand. He kicked the door shut behind him and placed the bags with the trays on the conference table. The file cabinets were lined up in a row behind the table. Ryan had numbered each file cabinet with a permanent marker in correlation to the order in their clever hiding spot before he and Hunter left Hardwicke. He did the same with the bags containing the plants to ensure their analysis would not be impacted.

Along with his private safe, Ryan had also installed an elaborate locking mechanism on the door to his office. Since there were no windows, the door was the primary way in or out. Before leaving for the evening, Ryan went through the usual security routine to prevent prying eyes from seeing the contents of his office during the night. Feeling satisfied the files and plants were safe, Ryan headed to his car to make the short drive home to what he hoped was an empty apartment.

After dinner and some mindless TV, Ryan decided to try to get some much-needed rest. Sleep had been something of a commodity these days, and Ryan was grateful for his past training, which allowed him to stay awake longer than most humans.

Ryan confirmed the alarm system was turned on, the door deadbolted, and he was still the only person in the dwelling. Still unnerved by Sue's visit, Ryan pulled back the sheets and looked under the bed. He still had visions of being killed in his sleep by some sort of venomous creature, courtesy of his unwanted guest.

After tossing and turning for several hours with only intermittent sleep, Ryan finally succumbed to a deep slumber. His dreams carried him to the depths of the Amazon rainforest.

The humidity clung to him like a second skin.

Fluffy white clouds floated above like they were traveling down a lazy river.

A symphony of wildlife sounds saturated the air.

Sunlight cascaded from the heavens above through a small opening in the tree cover, revealing a picturesque waterfall spilling its contents into the river below. Walking along the edge of the crystal-clear river, Ryan slowly walked toward the waterfall, trying to consume all his eyes were seeing.

This untouched world was painted with different shades of green in every direction.

The air was thick and smelled of damp vegetation.

Ryan walked at a snail's pace, trying not to slip on the moss-covered rocks dotting the water's edge.

As he crept closer, the spray from the waterfall gently caressed his face. Palm trees created a natural picture frame surrounding the water. Behind the water cascading into the pool below, Ryan thought he caught a glimpse of a cavern.

Curiosity drew Ryan even closer to the edge of the water. He treaded lightly across the rocks, which provided a bridge to the large pool before him. Some unknown force gently propelled Ryan forward in this quest. When he reached the final rock, Ryan slid into the cool water. Once submerged, he could feel the force from the water above.

Wiping water droplets from his eyes when he resurfaced, Ryan focused on the concealed secrets behind the wall of liquid in front of him. Swimming under the plummeting water almost forced Ryan deeper below. Using all his strength, he found himself in the underbelly of the waterfall. Stopping to catch his breath, Ryan held on to the ledge in front of him. Hoisting himself up, he landed in several inches of mud that acted like cement on his hands and knees.

Panic rose inside Ryan as he saw what looked like snakes reaching out from the depths of the water. Before he could break free of the mud, vines wrapped around every part of his body and began to pull him back into the pool below. Prior to being completely submerged, Ryan gasped at what was hidden at the edge of darkness. Thousands of bright pink plants appeared like a carpet in the cavern. Before he could examine the plants further, he was completely submerged in the deep depths of the reservoir.

Ryan abruptly sat up in bed, drenched in sweat and gasping for air. He flung the damp sheet off him and sat on the side of the bed, trying to catch his breath. With his heart racing, Ryan gulped in as much air as he could. Being in some of the most precarious situations during his previous career, Ryan was lucky to never experience night terrors like some of his colleagues. Although he didn't really know what would constitute a night terror, at this moment Ryan believed he had a better understanding.

The clock on the nightstand showed it was a little after two a.m. Ryan was wobbly when he stood up and noticed his lungs still burned. He wondered how the physical effects of a dream could be that real. Without turning on any lights, Ryan gingerly made his way to the living room.

Sitting on the couch in only his underwear, Ryan tried to remember all he could from his intense dream. Logically, Ryan understood dreams brought out thoughts from his subconscious mind and the events of the day clearly fueled his imagination.

Ryan had never been to the Amazon in all his travels. He made the mental note to conduct some internet research to see how accurate his dream was. Ryan surmised some of his visualizations were memories from watching *National Geographic* documentaries about lost cities and tribes in the Amazon.

Knowing he would never get back to sleep, and part of him not wanting to, Ryan decided to lay on the couch until he felt somewhat normal again. Staring at the ceiling, almost afraid to close his eyes, Ryan's mind drifted away from the Amazon and focused on Sue.

The open questions plagued Ryan about Sue's actual mission and how he fit into her and her employer's plans. Soon Ryan gravitated toward the more sensuous side of Sue as he drifted off to sleep. The smell of her distinctive perfume, her expertly toned body, and how her lips brushed against his.

CHAPTER 19

The faint sound of Ryan's alarm in the bedroom teased him awake. Sitting up on the couch, Ryan rubbed his bloodshot eyes and ran his hands through his hair. In one night, he went from the treacherous Amazon jungle to the sensuous Sue in what seemed like a matter of minutes in dreamland.

Ryan went straight into the shower, bypassing his typical workout routine. Opting for a lukewarm shower, he was in and out within ten minutes. Admittedly, the shower reminded Ryan of the waterfall that almost drowned him in his dream, which helped speed up the process.

Thankfully, the drive to work was uneventful, with light traffic during the early hour causing Ryan to arrive in record time. Choosing to use the elevator down to his fortress of solitude, Ryan caught a glimpse of the dark circles neatly residing under his eyes in the reflection on the stainless-steel doors. Rolling his eyes at himself, Ryan stepped into the elevator to begin the daunting task of sorting through four file cabinets' worth of information. Ryan prayed the tedious process would lead them down the right path of making the cancer-prevention drug a reality.

Around eight a.m., Hunter meandered into Ryan's office to find him surrounded by numerous piles of colored file folders. Deep in thought, Ryan didn't notice Hunter until he was directly beside him, startling Ryan.

"A little jumpy this morning, Ryan?" Hunter inquired.

"Geez. Are you trying to give me a heart attack?" Ryan clutched his heart for dramatic effect.

"Just thought I would pay my buddy an early morning visit to make sure he's earning his keep."

"Ha. Ha. There is a lot to go through in these files. I have only just begun trying to find some semblance of logic. And even then, I'm not sure if *my* logic is accurate," Ryan admitted, feeling exasperated.

Hunter looked Ryan up and down before asking, "How long have you been here? You didn't sleep here, did you?"

"I may look a bit disheveled this morning, but no, I did not sleep here. I came in around six a.m. Rough night sleeping."

"I slept like a baby, for the record."

"Well, I don't have a beautiful wife to share my bed with."

"Whose fault is that?" Hunter countered.

"Okay, we are getting off-topic," Ryan said impatiently.

"What topic are we supposed to be talking about?"

"Oh my God, you are in a mood this morning, Hunter."

"Just having a little fun with you, Ryan. What have you found out so far?" Hunter asked seriously.

"I definitely think these folders, like with the ones you found at Craig Sharpeton's house, are in chronological order. They are all dated and appear to tell a story. What the exact narrative is, I don't know yet."

Hunter peered at the colorful array of folders on the conference table in front of him.

"Are these just from the first cabinet?" Hunter questioned, astonished.

"Yes. My plan is to go in the order we found the cabinets to try to see what I can piece together. Although a lot of this might as well be in Greek. My hope is we can at least get some time frame and locations."

"Alright. I will leave you to it. Call me if you need anything," Hunter responded as he made his way to the door.

"Sure thing," Ryan answered, giving Hunter a thumbs-up.

Hunter disappeared into the elevator, leaving

Ryan on his own to examine the mountains of paper in front of him—files that potentially held a clue about this journey.

Ryan decided to take a short break to deliver the plants to his security crew at the research lab who would then hand deliver them to Dr. McGrady's team. To kill two birds with one stone, Ryan had decided to use the rental truck for this errand before returning it to the satellite location down the street from his office. Ryan briskly walked back to the office to continue attempting to decipher the notes from what he considered a madman.

Several more hours passed before Ryan made his cursory way through the final drawer in the first cabinet. From what he could tell, all the files were dated between twelve and fifteen years ago. The timeline roughly coincided with when Hunter indicated Philip first began to be interested in the Amazon.

It appeared Philip had sanctioned five expeditions into the Amazon during those early years in search of any botanicals his company could profit from developing. The first few trips were purely fact-finding missions based on the notes Ryan was able to decipher. Although cryptic, the notes were not coded. They were more of a catalog, with dates, rough coordinates, and vague descriptions of what was found.

A low rumble escaped from Ryan's stomach, signaling his lack of nourishment. He made a quick trip upstairs to the cafeteria to grab a sandwich. With a hot, shaved pastrami and spicy brown mustard on rye in hand, Ryan went back to his unusually cluttered office.

Before taking a bite of his mouthwatering sandwich, he decided to text his analyst. Ryan attached images of the pertinent files to see if she could create a map of the locations Philip had visited, up to this point, in the Amazon. Satisfied this chore was delegated, Ryan vigorously dove into the sandwich.

Within thirty minutes, Ryan's phone chimed, signaling he had an email. Wiping mustard and grease from the corner of his mouth and hands, he opened the email attachment from his analyst. The image on the screen showed a topographical map of the Amazon. There were several areas near the Columbia and Venezuela borders highlighted in yellow, with dates corresponding to the ones Ryan had provided.

Leaning back in his chair, Ryan stared at the map for another fifteen minutes. A hypothesis started to form in the depths of his brain. Ryan would either prove or disprove this theory once he reviewed the contents of the other cabinets. Philip Logan was the most methodical and calculated person Ryan had encountered in a long time. Given what he knew about Philip's personality, Ryan believed he was on the right track with his assumptions up to now.

Needing to take a mental break, Ryan punched the elevator button to bring him to the top floor of the building. When the doors opened, Hunter's assistant was conspicuously not at her usual guard station outside his office. Ryan said a silent "thank you" to the heavens for not being subjected to the barrage of questions he usually encountered.

Opening the door, Ryan sauntered into the office to find Hunter staring out the window at the calm Atlantic Ocean. Ryan stood there for a moment, wondering which of their numerous problems consumed Hunter.

"Anything interesting on the horizon?" Ryan queried.

Hunter turned to look at Ryan, not realizing his sanctuary had been infiltrated. "And to what do I owe the pleasure this afternoon?"

"I needed to take a break from inhaling dust from those file cabinets. I thought I was going to have some sort of respiratory ailment if I stayed down there much longer." Ryan coughed for effect.

"As I keep telling you, this is why I pay you handsomely. You get to do the dirty work, and I get to sit up here in my kingdom." Hunter waved his hands, showcasing his large office.

"Yes. And as I have stated repeatedly, we may need to renegotiate my salary." Ryan plopped down on the chocolate-brown leather couch in the corner of Hunter's office.

Wicked Nemesis of the Hunted   189

Hunter slowly walked to one of the matching leather chairs next to the sofa and sat down.

"Are you planning on keeping me in suspense?"

"Actually, I think I found something. I had my analyst start pinpointing the locations I was able to identify so far on a map. A picture is starting to emerge, but I need to keep looking at the rest of the files to see if I'm correct."

Hunter tilted his head and raised an eyebrow in Ryan's direction, with his curiosity stimulated.

"We know Philip was crazy-detailed about every aspect of his life."

Hunter nodded in agreement, allowing Ryan to continue.

"These files look like they are in sequence of dates. The first cabinet was from roughly twelve-to-fifteen years ago."

Hunter interjected, "Which is about the time we know my father became obsessed with exploring the Amazon."

"Yes! The next cabinet looks like it is from eight-to-ten years ago, so far."

"And?"

"*And* my guess is the other two cabinets will be similar from a date perspective. Notes from every few years up to about one to two years ago based on the condition of the plants we found."

Hunter stood up and began to walk back and forth.

"Ryan, this is all remarkably interesting, but what does it mean? My father spent years searching the Amazon. Great! We have solved the mystery," Hunter stated, annoyed.

"Hunter, think about what I just told you about the dates." Ryan pretended to pick a hangnail, waiting patiently for his response.

Hunter suddenly stopped and stared at Ryan.

"Holy shit! My father had already disappeared by the time the notes in the other three cabinets were created. They can't be from my father!"

Hunter had to sit down before he literally fell over.

"Exactly! And it begs the question—who the hell made these files and notes if it wasn't your father?"

The two men sat in uncomfortable silence as they pondered the repercussions of what Ryan discovered.

Ryan was the first to stand up and head to the door. Turning back to look at his best friend, he wondered how much more deception and secrets Hunter could handle.

"Hunter, there have been so many twists and turns since we began this journey. We don't need to keep pushing ahead. We can stop any time you want to."

Hunter did not respond and continued to sit quietly staring at the wall while Ryan closed the office door and waited for the elevator.

Once Hunter was alone with this latest information, he put his head in his hands. Swirling with crazy ideas, Hunter felt like he was on a runaway roller-coaster ride he was not allowed to get off.

How did the more recent files get into the basement of his family's estate?

Why did the handwriting look like his father's?

What rabbit hole was this leading all of them down?

And the big question—was Philip Logan actually dead?

Knowing he would not receive answers to any of these new questions now haunting him, Hunter packed up his belongings and decided to head home earlier than usual. One thing always managed to put his life into perspective—Emma. Although he had made the conscious decision to not reveal these recent findings to her, Emma still unknowingly found ways to soothe his conflicted soul.

CHAPTER 20

Hunter chose to take Emma to Mario's Ristorante for dinner. Emma was overjoyed at the thought of indulging in not only incredible Italian food but also spending time with her overworked husband. Luckily, Hunter had a standing reservation at Mario's as there was a line out the door with at least an hour's wait to get seated without reservations.

Memories of their intimate wedding reception at the restaurant popped into the couple's minds while Emma and Hunter made their way to their usual table in the corner. Within minutes, a bottle of their favorite Chianti was placed in front of them. Just as quickly, Kelly began pouring two glasses of the striking red liquid.

"Kelly, how are you?" Emma asked with genuine interest.

"Hi Emma, Hunter. I am doing well, although we have been crazy busy lately. I can't catch my breath!"

"We noticed the line out the door. Glad to see business is booming," Hunter commented.

Kelly spotted more people trying to make their way inside.

"Give me a few minutes. I need to grab Anna so she can herd the cats." Kelly sprinted like an Olympic medalist to the kitchen and then back to the entrance to provide the latest updates on wait times.

Hunter and Emma raised their glasses in unison and said "Salute!" before taking their first sip.

Once Emma gently placed her glass back on the table, Hunter reached over to hold her hand. Although Emma was slightly startled by the gesture, she embraced the human contact as she looked profoundly into Hunter's intense blue eyes.

"Hunter, you have seemed preoccupied lately. I don't want to pry. It just seems more than the usual work stuff. And I cannot help but worry about you," Emma commented, lovingly.

Hunter sighed before responding, still struggling with keeping the truth from Emma. This wasn't how Hunter wanted to start off his marriage and he wondered if this was how his parents' marriage began to unravel.

"I know. And I am sorry, love. Everything is fine. We are trying to do a few acquisitions that aren't exactly going as planned. It's nothing to worry about." Hunter paused, contemplating coming clean with Emma. "I appreciate you worrying about me. It warms my heart, knowing I can always count on you." Hunter gently kissed Emma's hand.

Before Emma could respond, Kelly flew back to their table to take their order, and the rest of their dinner conversation turned to the usual things couples discuss. Once they cleaned their plates, Emma and Hunter sat back in their chairs, contemplating if they had room for dessert. Deciding dessert is always a promising idea, the couple ordered Limoncello cake to enjoy with the remainder of their wine.

Mario, pleased with his dessert creation, delivered the cake personally to his favorite patrons.

"*Godere dolce!*" Mario exclaimed, before vanishing to the kitchen to continue supervising the evening's food preparations.

While Hunter and Emma enjoyed a carefree evening, Ryan opted to stay in to relax. Just as he was cracking open a Guinness, there was a knock at his door. Instinctively, Ryan grabbed his Glock from its hiding place before peering out the peephole. He felt relieved when he saw who his unexpected visitor was.

Unlocking and opening the door, Ryan greeted his visitor.

"No hot date tonight, so you decided to pop in to see me?"

Making his way to Ryan's kitchen to deposit the twelve-pack of Guinness into the refrigerator, Frank replied, "I figured you may need some protection from unwanted visitors. Plus, you have a better TV than I do to watch the Bruins game."

Ryan laughed. "I knew it had to be more than my sparkling personality that brought you over here."

Grabbing a beer and settling in on the couch, Frank quickly took control of the remote to watch the Bruins and Montreal Canadiens game.

"Anything new on the Greg Smythe front?" Frank asked, before taking a long swig of his cold beer.

"The usual. The more we learn the more we don't know."

"That is cryptic even for you, Ryan."

"Haven't found any new info on our friend Greg. However, we did find some files we assumed were from Philip Logan, hidden in a secret room in the basement of the Logan Estate."

"A secret room? Guessing it's a safe assumption the files are Philip's." Frank asked, thoroughly confused.

"Yes. Long story short, there was a hidden door in Philip's home office leading down to a perfectly preserved basement room full of files. One catch—the dates on the files are suspect. The majority were dated *after* Philip disappeared." Ryan left out the part about the dead plants, although not sure why.

"Okay, that is beyond baffling. What are you thinking, Ryan?"

Frank lowered the volume so he could concentrate on what Ryan had to say.

"Honestly, man, I just don't know."

Frank pushed. "Come on, Ryan. I know you better than you know yourself. You have an idea rattling around in that skull of yours."

Ryan went to the kitchen to grab two more beers and give himself time to decide how much he should divulge to Frank.

Strolling back into the living room, Ryan explained, "Well, one obvious conclusion would be the dearly departed Philip Logan isn't all that departed."

"That is one clear option but how could that even be possible? I mean, was he living in this subterranean hideaway all these years, and no one noticed him?" Frank questioned in disbelief.

Ryan chuckled as he set the two beer bottles on the coffee table. "Hey, it would not surprise me with this sadistic bastard. He was one slippery asshole. My gut tells me it is something else, though."

"His body was never found with the plane crash, correct?" Frank recalled from the news coverage at the time.

"You got it. There are all these neon flashing arrows pointing us in this direction, but I just don't quite buy into it. There is something I'm missing. I just haven't figured out what it is yet." Ryan slouched back on the couch and inhaled half his beer.

Frank contemplated what Ryan divulged and admitted to himself this was an unexpected turn of events, to say the least.

"Alright, let's table the 'Philip rose from the dead' theory for now. What else you got?" Frank asked, intrigued.

"Philip had…or has…a partner." Ryan let this idea hang in the air for a moment before continuing, "Someone else not only knew about the cancer plants but helped Philip with his little venture both in life and death."

"If what you said is true, I wonder if this partner is still around and continuing the work?" Frank nudged Ryan in the direction neither wanted to go.

"If you're hinting at this being the connection with Sue, I don't know. It's plausible, I guess. Hell, anything is conceivable with that vixen on a good day. But as you told me a while ago, it always comes back to the money trail. And so far, there is absolutely no trail. Zilch!" Ryan swallowed his beer hard.

Frank opened his next beer and leaned back on the sofa, casually glancing at the Bruins game.

"We both know Sue is a master at playing hide and seek." Frank noticed Ryan winced. "And there aren't any other long-lost relatives in the Logan clan?"

Ryan stared at the TV before answering. "That is a good question. We never thought Hunter had a half-sister, so who-the-fuck knows. The Logan family tree is a mystery in itself. Which, by the way, I warned Hunter about if we continued to pursue this. He may not like what else we uncover."

Inconspicuously, Frank's eyes watched the Bruins sink the puck into the net for another goal in the preseason game.

"The thing bothering me is Hunter was so sure the notes in those files were in his father's hand-writing." Ryan held up his hand when Frank tried to interject. "I know handwriting can be forged, but why would someone do that? I mean this was a room hidden in the depths of the Logan house that we just uncovered. Would someone from five or seven years ago know enough to anticipate need-ing to disguise the handwriting? And, trust me, no one had been in that room for a few years at least."

"Excellent questions, my friend. You could have some of our old pals do a handwriting analysis."

Ryan recoiled at the thought of getting in deeper than he already was with their former employer. "I am not ready to do that yet."

"Categorically, a lot to think about. My advice—sleep on it for now and see what pops the more you investigate those files. Let them guide you."

"Aren't you just full of divine wisdom tonight?" Ryan responded, mockingly.

"Now, can we get back to the hockey game? You have already made me miss the entire first period."

"I am so sorry I burdened you with my troubles, considering I didn't invite you over to watch the game." Ryan managed to chuckle.

For the rest of the game, Ryan and Frank talked about player statistics and the chances of the Bruins winning the Stanley Cup. After the game ended, Frank gathered his empty beer bottles and disposed of them in the recycle bin in the kitchen.

Before departing, Frank reminded Ryan, "As I keep telling you, watch your back. There is some strange juju going on with the Logan family, and I don't want you to get sucked into their quicksand."

"*Juju?* I can't totally disagree with you. Although I never thought Hunter's family was something out of a suspense movie."

Once Frank closed the door, Ryan immediately enabled the alarm system and deadbolt. The conversation with Frank had him on edge. After last night's incredible dreams, Ryan did not need to feel any more trepidation about going to sleep tonight. His only saving grace might be the combination of several beers and the fact his body was completely exhausted.

Ryan slid into much needed sleep quickly and commenced the repeat journey into the Amazon jungle. The setting was the same as the previous night—a cascading waterfall, thick vegetation, and a mysterious cavern holding secrets of the past. Unlike the prior night, Ryan was not attacked by deadly vines trying to drown him.

Instead, he was able to enter the cavern, which was now completely dry versus the thick mud in his last nighttime adventure there. Ryan drew in a breath and exhaled slowly as his eyes darted around the shadowy space. Inching his way further into the darkness, a faint light glowed ahead of him.

Cautiously advancing toward the light, Ryan examined the tunnel. To his novice eye, the cave looked like it was naturally occurring versus something manufactured. Water trickled down grooves in the rock walls, forming small stalagmites that played off the light in front of him. As he moved further down the tunnel, the light became brighter until it almost hurt his eyes.

In front of him was a field of bright pink plants for as far as he could see. Looking up, Ryan noticed sunlight was beaming down on the plants from an opening in the cavern. Crimson topaz hummingbirds fluttered around him while he took in the view. The air no longer smelled musty or damp—it felt alive and pure. A gentle breeze from above rumpled Ryan's hair.

Soaking in the rays of sunlight, a whisper was carried by the breeze.

"Secrets are hidden close."

CHAPTER 21

———

Ryan's eyes slowly blinked open. Looking around, he was relieved to be safely tucked in his bed. Dawn began to encompass the city. He rubbed his eyes to make sure he still wasn't dreaming. Throwing the covers off to the side, Ryan sat on the edge of the bed, still trying to get his bearings.

"At least the damn rainforest didn't try to drown me this time," he said to an empty bedroom.

Trying to stick to his normal routine, Ryan threw on his running clothes and headed out the door. Given he was more than likely being watched at any given time by unknown friends or foes, he took a completely different route. Although a new path, Ryan still managed to end up at Kerns for much-needed coffee.

Back in his apartment, Ryan couldn't shake the haunting message in his dream. Logically, he knew these dreams were just part of his mind being in overdrive for months. But Ryan still felt the two nights of Amazon dreams meant something—especially since they happened after finding Philip's files. He just couldn't put his finger on it.

The hot shower did little to jiggle free the piece of the puzzle Ryan felt would put everything else into perspective on this journey. Dressed in only a towel, he rummaged through his closet to find clean clothes.

"Ryan, I might suggest you do some laundry. Your closet is looking rather dismal even for you," a sultry voice echoed through the apartment.

Almost jumping out of his skin, Ryan stormed into the living room to find Sue, once again, making herself at home on his couch.

"Well, I must say this is a pleasant surprise, Ryan. That is an outfit I most *definitely* approve of," Sue commented as she eyed Ryan like a lioness examining her prey.

"What the fuck, Sue? How is it you keep getting in here?" Ryan did not bother to hide his anger.

"My. My. A bit testy, aren't we?" Sue gracefully left the couch and stood nearly nose to nose in front of Ryan.

Their bodies were so close that each of them could almost feel the other's heartbeat.

"I will ask you one more time, Sue, how did you get in here?" Ryan demanded through gritted teeth.

"The same way I always do, Ryan. Now, shall we dispense with all this nonsense and get down to business?"

Sue let her index finger gently glide down Ryan's chest to the top of his towel. Ryan's skin involuntarily tingled at Sue's touch. The sensation rippled through his body. His normally passive face flashed a hint of pink in his cheeks.

Knowing the effect she had on Ryan, Sue also knew it would go one of two ways: Ryan would push her away or give in to the burning desire that still consumed both of them. Ryan chose the first option and moved Sue's hand away before he was past the point of no return.

Escaping into his bedroom, he forcibly slammed the door shut behind him, causing the apartment to shudder. Rummaging through his drawers, he found a clean pair of running shorts and a T-shirt. Feeling less exposed, Ryan strode back to the living room to find Sue sitting in what was becoming her spot on the couch.

"You're still here? Guess you can't take a hint," Ryan said, barely looking in Sue's direction on his way to the kitchen to grab a bottle of water.

"Ryan, you can try to drive me away all you want, but you know as well as I do there is an unbreakable bond between us. The more you fight it, the more it intensifies."

"You are seriously delusional."

"And the more you protest tells me how right I am." Sue crossed her long legs for effect.

"What do you want?" Ryan asked curtly, with

flaring nostrils.

"Can't I just stop by to see how a close friend is doing?"

"No."

"Okay. How about I missed you?"

"Try again," Ryan said, bluntly.

"The part about missing you is true. Whether you believe it or not. Do you dream about me, Ryan? Because I dream of you…frequently. I miss your body intertwined with mine. I miss our hearts synchronized as one. Do you hate me so much that you have erased all memories of me in your mind?" Sue inquired with soft emphasis.

Ryan knew he would not be able to continue this conversation much longer before he lost all control.

"Sue, you have ten seconds to tell me what the fuck you want, or I will remove you from this apartment."

Ryan started toward Sue before he forced himself to calm down.

This was the woman he was willing to die for years ago.

The woman he had fallen in love with before she betrayed him.

The woman he contemplated spending the rest of his life with until she shredded his heart into tiny pieces.

"No need to get all huffy, Ryan. I just came to check on your progress with our little project."

"I did not realize *we* had a little project, Sue," Ryan replied through a clenched jaw.

"Being coy does not suit you, Ryan. I do know you spoke with our former handler the other day." Sue waited to gauge Ryan's reaction. When she didn't see one, she continued. "It was very brave of you to join forces with the evil-doers, as you had once referred to them," she commented with an air of arrogance.

"My alliances are none of your concern, Sue. Since you are on a fact-finding mission and do not have anything to provide me in return, I will escort you to the door."

Ryan grabbed Sue by the wrist and pulled her off the couch. Slightly off-balance from Ryan's brute force, Sue instinctively grabbed onto Ryan's shoulders so she didn't hit the ground. At that moment, the memories came rushing back, and Ryan could not fight his urges any longer.

Grabbing at each other's clothing, throwing all garments haplessly around the living room, the pair fell to the area rug. For the next few hours, Ryan became reacquainted with Sue in a way he never thought would happen again. Sue did not disappoint in her enthusiasm as they succumbed on more than one occasion.

During the couple's last exploration, they decided to move to the couch. Breathless, Sue rested her head on Ryan's sweat-dampened chest. Ryan didn't think beyond the immediate moment as he caressed Sue's bare back with his fingertips.

CHAPTER 22

———

Formidable gray clouds announced the arrival of afternoon rain in Boston when the pair finally broke free of each other.

"That was certainly unexpected but completely worth it," Sue commented as she was gathering her clothes.

Ryan's eyes traveled up and down Sue while she was getting dressed. Heat, desire, and passion were never an issue for the pair. It was honesty and trust that extinguished the flame long ago, or so Ryan had thought. Sue threw Ryan's shorts and T-shirt in his direction, which he caught with one hand.

"I hope you know what happened here today does not change anything between us."

"Nice way to ruin the mood, Ryan," Sue replied flippantly.

"What happened today was just two people scratching an itch. Nothing more. Nothing less."

"Fine. Whatever you say. Although it sounds like you're trying to convince yourself and not me. I will follow your lead on this, Ryan," Sue responded as she pulled her sweater over her head.

"That will be the day that you follow anyone," Ryan mumbled while putting on his shorts.

"Unfortunately, you don't know me as well as you think you do."

Sue grabbed her purse from the ottoman and headed toward the door. Before leaving, she turned and kissed Ryan on the cheek.

"I very much look forward to our next encounter, Ryan."

Sue closed the door and waited for the elevator. Once tucked in the elevator with the doors closed, she exhaled while a tear gently slid down her face.

Still sitting on the couch, Ryan replayed the events of the day. He knew Sue was right about one thing—this was not just a casual encounter like others he had experienced. Their relationship had always been complicated at best. There was a reason rules were in place regarding fraternizing with teammates. It could mean the difference between life and death.

Ryan closed his eyes and remembered the first time he met Sue. One morning, he and Frank were informed they were going to be training a new female agent. When she walked into the conference room, Ryan felt immediately drawn to her. For the first few seconds, he and Sue gazed at each other like no one else was in the room. Frank broke the trance when he began introducing Sue to the team.

During the briefing for their upcoming mission, Sue purposely chose to sit next to Ryan. The close proximity electrified the pull between them. Although never touching, even accidentally, Ryan recognized Sue felt the same heat he did.

That night, Ryan did some research on his new teammate, which revealed her parents had died several years earlier and, besides some distant relatives, she was alone in the world. This wasn't anything out of the ordinary—it was almost a prerequisite for a job there. She had graduated from college with a degree in art history and, like many others, was recruited during a career day before graduation. Sue spoke several languages fluently including Arabic.

The next day, the team prepared for their overseas mission of gathering information about priceless artifacts being smuggled into the United States. Normally, this wasn't something Ryan's team would be involved in except there were suspected terrorist ties. It had now made sense to Ryan why Sue was selected, given her art history background.

From that point forward, a kinship formed. Ryan took Sue under his wing and became her protector in the field. Frank watched closely, noticing the warning signs. Ryan was heading down a dangerous path. It wasn't until several months after their initial encounter that Ryan's and Sue's relationship progressed past the forbidden gate.

When their latest job was completed in France, Ryan asked Sue to join him at the Louvre for a private tour. He knew Sue wouldn't be able to pass up the opportunity to enjoy the priceless art without other tourists. After their visit ended, the couple dined in one of the romantic restaurants on the River Seine. Ryan and Sue barely made it back to his hotel room, signaling the beginning of the end for the couple.

A year after that liaison, Sue betrayed Ryan to the point Frank wasn't sure if Ryan would completely recover from the emotionally deep scars. Shortly after the incident, Ryan decided to leave the agency and move to the private sector, working for the Logan conglomerate.

The wounds eventually healed, and Ryan settled into his new life—until now. Ryan silently vowed this time would be different. He knew the lengths Sue would go to in order to get what she wanted, something he was not prepared for previously but was fully aware of now. And Ryan knew he could beat her at her own game. The tables had been turned and he was now the one in control.

CHAPTER 23

Every time Ryan closed his eyes, flashes of Sue popped into his head. This continued off and on for the remainder of the night. Ryan's veracious tossing and turning made it look like he had been fighting to the death with a wild beast in bed.

Dawn illuminated the apartment, announcing the final day of the weekend had arrived. Ryan's plan for the day was to clean his apartment while watching whatever football games were on. Although cleaning was never at the top of his list of pleasant tasks, he had an overwhelming desire to disinfect the place from top to bottom.

Throwing a load of laundry into the washing machine, Ryan filled a bucket with warm, soapy water and scrubbed the bathroom and kitchen until they gleamed. Hearing a faint rumble in his stomach, Ryan looked at the clock on the wall in the kitchen and noticed it was time for lunch. Rummaging through the refrigerator, Ryan found sliced

American cheese. In a short time, he was sitting on the couch eating a grilled cheese sandwich.

After putting his dirty dishes in the dishwasher, Ryan found a can of disinfectant spray advertising a fresh-air scent. He made a beeline to the couch and sprayed every surface until he was almost choking from the mist in the air.

"Fresh air, my ass," Ryan commented aloud.

After the laundry was dried and folded, the cleaning supplies put back in their appropriate places, and the alarm system enabled, Ryan fell into the couch to mindlessly watch football. He was praying for a nail-biter Patriots' game to keep his mind from wandering down the path of carnal pleasures.

With his feet propped on the coffee table in front of him and a Guinness next to him on the end table, Ryan focused his attention on the television. A chime on his phone immediately caused him angst.

His mood changed when he saw the text was from Hunter inviting him to dinner at Mario's Ristorante at six p.m. Although he enjoyed spending time with his close friends, Ryan wasn't in the mood to socialize this evening. He sent Hunter a text politely declining the offer, with an excuse of having other plans.

Ryan knew Hunter would more than likely accept the excuse. It wasn't the first time Ryan had begged out of last-minute invitations. The truth of the matter was Ryan needed tonight to try to gain his composure. He had been out of the spy game for too long, making it hard for him to fool someone like Hunter. The last thing Ryan wanted was to have to try to explain the encounter with Sue.

A gentle knock on the door startled him. On the way to the door, Ryan detoured to his bedroom to get his firearm just in case. Looking through the peep-hole, he breathed heavily before unlocking the door.

"At least you knocked this time," Ryan said as he opened the door.

"I didn't want to intrude."

"That has never stopped you before."

Ryan headed back to the living room to claim his spot on the couch.

Sue hesitated for a second before following Ryan.

"Umm. Did you happen to find a gold bracelet here?" Sue casually looked around while standing at the edge of the kitchen.

"A gold bracelet? No. I haven't," Ryan replied, keeping his eyes squarely focused on the game.

"Would you mind if I looked on the floor and couch for it?" Sue asked, meekly.

Ryan sighed. "Fine. Make it quick," he replied, not hiding his annoyance.

Sue began scouring the floor including under the area rug. She could sense Ryan's impatience and eyes staring at her with every move she made.

"Do you mind if I look under the cushions?" Sue asked, standing in front of Ryan on the couch.

Ryan scowled and stood up. Both overturned the cushions until Sue squealed in his ear.

"What the hell?" Ryan snapped.

"Found it!" Sue exclaimed, with the delicate piece of gold craftsmanship dangling from her index finger.

Ryan couldn't help but notice the bright smile on Sue's face. It reminded him of Paris and watching her admiring the priceless works of art.

"Sorry, I didn't mean to scream like that. This is something especially important to me and it would pain me if I lost it. I will leave you to watch the football game."

Sue turned to leave, holding back tears.

"Wait," Ryan said against better judgment.

"Ryan, it is best if I just go. I didn't mean to disturb you," Sue responded shakily.

Ryan immediately picked up on her quivering voice and her need to vacate the premises quickly. This was different than her usual cat-and-mouse game. This was something more real and heartfelt. Part of Ryan didn't know if it was yet another trick by the temptress, but his senses told him this was something else.

Ryan's hand gently touched Sue's arm when she reached for the door handle.

"Please look at me."

"Ryan, I need to leave. Please just let me go," Sue declared through tears.

"If you won't look at me, at least listen to me," Ryan pleaded.

Sue let her hand drop from the door handle, but she didn't turn to face Ryan.

"I can see this is more than some random bracelet. *And* I can also tell you aren't playing some wicked game. Right now, you're desperately trying to control your breathing, which leads me to believe you are crying. You want to bolt out that door like a gazelle fleeing a lion."

Slowly, Sue turned to face him.

Ryan noticed a steady stream of tears trickling down her pristine face. Instead of her eyes looking bloodshot or puffy, the tears glistened, highlighting the brown color. Without hesitation, Ryan encircled Sue in his arms and the flood of emotion escaped Sue like a tidal wave.

Time passed slowly. Ryan wasn't sure how long they had been standing in the hallway nor was he sure what his next move was going to be. This was unfamiliar territory for him and completely unexpected. Ever since the betrayal, Ryan thought of Sue as being like the Tin Man in the *Wizard of Oz*—without a heart.

"Come on. Let's go sit down."

Ryan guided Sue to the couch. Once Sue was situated, he ran to the bathroom to get a box of tissues and handed them to her.

"Thank you," Sue whispered.

More time passed without either of them talking. Sue's head was nestled on Ryan's shoulder. He could still feel her trying to control her emotions and her body trembling.

Suddenly, Sue sat up and looked at Ryan.

"I can only imagine what you are thinking about me right now. All I can say is this isn't some calculated ploy to win your trust. I guess I just lost it for a bit."

"I believe you."

"You do?" Sue asked with skepticism.

"There are some things you can fake and some you can't. That amount of raw emotion is nearly impossible to fake. I won't pry. If you want to talk, I am willing to listen."

Sue inhaled a deep breath before responding. She replied softly, "The bracelet has a lot of sentimental value."

Ryan stayed silent.

"It was the bracelet my father gave my mother on their first wedding anniversary. My mother had given it to me."

Ryan was a little confused. "I thought your parents died when you were young."

"They did. In a car accident. The bracelet was left in my parents' safe deposit box with a note it was to be given to me on my sixteenth birthday."

Trying to put the pieces together, Ryan did not want to come across as interrogating her.

Sue smiled at Ryan. "I can see the wheels turning, Ryan. You are showing a great deal of restraint in not peppering me with questions."

"This goes against my nature, but I am trying to understand."

"I have always thought my parents' car accident was suspicious even though the police did a thorough investigation and found no evidence of foul play. Growing up, I never considered us wealthy. We had a nice house. My parents always took care of all my needs. Then came the accident and my world changed forever.

"How does a ten-year-old little girl recover from losing the only two people her world revolved around? My aunt and uncle were kind enough to become my guardians. They weren't able to have children of their own so, in some ways, it was a miracle for them."

Ryan focused all his attention on Sue's story. These details were never part of her agency file he had access to. He knew at a high level about the car accident and how Sue went to live with her mother's sister and husband.

Sue cleared her throat before continuing. "The years with my aunt and uncle were good ones. They took care of me like I was their own daughter. I never lacked love or attention. On my sixteenth birthday, after a grand party with all my friends and the neighbors, my aunt asked to see me in my bedroom. I thought something was wrong. I will never forget the look on her face when she handed me a small jewelry box. Inside was this bracelet."

Sue held it up for him to take a closer look. Ryan had to admit it was stunning, and the design was intricate and beautiful.

"My aunt told me it was in the safe deposit box with explicit instructions in their wills to be given to me on my sixteenth birthday if they had passed prior to it. She then told me the story of how my father had given it to my mother. My aunt remembered when my mother first showed the bracelet to her. My mother was giddy and grinning from ear to ear at the extraordinary gift."

Ryan was beginning to understand the more human side of Sue, which caught him by surprise.

"The bracelet is magnificent. I don't think I've ever seen a design like this in all my travels," Ryan admitted.

"I know what you mean. It's unique and original and handmade. And the perfect symbol of the love between my parents. They were remarkable people. Even at ten years old, I knew that."

Sue took a tissue to wipe the side of her eyes.

"If this is too much, you don't need to tell me anymore."

"It's fine. Besides my aunt and uncle, no one else has ever heard this story. And for the longest time, I kept the bracelet in a jewelry box. It wasn't until

Wicked Nemesis of the Hunted   219

recently that I started to wear it. For some reason, I needed to have something to help me feel close to my parents. Corny, huh?"

"Not at all. Having ties to your past isn't corny— it's human."

Sue cocked an eyebrow at Ryan.

"Okay. It is human for everyone but me," Ryan responded with a smile.

"When I couldn't find the bracelet, I panicked. I did not want to lose the last connection to my family. I am sorry I dumped all of this on you. That was not my intention," Sue expressed sincerely.

Ryan cupped Sue's face in his hands and stared into her brown eyes. "What's really going on, Sue?"

"What do you mean?" Sue asked, trying to dodge the question.

"I have never seen you emotional like this. In my experience, there is usually some sort of trigger to bring on a flood of emotions like this."

"Always the profiler, aren't you?" Sue wiggled out from Ryan's warm touch.

"It's a curse. As I said before, I'm not going to pry."

"I wish I could tell you the full story, Ryan. You don't know how much I yearn for that. It is too dangerous for both of us. I am doing my best and that might not be enough, to protect us. There are many things in my past I regret and wish I could change. I just need you to know decisions were made under duress to protect everyone I cared about. And the same holds true in the present."

Ryan had a quizzical look on his face when he responded. "I am not following you."

"I know. Just know that someday I hope to be able to tell you everything. Until that day, we will have to figure out a way to coexist in this tangled web in which we are caught."

Ryan stood up and rubbed the bristles on his chin, trying to absorb the events of the roller-coaster weekend with Sue. The couple went from hatred to carnal pleasures to raw emotion in less than forty-eight hours.

Sue approached Ryan cautiously. "I think I should go. Thank you for listening."

Ryan knew at that moment he was never going to let Sue out of his grasp again. The moments they just shared were more intimate than all their previous liaisons combined.

"Don't go. Stay the night. No expectations on my part. Just comfort."

This was a first for Ryan, and Sue knew it.

"I'm not sure if it is such a good idea, Ryan. You and I have never been the comforting types."

Ryan laughed, "Well, consider this a new beginning. We go slow and see where it leads."

Sue caressed Ryan's cheek with her hand and let her lips gently kiss Ryan's.

Not knowing where this was going to lead them,

Ryan decided to start by making dinner, with Sue watching him intently. He smiled to himself about how thankful he was he declined Hunter's invitation for dinner this evening.

Luckily, Ryan had a roasted chicken in the refrigerator he only needed to reheat. Adding a mixed medley of frozen vegetables and baked potatoes, in an hour they were dining on a filling meal Ryan was proud of.

Sue cautiously took a bite of each item from the plate that had been placed in front of her.

"Who knew you could cook? This is delicious, Ryan," Sue acknowledged, with a hint of amazement in her voice.

Ryan bowed in his chair at the kitchen island, trying not to fall off.

After their meal had been devoured, Ryan cleaned up the minimal mess he had made in the kitchen while Sue tried to relax on the couch. She had not taken her eyes off Ryan tending to his kitchen duties. Fear was rippling through her body at an almost uncontrollable pace. Every choice she had made since walking into their previous employer's office that first day led to this moment.

The insurmountable lies.

The devastation of walking away from love.

The quest to find answers.

Ryan broke Sue's runaway train of memories, "Everything alright?"

"Sorry. I was amused by how domesticated you have become." Sue tried to deflect from answering.

Sitting next to Sue on the couch, Ryan wrapped his arm around her shoulders. Based on her facial expression, he knew Sue was lying about the thoughts swimming in her brain. Ryan did not respond and only lightly kissed her temple.

The rest of the evening looked as if it was something out of a Hallmark Channel movie—Ryan and Sue snuggled on the couch watching a romantic comedy movie, with a bottle of Holloran Vineyards pinot noir and buttered popcorn.

After the movie ended, the couple wasn't exactly sure how to proceed. *This is like an awkward first date in junior high school*, Ryan thought to himself. He slowly sat up, partly because his arm had fallen asleep.

A wave of fear washed over Sue's face.

"Just need to move my arm. It's all tingly."

"Sorry," Sue replied.

"It isn't your fault. I was extremely comfortable," Ryan reassured her.

"I need to use the loo," Sue announced.

Ryan's chuckle was met with a questioning look from Sue. "You said 'loo' and it sounded very British of you. It was cute."

Sue relaxed a little but knew she had to remember not to make that mistake again. "Old habits."

While Sue was in the bathroom, Ryan's phone chimed with a text message.

Wicked Nemesis of the Hunted   223

"Just checking in to see if there are any new developments."

Ryan had a mild heart attack, thinking there was surveillance in his apartment, and scolded himself for being paranoid.

"Nothing new on this end," Ryan replied to Frank.

Another chime sounded a few seconds later. "Anything from our favorite stalker?"

Once again, Ryan replied, "Nope. All quiet."

Before any more texts populated at an imperfect time, Ryan shut off his phone. It scared him how easily he was able to lie to Frank, without even the slightest pang of guilt. The tricks of the spy world were slowly coming back to him. Something he did not relish.

Getting a little concerned about the amount of time Sue had been gone, Ryan ambled to his bedroom where he found her waiting for him. The dimly lit room provided the perfect backdrop to highlight her silky skin strategically positioned on top of the comforter. A sly smile formed when Sue noticed Ryan leaning against the door jamb, soaking in the view.

"Well, it took you long enough."

"As I said earlier, I didn't want to invade your space."

"This is me asking you to invade my space."

Within seconds Ryan was undressed and next to Sue. For the next several hours, the two bodies, once separated, were now intertwined as one without a beginning or an end.

CHAPTER 24

The couple's nocturnal activities continued into the early morning after a few breaks to regain their strength. Burning off all nervous energy from the day before, Ryan and Sue fell asleep in each other's arms, oblivious to the morning slipping into the afternoon of the holiday weekend until Ryan's stomach nudged him awake.

Rolling over and stretching, Ryan noticed the clock said noontime. He could not remember the last time he had slept half the day away. With a bright smile, he remembered every detail of why he had been in a state of utter exhaustion.

Careful not to wake Sue, who was still in dreamland, Ryan edged himself out of bed toward the kitchen. Panic rose inside him when he couldn't remember if he had any food for breakfast or, technically, lunch. Normally, on the weekends, he would grab a protein bar and call that a well-balanced breakfast.

Quietly rummaging through the refrigerator, Ryan found eggs not yet expired, some cheddar cheese, and a lonely pepper. Grabbing an apron from the drawer after noticing he was completely naked, Ryan got to work on making omelets with toast and coffee. Hunter had bought him a Keurig a couple of years ago for Christmas, and he kept a small supply of pods on hand for emergencies like this.

The aroma of eggs flowed into the bedroom, awakening Sue. Getting her bearings, she grinned when she remembered the evening filled with emotional and physical exploration. Reality hit Sue suddenly. Her job was to keep Ryan safe. Being emotionally involved was more than dangerous—it could be deadly. She made a deal with herself to allow herself this weekend, but under no circumstances could it happen again until the situation had been utterly resolved for the last time.

Grabbing one of Ryan's long-sleeved button-down shirts in the closet, Sue covered herself and tiptoed through the hallway to the kitchen. It was her turn to lean against the wall and admire the view.

"Will totally be giving this bed and breakfast a five-star review." Sue's sultry voice echoed through the kitchen.

Startled, Ryan turned to look at her. "You may want to hold off on your review until you taste the omelet. And I'm using the word 'omelet' loosely."

"I wasn't talking about the omelet," Sue commented as she stood next to Ryan and kissed him on the cheek.

Ryan almost dropped the omelet pan and laughed. Gently maneuvering Sue to her seat at the island, Ryan slid the omelet onto the plate he had already set up.

"Toast will be ready momentarily. I only have butter and no jelly. Hope that is alright."

"Ryan, you don't need to do this to impress me. I was impressed with you the first time you said 'hello' to me all those years ago," Sue responded earnestly.

Blushing, Ryan quickly made his own omelet, retrieved the darkened toast, and sat next to her. Neither spoke while enjoying their breakfast. Ryan's thoughts drifted to the realization this was what Hunter kept talking about. When you find the right person, your world is turned upside down in a good way.

Sue's thoughts focused on if she would be able to let Ryan go for the second time in her life, knowing it would more than likely be the final time.

Once the breakfast cleanup was completed, Ryan looked into Sue's big brown eyes, trying to search her soul for guidance.

"I have to say, I'm a bit of a fish out of water here. Not really sure what to do next. I honestly do not want you to leave, yet I get the distinct feeling this amazing weekend is ending. Am I wrong?"

Sue inhaled sharply. "Unfortunately, I need to leave to tend to a few errands demanding my attention. Please don't take that as my excuse to hightail it out of here." Sue cupped Ryan's face in her hands. "I truly want nothing more than to stay here and continue with our escapades."

Ryan pulled Sue in for a passionate kiss, leaving them both wanting more. Before the inevitable happened as it had throughout the weekend, Ryan pulled back.

"I understand. I won't be offended. I might cry a little bit that you're choosing the doldrum of errands over this," Ryan said while he waved his hand up and down his body.

Sue tried to not burst out laughing. "Thank you for understanding. I am going to grab a quick shower and get dressed."

"I could join you if you would like. Think of it as dessert after breakfast?" Ryan shouted in Sue's direction before she closed the bedroom door.

The lack of response and the shower running told Ryan all he needed to know. Sue was like a wounded animal, and Ryan needed to continue with caution. Wounded animals were sometimes the most dangerous of all creatures.

Within twenty minutes, Sue joined Ryan in the living room, completely dressed and refreshed. Ryan observed he still wasn't dressed in anything but the apron he had put on earlier.

Ryan chuckled. "Seems as if I am a bit underdressed."

Sashaying over to Ryan in only the way Sue could, she kissed him hard as though her life depended on it, and in some respects, it did.

Ryan walked Sue to the door and, before opening it, reminded her, "You know I am here for you. And I don't mean just for pleasure. If you need me, I will be there."

A slight smile formed, and Sue brushed her hand across Ryan's face before opening the door and disappearing into the elevator.

CHAPTER 25

Deciding he also needed a shower, Ryan quickly slid under the hot water and contemplated the meaning of the unanticipated and complicated past few days. The feeling Sue was holding back vital details had bothered him throughout their time together. This was different than their last mission together. It was something more personal and dangerous, Ryan postulated.

Wiping himself off and throwing on a pair of lounge pants paired with a long-sleeved Patriots T-shirt, Ryan elected to call Hunter to occupy his mind with other thoughts than those he was having.

"Hello, Ryan. To what do I owe this pleasure on an overcast afternoon?"

"It's overcast? Huh. I didn't even notice," Ryan unenthusiastically stated.

"That is a bit concerning. Are you ill?" Hunter asked with a hint of concern.

"No. Just haven't had a chance to look outside today yet."

"That is a bit unusual for even you, Ryan. Is there a specific reason you have been cooped up in your apartment?" Hunter questioned with a sly smile.

"If you are asking if there was a lady here this weekend to occupy my time, the answer is you will need to come over here to learn more."

Immediately Hunter sensed there was more to the story than just some dalliance with a random beauty Ryan had picked up.

"Give me about an hour. I must say—I am intrigued," Hunter responded.

"See you then, Hunter," Ryan confirmed and disconnected.

Ryan had an hour to decide how much he was going to recount to Hunter. If his intuition was correct, Sue was in trouble, and he might be the only person who could save her. Although there was still a tiny part of him thinking this might all be part of a rouse, and Sue was a pawn following orders.

Precisely forty-three minutes later, a knock at the door alerted Ryan his guest had arrived.

"Wow. You are even punctual on a long weekend. That must drive Emma crazy." Ryan greeted Hunter when he opened the door.

Hunter followed Ryan silently into the kitchen and unknowingly selected the same stool Sue occupied earlier.

"Now that I have left my beautiful and remarkable wife to come over here, this story had better be a good one." Hunter feigned annoyance.

Ryan poured two fingers of Angel's Envy bourbon into two glasses. Hunter swirled the rich, amber-colored liquid in the glass before taking a sip.

"I had a femme fatale visitor this weekend."

Hunter looked at Ryan, waiting for him to explain further.

"Do you remember when I told you about Frank and my last mission?"

"Yes. You were shot by your female comrade."

Ryan chuckled. "Correct. Well, this female comrade, as you put it, spent the weekend."

Hunter was not sure what Ryan was leading up to, so he stayed quiet, hoping he didn't come over only to hear about Ryan's nocturnal escapades. Hunter took another sip of his bourbon.

Ryan continued. "It was unexpected. I won't go into the details."

"And I appreciate that." Hunter noticed Ryan was struggling. "Ryan, let me ask you this. Do you think this woman is caught up in our little puzzle?"

Ryan swallowed hard. "My gut tells me she is involved in some capacity. I am not sure to what extent."

"And do you think it's wise to, shall we say, get involved with her?" Hunter tried to be delicate.

"Look, Hunter, I know better than anyone how dangerous it can be to get involved with a teammate or enemy or both. This feels…different." Ryan snipped.

Changing tactics, Hunter asked, "What does Frank think?"

"He doesn't know. And, for now, I am not going to tell him. I can't put my finger on it, but my gut tells me it will be more dangerous if he knows."

A blank look washed over Hunter's face.

"I know. It sounds stupid to say that. He has saved my ass more times than I can count. Something just feels off. That is the only way I can describe it." Ryan examined his glass, noticing how the liquid glided down the sides after his last swallow.

"Okay. Let's leave Frank out of the equation for now. Do you love this woman?"

Ryan finished his bourbon in one swallow. "I don't know. The pull between us is fierce. Like nothing I have ever felt before. But it is more than just the physical draw. I feel the insane need to protect her. To make sure no harm comes to her. Which defies all logic."

"Would you take a bullet for her?"

Without hesitation, Ryan answered, "Yes."

"Then you have your answer."

Ryan sighed. "Let's switch gears for a minute. One thing she mentioned was how she couldn't tell me the full story. That it was too dangerous for both of us, and she was trying to protect us. Then she mentioned something about having to 'make decisions under duress.' I am struggling to remember every conversation or moment with her from back then to attempt to stitch together the pieces and make some sense out of all of it. Oh, and she alluded to the fact that the danger is still alive and well."

Hunter rubbed his hands over his face, absorbing what Ryan said. "Ryan, I am not a spy, so I don't understand the world you came from. Based on what you just said, it sounds like she is trying to manage a lot of conflicting balls in the air right now. Including her feelings for you. Which seem to run deep."

Ryan leaned against the countertop behind him with his head hung low, feeling a mix of emotions he never thought were possible.

"For the first time since I have known her, I saw this raw emotion, which would be difficult to fake. And I admit…this weekend stirred reactions in me I didn't know even existed. Ain't love a bitch?" Ryan managed a half-hearted laugh.

"Look, my best advice to you is to be extra careful…*especially* if you think she may be caught in this evil web of ours. My concern is *you*. No offense to her. You are my best friend, and I don't want you going off half-cocked and doing something utterly foolish," Hunter declared with candor.

"You are right as always, my Jedi master."

Hunter swallowed his laughter, partly relieved his friend still had his sense of humor.

Changing topics slightly, Hunter asked, "Any news on our project?"

"Nothing of any consequence. I still believe there are answers in your father's files. But answers to which questions, I have no idea. What about the scientists?"

"They are still working on their own theories. The dead plants may be the keys to unlocking some of those answers, but it is slow going right now. The team doesn't want to rush or jump to any conclusions. I did get an email from them saying they had found some unique mineral deposits in the soil. Whatever that means." Hunter unconsciously rubbed his brow.

"Did they say which batch of plants?" Ryan's posture perked up.

"No. I did not ask either. I will call Dr. McGrady in the morning. Feel free to join me if you would like to."

"Sounds good. I'm interested to learn if the mineral deposits are in all the batches or just certain ones."

Hunter raised an eyebrow.

"If those plants were in chronological order and the corresponding files are in chronological order, then we may be able to narrow down some locations."

"Seems logical. But you of all people know nothing with this ordeal has been rational."

"True, except your father was the poster child for OCD. He needed to keep things neat, tidy, and in a specific order," Ryan countered.

"And you are forgetting that, if you are correct with your assumptions, my father's ghostly spirit must have come back to organize the last set of files and plants since he was presumed dead somewhere in the Amazon."

"The key word being '*presumed*,' Hunter."

Hunter's eyes bulged. "Are you seriously saying you now believe my father is amongst the living?"

"I would say it is a possibility but not probable. I still think he had a partner, and that partner has been carrying on this project after Philip took the express elevator down to hell."

"I am sure you have thoughts on who this partner could be?" Hunter rubbed his temples as a headache started to form.

"Well, we have our favorite foe, Greg Smythe— who, by the way, has fallen off the earth without a trace."

"I am not completely convinced he seems like the partner type, with all we know about him. For one, he is a newer player coming on board well after my father's demise. And although he has a certain skill set, Greg Smythe gave the appearance at least of being more of a puppet versus the puppet master. With that being said, let's still keep him on the list, given what he was able to accomplish up to this point."

"Next would be my female liaison. She has many of the skills required for this type of job. I don't know if she would truly sell her soul to the devil purely for monetary reasons."

"I will trust your intuition on her as I have not had the pleasure of meeting the lady."

"And then there is the most menacing scenario of them all—an unknown player who has not introduced themselves yet. Someone hiding in the shadows."

Ryan poured two more drinks, while both men sat in silence mulling over the possibilities. After several minutes, Hunter finished his drink and stood up.

"I need to get back home. Meet me in my office around nine a.m. and we can call the research team. Hopefully, they will have some good news for a change."

Hunter showed himself out and headed back to his sanctuary and Emma.

Ryan, alone once more, sat on the couch and stared at the wall in front of him. His mind was doing summersaults trying to make sense of any nugget, without much luck. Ryan was missing a key piece of information, and it was hidden somewhere within the depths of his mind. And he was not sure how to retrieve it. Every one of Ryan's instincts pointed toward danger hovering in the peripheral. The longer it took for Ryan to identify the missing pieces, the more the danger inched closer.

CHAPTER 26

A restful sleep overtook Ryan's exhausted body. Without any clandestine trips to the Amazon or elsewhere in his dreams, Ryan was gently nudged awake by the vibration of his phone alarm on the nightstand. Rolling over, he stretched like a cat arching its back.

Within thirty minutes, Ryan was showered, shaved, and dressed in jeans and a lightweight navy V-neck sweater. Ryan entered Hunter's office at 8:50 a.m. to find a blueberry muffin and black coffee waiting for him.

"You know me too well, my friend," Ryan admitted before taking a bite out of the muffin.

"Geez, Ryan! You are like a great white shark biting into that thing." Hunter handed Ryan a napkin before his desk was sprinkled with crumbs.

Ryan finished the medium-sized muffin in two more bites and wiped his mouth with the napkin. Before reacting to Hunter's comment, he washed the muffin down with a large mouthful of coffee.

Ryan sat back in the chair to let his breakfast settle.

"Now that you are fed, can we get down to business?"

"You're the boss!" Ryan crossed his legs at his ankles and sat back in the chair.

Without responding, Hunter began clicking on his laptop and within a few minutes, the research team materialized on the large screen on the wall next to Hunter's desk.

"Good morning, ladies and gentlemen," Hunter greeted the team.

"Good morning, Mr. Logan," the team responded in unison like a church choir.

"You know my chief of security, Ryan Donovan."

Heads on the screen acknowledged their recognition.

"I am hoping you can provide a progress report on the plants and soil samples."

Dr. McGrady took on the role of spokesperson for the team. "We have been making slow progress as I outlined in my last email. This morning, we began to run a marathon of additional tests on the soil the plants were in. I do not have anything conclusive yet." Dr. McGrady hesitated. "We are seeing some unusual mineral content not typical of the Amazon region, requiring a more in-depth analysis."

"Can you offer any details, Dr. McGrady?" Hunter did not want to put undue pressure on the team but knew the clock was ticking.

"All I can say definitively is this soil is not from the Amazon," Dr. McGrady confirmed.

Hunter and Ryan almost gave themselves whiplash turning to look at each other.

Ryan was the first to speak. "Did we hear you correctly? The dirt isn't from the Amazon?"

"Yes, Mr. Donovan. That is correct. We have tested and retested multiple times. This soil is not indigenous to that region. Let me explain. First, there are traces of insecticides, which are not naturally occurring. And secondly, the soil found in the Amazon is virtually devoid of nutrients but is rich with iron and aluminum oxides."

Hunter responded, "Go on, doctor."

"These oxides should be extremely high if the soil came from the Amazon. We have only been able to find trace amounts." Dr. McGrady patiently waited while this admission sunk in.

"So, what you are saying, at this point in your research, is the soil we found the plants in did *not* come from the Amazon rainforest."

"Yes."

"I don't mean to put you on the spot, doctor, but if the soil is *not* from the Amazon, where the hell is it from?" Hunter's cheeks started to turn crimson.

Ryan was at a loss for words watching the back-and-forth exchange between Hunter and Dr. McGrady. This was not an outcome either man expected. All the evidence to date pointed to the plants being retrieved from the Amazon.

The research team visibly became uncomfortable, knowing they were going to need to provide answers soon to their employer.

Clearing his throat before answering, Dr. McGrady continued. "Well, there are significant traces of quartz."

"And this means what? The plants like shiny soil?" Hunter demanded.

"Based on the data we have, the team feels strongly about their hypothesis."

"Which is?" Hunter's eyes narrowed.

"The soil you found came from the southern portion of the United States."

Ryan's eyes almost popped out of his head at this admission. Hunter's mouth dropped open.

"Wait a minute. Are you saying my father did not find the plants in the Amazon as all evidence suggests and, instead, he took a side trip to Florida and stumbled across them?"

"All I can tell you right now is the soil is not from the South American Amazon rainforest. The higher-than-usual concentration of quartz could suggest Florida. Keep in mind other regions also have quartz in their soil. We need to now go through the painstaking process of eliminating other possibilities."

Hunter closed his eyes wishing he was back in Europe on his honeymoon when, for a few brief weeks, all this nonsense did not exist. Ryan watched Hunter closely, knowing this was another unexpected outcome.

"Dr. McGrady, forgive my ignorance, just because the soil is from a different location, it doesn't necessarily mean the plants are from that same area, correct? The plants could still be from the Amazon and were just put into soil from someplace else."

"Yes, Mr. Donovan. You are correct. We are conducting additional tests on the plants themselves as minerals and nutrients would be absorbed by the plant. This should give us a better indication if the plants are also from a different region than originally thought."

"Very well. Please let me know as soon as you have more information, Dr. McGrady." Hunter abruptly disconnected the video call.

"What the bloody hell is going on, Ryan? All the notes indicate the Amazon. For God's sake, my father's plane was found crashed in the Amazon!"

Before answering, Ryan placed his coffee cup on one of the custom reclaimed-wood coasters from Walden Hill Woodworks and inhaled sharply.

"Ok, buddy, looks like we need to really start reviewing those files." Hunter began to respond until Ryan exclaimed, "Damn! The reason for the call was to find out which batch of plants and dirt they were testing."

"I will email Dr. McGrady about that. How quickly do you think you can do a cursory review of the remaining files?" Hunter probed.

"It will be my priority today. What is it you are hoping to find besides the proverbial 'X' marks the spot, Hunter?"

"I am wondering if you will see a change in the notes. You said the first files you examined provided a rough map of areas my father had scoped out. And locations were in the Amazon. I am wondering if at some point he gave up on the Amazon."

"Gotcha. The same thought was going through my head when the good doctor was talking. I guess Florida would be considered a subtropical rainforest, although I'm no botanist."

Hunter stood and walked to the windows as his way of coping.

Ryan paused, then decided it best to ask the one question that was the elephant in the room.

Before Ryan could open his mouth, Hunter instinctively answered, "No, Ryan, I do not know what this means regarding my father's presumed demise. I know that was going to be your next question." Hunter continued without turning to look at Ryan. "Could he have faked the plane crash? Absolutely. Is it possible he survived the plane crash and made it back to the United States? Absolutely. Could he have been swallowed up by the rainforest and his evil twin is the one wreaking havoc? Who the hell knows!"

"Hunter, before we jump to unnecessary conclusions and this becomes the dog chasing its tail, let's take this one step at a time. I will work on the files today to see what I can come up with. At the end of the day, we can regroup to see where we are."

Hunter turned, retreated to his desk, and tilted his head in Ryan's direction as a sign of both approval and dismissal.

The express elevator down to Ryan's lair never gave him enough time to decompress from the meetings with Hunter. The news this morning opened a whole new can of worms in Ryan's opinion. Previously, they were concentrated on one region, although an exceptionally large area. Now, these plants could be anywhere in the Southern Hemisphere, Ryan theorized as the elevator slowed and came to a stop.

Unlocking the door to his office, Ryan glanced around the room filled with filing cabinets. He had already gone through the first cabinet, which yielded a few morsels of information. The second cabinet was virtually identical to the first, with various colored folders and cryptic notes when he slid open the drawers.

"No use procrastinating," Ryan said aloud and locked the door behind him.

Halfway through the plethora of files, Ryan stood up. Every muscle in his body ached. Raising his arms above his head and rolling his head in either direction, some of the tension started to trickle out of Ryan's body. The grumbling in his stomach signaled it was time to head to the cafeteria to grab a sandwich.

Upon his return, Ryan dove into the toasted BLT like he hadn't eaten in days. With only a few crumbs left on the paper plate, Ryan wiped the grease from his hands before clearing out several emails from his inbox over the last few hours.

Ryan maneuvered his chair back over to where filing cabinets stood like sentries guarding a treasure. As if on cue, Ryan's phone chimed with a text message. Rolling his chair across the room to his desk where his phone rested, Ryan's body tingled, wondering if the object of his nocturnal activities would be the messenger.

To his disappointment, the message was from Frank asking how the investigation was going. Without hesitation, Ryan responded, "Moving at snail's pace."

Seconds later, a snail emoji popped up in Ryan's messages.

Continuing his hunt to decipher the files by the end of the day, Ryan ignored all additional messages of any kind from anyone. Unbeknownst to Ryan, the yellow folders nagged at him as they had with Hunter back in Hardwicke. Something about their contents was different, although Ryan could not explicitly say how or why.

By four o'clock, Ryan had inspected every folder in each cabinet, careful to keep them in the exact order in which they were found. Sliding in his chair back to his desk, Ryan leaned back and stared at the ceiling, closing his eyes.

Without realizing it, Ryan had dozed off and nearly fell out of his chair when his phone rang.

Looking at the caller identification, Ryan answered, "Hello, detective."

"Hey, Ryan. I wanted to make sure you were still part of the living."

"As of right now, I am. Were your lab folks able to find anything?" Ryan asked, purposely sounding vague.

"It was just like we suspected—no prints, no smudges."

"I am definitely not surprised."

"Even though we weren't able to identify a specific perpetrator, we did find something a bit odd."

Ryan almost didn't want to ask. "Do I even want to know?"

The detective chuckled. "Well, there was the tiniest trace of dirt on the edge of the photograph. Any chance you could have transferred it when you examined it?"

Ryan considered the question before answering. "I can't say with one hundred percent certainty, but I think it is extremely doubtful. Do you know what kind of soil?"

Wicked Nemesis of the Hunted   247

"The sample is so small it will be tough to tell. I can send over the report and Hunter's people can look at it. They will have more sophisticated equipment than we do."

"Sure. Send it over. Could be nothing or it could be something."

"Ryan, I must ask. You don't seem surprised, and I am wondering why."

"Sorry. There have been a lot of conversations around dirt today. I, unfortunately, know more than I ever wanted to about minerals in dirt."

"Okay. You don't need to elaborate. I think I understand what you are saying," Detective O'Reilly responded cautiously.

Ryan joked. "Just more questions and a lack of answers per the usual. Another day in paradise."

"I hear you, my friend. I have to run. Ryan, I know I say this a lot lately, please be careful. My gut is telling me things are about to heat up, and I don't mean the weather."

"Right back at you, detective. Stay safe out there."

Ryan's expression naturally tensed, not knowing what to make of his conversation with Detective O'Reilly. What were the odds it was a pure coincidence the stalker's photo had soil deposits on it?

Hunter knocked softly on the locked door after he tried the handle without any luck.

Ryan unlocked the door and looked a little dazed. "Hey."

"Hey. You seem a bit off your game if you don't mind me saying."

Hunter took a seat in his usual spot.

Ryan hesitated before responding solemnly, "Hunter, I need to tell you something but wanted to gather as much information as I could first."

"Ryan, by your expression and demeanor, I can tell I'm not going to like what you have to say."

"You are very astute, my friend." Ryan took a deep breath. "A few days ago, I decided to burn off some steam with a run in the common."

"Okay. Sounds like you. Go on."

"The run was peaceful and uneventful until I returned to the parking garage."

"Let me guess. This is the part I'm not going to like."

"You really do know how to spoil the mystery, Hunter. *Anyway*, when I reached my car, I noticed something on my windshield—a white envelope. Inside was a picture of me running a few minutes prior."

Ryan waited for Hunter to catch up.

Suddenly Hunter exclaimed, "Oh, fuck!"

"My thought, exactly."

"Ryan, with our cutting-edge security, how could someone get into the underground garage?"

"I reviewed all the surveillance footage multiple times and honestly don't have a clue. Except…"

"Except what, Ryan?"

Wicked Nemesis of the Hunted   249

"Except if it was somehow, partially, an inside job."

Hunter rubbed his eyes but stayed silent.

"I sent the photograph to Detective O'Reilly to see if his team could get anything from it. The detective called to let me know there weren't any fingerprints on the photograph."

"Forgive me, but that doesn't sound unusual. If this was from the same people we have been dealing with, then I would expect them to be very careful at covering their tracks."

"I tend to agree. The interesting thing the detective *was* able to find was a minuscule sample of dirt particles on the photograph. It was too small for his lab to do any analysis, so he thought your lab might be better equipped for that sort of thing. He's sending me the report and sample."

"Why is every conversation today revolving around dirt?" Hunter questioned, starting to feel jittery.

"If this sample turns out to be the same as what the plants were in…" Ryan's voice trailed off.

"Then things just got kicked up a notch. What is your intuition telling you, Ryan?"

"My gut is telling me this web is getting even more tangled, and we need to figure this out soon."

"And to satisfy my own questions, you still don't think this could be Greg Smythe? He is an experienced stalker."

"Although he does have that particular skill set, I'm not convinced it is him. Here is my prediction as it relates to Greg. He no longer serves a purpose and is dead by now or has been reassigned until he is needed again."

"Alright. I trust your judgment. So, I guess we need to follow the dirt for now."

Ryan stifled a laugh. "Never thought I would hear those words come out of your mouth, Hunter."

"Glad I could be entertainment for you. Did you find anything in the rest of the files?"

"As I originally suspected, they positively outline a chronological timeline."

"I thought we had already established that fact, Ryan, or am I hallucinating?"

"Yes, we did. I just wanted to double-check to make sure I didn't miss anything. I did notice something else while I was combing through the years of files."

"Please don't keep me in suspense, Ryan."

"Something seems a bit off with the yellow folders compared to the other colors. I need to spend some more time examining those," Ryan admitted.

"Funny you should mention that. When we were in Hardwicke, and you had left to go grab the rental truck, I started skimming those and felt the same thing. It wasn't something I could clearly articulate—just a feeling I had."

"Exactly! My inner voice is telling me a clue is hidden in those folders. I will pick them up again tomorrow to see what I can decipher."

"Before you run off to whatever clandestine plans you have this evening," Hunter said, "I spoke to Dr. McGrady again."

Ryan had forgotten Hunter was going to follow up with the science team.

"And what did the good doctor offer?"

"They started testing the plants and soil in backward order, chronologically."

"So, the dirt they said could be from Florida was what we think are the most recent samples?"

"Bingo! I asked Dr. McGrady to have the team quickly do some preliminary testing of the other samples. Just for initial chemical makeup."

"Hmm," Ryan mumbled.

"Hopefully, we can determine locations along the timeline."

Ryan stared at Hunter.

"Yes, Ryan, I understand what the implications of this are. My father may not be as dead as we assumed."

"Or…"

"*Or* he has a helper. A prodigy following in his footsteps. Such a lovely thought," Hunter remarked, curling his lip.

Without responding, Ryan packed up his belongings, hoping to give Hunter a not-so-subtle hint he wanted to head home. Hunter rose and walked to the door.

"See you tomorrow, Ryan. Be careful. Especially if you have any unanticipated visitors tonight." Hunter chuckled all the way to the elevator.

Ryan rolled his eyes then shut off the lights and locked the door.

CHAPTER 27

The drive home was ordinary for Ryan. The music surrounding him in the car, usually a calming effect, wasn't able to deflect his thoughts away from the events transpiring over these last few days. Through the filthier-than-normal windshield, plumes of storm clouds were building in intensity like an atomic explosion. Ryan hoped he would be able to make it home before the downpour saturated the streets, slowing traffic even further.

With a few minutes to spare, Ryan was safely tucked into the hideaway he called home when the first roll of thunder announced the arrival of the barrage of water encapsulating the city. The time had come for Ryan to contemplate the dinner menu, with pasta and garlic bread being the clear winner.

Boiling the water to the precise temperature before emptying the penne pasta into the pot, Ryan donned an apron while he poured the marinara sauce into a second pot. While the main course was on its way to being a worthy dinner, Ryan retrieved two pieces of garlic bread from the freezer and placed them in the toaster oven.

Satisfied he had everything under control, Ryan made his way to the couch to relax for a few minutes. Closing his eyes for a moment, he visualized the yellow folders sitting in his office. The clue that had been eluding him was just out of reach—like how a word at the tip of his tongue often eluded him. Something was subtly different about those files, and if Ryan could figure out what it was, it might be the break they needed.

Suddenly, water gushed from the pasta pot, startling him.

"What a damn mess!" Ryan yelled at himself for being so careless.

Grabbing a roll of paper towels from under the sink, Ryan tried to soak up the mess on the stove top as best he could. Adding insult to injury, smoke slowly began to spill out of the toaster oven where the garlic bread was now burnt. After ten minutes, the stove was cleaned, and Ryan sat at the counter eating a more well-done dinner than he had hoped for.

Once the mediocre meal was consumed and Ryan finished cleaning the kitchen to a pristine state, he flopped on the couch to watch hockey. Dozing off, Ryan's thoughts slowly made their way to tropical rainforests and yellow folders.

Ryan tried to make sense of the random thoughts floating in his mind. The colors of the rainbow plagued Ryan's dream. The movie in his head ended abruptly with the bright yellow sun shining down on a pot of gold and a yellow brick road.

Sitting up on the couch, Ryan noticed the clock on the stove in the kitchen said midnight. Still groggy and trying to shake the fog from his head, Ryan stumbled into his bedroom and fell face down onto the bed still fully clothed.

Six hours later, Ryan awoke more refreshed than when he entered the bedroom.

Clasping his hands behind his head resting on the pillow, Ryan stared at the ceiling trying to make sense of the many vivid recent dreams. His subconscious mind was working overtime trying to solve the growing number of problems. Ryan needed to think of something completely different than yellow folders, cancer-prevention drugs, and the Amazon.

Unfortunately, the one avenue he needed to focus on still led him down the same path. *Could Sue really be involved in this mess?* Ryan wondered. He once again began to second-guess all his decisions during that fateful last mission with Sue and Frank.

What if he had been able to retrieve Sue before she ran off to parts unknown?

Could things have turned out differently?

Would that have impacted the here and now?

Ryan swung his legs over the side of the bed and retreated to the shower. This was going to be another day of trying to decipher files no one had seen in several years, or so he thought.

The winds were howling like a phantom locomotive barreling down the tracks when Ryan exited his apartment on the way to his car in the adjacent parking garage. With the windshield wipers on high, the Mercedes crawled to the Logan headquarters. Literal sheets of rain washed over the car the entire drive until Ryan safely entered the parking structure.

Ryan had bypassed his standard routine of stopping for coffee at Kern's and opted to head straight to the office, given the inclement weather. One habit Ryan was unable to evade was grabbing his usual muffin in the cafeteria. Glancing at his watch, he noticed it was just after seven a.m. Although there were a fair number of early birds in the office at this hour, it was quiet and peaceful.

Unlocking his office door while balancing coffee and a chocolate-chip muffin, the lights automatically illuminated the space after Ryan crossed the threshold. He stopped in his tracks when the faint smell of stale cigarette smoke permeated his nose. The smell was weak but distinctive. Since Ryan didn't smoke, he knew someone else had been in his private domain not that long ago.

Haphazardly dropping his belongings on top of his desk, including almost spilling his coffee, Ryan checked the desk drawers and the file cabinets as quickly as he could to determine if any had been broken into. The desk drawer with its secret compartment was undisturbed and had no signs of an attempt to forcibly unlock it. The file cabinets were in their rightful places and, on the surface, looked as though they too were undisturbed.

Looking at the cabinets more closely, the third one caught Ryan's eye. He peered closely at it from various angles and noticed the second drawer down was ever so slightly askew. Tilting his head to get a closer look, Ryan noticed a few nicks in the metal around the lock. In normal circumstances, Ryan would have chalked it up to regular wear and tear, except for two things. The knicks looked fresh and there were lingering remnants of cigarette smoke.

The other three file cabinets seemed untouched. The only one with any indication of tampering was the third cabinet. Ryan grabbed his phone from his bag and took several pictures including close-ups of the scratches.

Before Ryan alerted anyone else to the presumed break-in, he logged on to his computer and replayed the surveillance footage from when he left the office last night until he came in this morning. Cameras were strategically mounted in almost all areas of the building, with a special focus on all entrances and exits. It was no different in the security office.

Fast-forwarding through the boring overnight hours, Ryan paused the footage at around five a.m. The angle of the camera wasn't perfect and the frame looked a bit obscured, although Ryan thought he saw a glimpse of movement in the shadows on the corner of the screen by the emergency-exit stairwell. The video never showed anyone breaching the door to his office, which stumped Ryan.

"What the hell is going on?" Ryan whispered, still staring at the film playing before him.

Fifteen minutes later, movement once again showed up in the same corner of the screen, and then nothing until Ryan was seen unlocking his office door.

"Maybe I really *am* starting to lose my mind, or we have a ghost," Ryan muttered.

"Did you say something?" Hunter inquired from the open doorway.

Ryan jumped, alarmed at the sound of Hunter's voice behind him.

"What the fuck, Hunter? Are you trying to put me in an early grave?" Ryan roared.

"Whoa. Easy there, buddy. Did you not have your morning jolt of caffeine yet?" Hunter did not move from the doorway.

"Do you smell anything in here?"

Hunter inhaled deeply. "No. What am I supposed to smell? If all of this is because of a dead mouse, then I may have to reevaluate my selection for head of security."

"That may happen anyhow," Ryan mumbled.

Hunter cautiously entered the office and chose to stand instead of sitting in his usual spot. Searching the area for any anomalies that would have caused Ryan to be this much on edge, Hunter came up empty.

"Ryan, what is going on with you this morning?"

Dodging the question, Ryan cursed under his breath.

"Earth to Ryan. There is obviously something not quite right with you."

"Fine. When I unlocked my office door this morning, I caught a faint whiff of cigarette smoke."

"And?"

"And what? Isn't that enough? I don't smoke! No one in the security area smokes. So, why the fuck did I smell smoke?" Ryan exclaimed.

"How about we dial the tone down a few notches, Ryan? Could the smoke have been on someone's jacket? Could they have picked it up in a bar or on the train platform?"

It took all the restraint Ryan had to hold his composure. "Hunter, let me try this again. I *did not* smell the smoke in the hallway on the way to my office. I *did not* smell the smoke until I physically

260   *Tracey L. Ryan*

entered my office. If it was on someone's jacket as you had suggested, I would have smelled it outside of my door and *not* inside."

"Look, I was just trying to come up with plausible explanations for what you had told me." Hunter inhaled sharply and continued. "Where do you think the smoke smell came from? The air vent?"

"I don't fucking know! If I did, I would not be having this conversation with you right now," Ryan bellowed, speaking so fast it was almost hard to understand.

"There must be more to this incident than you are telling me."

"The third filing cabinet may have been tampered with."

Hunter's eyes bulged in response to Ryan's comment. "What do you mean 'tampered with'?"

"There are scratches and nicks around the locking mechanism, and the second drawer down was slightly open."

Closing his eyes, Hunter counted to five before responding. "Are you sure you locked the cabinet before you left last night and closed all the drawers tight?"

"I am fairly certain but not one hundred percent," Ryan admitted sheepishly.

"Okay. These cabinets are, perhaps, twenty years old. Could these marks be from a different time and not recent?"

"Again, it is possible, although they look fresh."

"Don't bite my head off, but how can you tell?"

"The metal in the grooves is very shiny. If these were several years old, dust and dirt would get in there and they would be duller-looking," Ryan explained more calmly.

Hunter strode over to the cabinet and looked for himself. "I guess I can understand your logic."

"That's it? You can see my logic?" Ryan's cheeks flushed and his pulse quickened again.

"Ryan, I am not sure what an appropriate response should be in this situation," Hunter responded, at a loss for what else to say.

"An appropriate response would be to react as dumbfounded and angry as I am. Hunter, let me clearly spell this out for you since it does not seem to be getting through your thick skull. There is a possibility—*an incredibly good possibility*—that an unauthorized person was inside my locked office with these ultra-secret files that could very well hold the key to ending cancer." Ryan began to pace around before finally slumping in his chair.

Hunter decided it was safe to take his regular seat. Silence filled the space while Hunter tried to innocently look around, noticing the untouched coffee and muffin on Ryan's desk.

"I understand your concern, Ryan. I am trying to be the voice of reason. Right now, you have a lot on your shoulders between the countless aspects of the mess we are in. I worry you are beginning to see conspiracies where none exist.

"This building has the best security in the world. You should know since you oversaw many of the upgrades. I am not saying it is foolproof, but what are the odds some unauthorized person was able to skirt all the security measures in place?"

"Slim to none, although I should remind you of the recent incident in the garage," Ryan said, with his head slumped forward.

"Okay. Say there is someone out there with the skills necessary to get in and out of this building undetected. Was anything else disturbed? Anything taken?"

"From what I could tell, everything is in its rightful place. I haven't looked inside the cabinet yet. Was about to do that when you caused me to jump out of my skin."

"Well, before we go any further down the road of assumptions, how about we look inside the cabinet?"

Ryan opened one of his desk drawers and pulled out a pair of latex gloves. After putting them on, he pushed himself out of his chair and went to the cabinet in question. Looking back at Hunter, who nodded in consent, Ryan started to gently pull the second drawer open.

Shaking his head, Ryan scolded himself, "Damn, I shouldn't have done that."

Wicked Nemesis of the Hunted   263

Perplexed, Hunter inquired, "What do you mean?"

"This thing could have been booby-trapped and blown us to bits. That was an amateur mistake. Many I am making lately."

Hunter decided it was best not to respond. He had noticed Ryan had not been in top form lately and wondered if it was because of his former flame resurfacing.

Gently pulling the drawer open a millimeter at a time, Ryan looked closely to ensure there wasn't an incendiary device hidden deep within it. Satisfied the drawer was safe, Ryan pulled it out the full length. The files seemed to be in order, but Ryan could not say with certainty.

"Well, is anything missing or not in the order you left things?" Hunter asked anxiously.

Ryan scratched his head before answering. "I can't say for sure. Looks in order. Let me check something."

Pulling out his phone, Ryan quickly scrolled through his photo gallery until he reached the day they had uncovered these cabinets hiding in Hardwicke.

With a little chuckle, Ryan said, "Good thing you were so conscientious with your assigned job in Hardwicke, Hunter. I think you took photos of almost every file. So, let's do a little compare, shall we?"

Hunter got out of his chair and moved next to Ryan. Both men looked at the photos of the cabinet in question and then at the specific drawer. Ryan silently counted the number of files in the photo clearly visible and arrived at the number thirty-three.

Without touching the files, Ryan counted the actual files in front of him and came up with the number thirty-two. Repeating these steps two more times, Ryan still ended up with thirty-two files in the drawer and thirty-three in the picture.

"What is it?" Hunter queried.

"When I count these, I get thirty-three in the picture and only thirty-two in the actual drawer."

"Hmmm. Could one file have slipped so it is underneath?"

Ryan peered inside once again, using the flashlight on his phone for more light.

"Nope. Nothing on the bottom. I don't want to touch these too much since it's looking more and more like someone was here who shouldn't have been."

Hunter was desperate to find a logical explanation otherwise the ramifications could be catastrophic.

"Can you tell which color file is potentially missing?"

Ryan held the photograph up next to the drawer and reviewed it file by file, checking it twice for good measure.

"Looks like one of the yellow folders is the one unaccounted for." Ryan's senses tingled once he admitted this out loud to Hunter.

"Figures it had to be a yellow one."

"The problem is we don't know exactly which yellow folder was taken or its contents. The folders never had any information on the tabs, just inside them. And I still can't figure out how this person got in here, to begin with."

"Could the surveillance footage have been tampered with?"

"Anything is possible, I guess. There were a few seconds when I thought I saw movement in the shadows of the camera frame. But it could have been the heat kicking on and moving the majestic palm plants in the corner of the security room."

"Ryan, do you really believe it was the heat?" Hunter cocked an eye in Ryan's direction.

"No, I guess not. Not really. Unless this person was a ghost or invisible, no one except me came through my office door." Ryan pointed in the direction of the door, which currently stood wide open.

"I should know this since I own the building, but is there another way in here?" Hunter looked around and only saw concrete walls.

"Well, actually there is."

"Are you sure? I only see concrete walls in here," Hunter commented while his eyes darted around the room once more.

"Let me check the closet where I had an emergency escape hatch installed just in case it was ever needed."

Hunter's mouth dropped open at this admission from Ryan.

Ryan darted out of his seat like a cannonball and opened the closet door to find the reinforced steel door closed but not secured. When Ryan had the closet installed, he had it designed as both a safe room and an escape route. All four of the closet walls plus the ceiling, including the main door and the escape hatch, were made of reinforced steel that would withstand not only a breach but also fire.

Opening the small hatch and crawling through into the adjacent utility closet, Ryan entered the security office. He joined Hunter again by coming through his office door.

Hunter got whiplash when Ryan reappeared. "How the bloody hell did you do that, Ryan?"

"Come with me. Apparently, a large rat both entered and exited my office through a door no one knew about except myself. *Or* so I thought."

Ryan showed Hunter the entrance and escape route, causing Hunter to scratch his head.

"Hunter, I need to declare this a crime scene. This escape door is always secured, and it wasn't a few minutes ago. I think the question about if there was an intruder has been answered. Now we need to figure out who it was and which file was taken."

Wicked Nemesis of the Hunted   267

"By crime scene, do you mean calling the police? The publicity could be devastating."

"Not the entire police, just one person within the ranks of a detective who can be trusted." Before Ryan dialed Detective O'Reilly, he reminded Hunter, "I need you to understand the ramifications of what has happened, Hunter. Your top-notch secure building has been breached twice now. We don't know by whom or who they are affiliated with. This is more than someone getting into the underground garage. This could be something simple like corporate espionage and stealing trade secrets or it could be more threatening."

Hunter nodded and stayed silent, allowing Ryan to continue.

"And I hate to even say this aloud, but between this incident and the one in the garage, we are not only dealing with professionals, but I am leaning toward believing it's someone with inside knowledge."

Hunter remained silent and looked at Ryan with a furrowed brow.

"Hunter, in that big brain of yours, you must be thinking some of the same thoughts as I am. How did this person get in here unseen? No reports of any suspicious activity have been conveyed. No fire or security alarms were triggered. The cameras, in essence, saw nothing unusual."

With a stone expression on his face, Hunter continued to stand in front of Ryan, silently.

"This person was able to do all of this because they were, and more than likely have been, hiding in plain sight."

With the last statement hanging in the air, Hunter retreated to his office high in the clouds while Ryan dialed Detective O'Reilly.

CHAPTER 28

After several rings, the detective answered. "Ryan, don't take any offense to this, but I cringe every time I see your number pop up."

Ryan exploded in laughter. "I tend to have that effect on people. Crazy weather we are having, huh?"

"Did you really call me to talk about the weather? But to answer your question, yes, it is insane. The winds blew down some trees and almost derailed the commuter rail from Worcester. And traffic lights are out in the Financial District. So, it has been a lovely morning."

"Sounds like you have your hands full today. And I hate to bother you with something as trivial as a break-in."

Detective O'Reilly sat up in his squeaky office chair. "Break-in? Where?"

"At the Ares Logan building."

"Ryan, is this your secret admirer again? And if it is, I seriously don't have time to chase away your love interests."

Ryan noticed the detective was grouchier than usual. "I wish it was my admirer. Well, I guess it could be technically. But I'm not really sure," Ryan said, with his voice trailing off.

"What the hell are you talking about? You're not making any sense and are talking in circles, Ryan."

"Sorry. Someone broke into my office in the building. And once again, they were very stealth, getting in and out without being seen."

The detective let a sigh escape. "And you want me to come over and check it out?"

"That would be swell. And just you—not a team. I am trying to keep a lid on this."

Hearing the alarm in Ryan's voice, Detective O'Reilly agreed to meet Ryan at the Logan building in thirty minutes.

Ryan waited in the main lobby by the koi pond with a cup of dark roast coffee in hand. Trying to look unnerved, he pretended to read a magazine that had been left on the bench. All types of people came and went through the lobby—employees, prospective employees, vendors, and delivery personnel.

A middle-aged man dressed in the standard brown khaki delivery uniform almost ran by Ryan with a letter-sized parcel in his hand. Already on edge, Ryan snapped to attention and was ready to pounce while he watched the man. He exhaled in relief when the deliveryman caught up to his intended target, a young woman Ryan recognized from the legal department.

Just as Ryan sat back on the bench and crossed his legs, trying to get comfortable, he noticed Detective O'Reilly heading in his direction. The detective was in awe of the building and still couldn't believe there was an actual park inside the lobby. Sitting next to Ryan on the bench, the detective admired the koi in the pond behind him.

"Thanks for getting here so quickly, detective."

"It's not like I had anything else to do this morning, Ryan." Still looking around, the detective continued. "This building still amazes me. Who would have thought you could have a pond with fish inside a high-rise in Boston?"

Ryan chuckled. "Very true, my friend. C'mon. Do you want any coffee or a muffin before I take you down to the scene of the crime?"

"No, I'm good. Thanks, though. Let's see what has you so spooked."

Ryan looked at Detective O'Reilly and took a step back.

"Ryan, I'm a detective. I can tell when people are lying, genuinely upset, or spooked. And you were unequivocally spooked when you called me this morning."

"I can't argue with you. All this shit has me on edge. Let's go."

The two men walked to the elevator, and Ryan pressed the down button to take them to the basement. When they exited the elevator, Detective

O'Reilly was astounded at the security office with a twinge of jealousy. He fantasized about working in this type of place when he retired from the Boston Police Department.

Ryan noticed the look on the detective's face. "You have a job here anytime you want, detective."

Detective O'Reilly grinned. "I appreciate that. Let's make it through this situation unscathed first and then we'll talk."

"Fair enough. While we are here, let me give you the five-cent tour."

Ryan proceeded to point out the state-of-the-art surveillance equipment, which groups were doing what tasks, and the armory. Finally, he ended the impromptu tour at his office where he found Hunter waiting for them.

The detective immediately held out his hand in Hunter's direction, which Hunter gladly shook.

"Detective O'Reilly, it is nice to see you again. Although I do wish it was under better circumstances than this."

"Likewise, Mr. Logan."

"Please, call me Hunter. We have been through too much for you not to."

Detective O'Reilly remembered the first time he had met Hunter, Ryan, and Emma. Someone, which they later found out was Greg Smythe, had broken into Emma's office and vandalized it, including writing nasty words on the walls. The last thing Detective O'Reilly wanted to do that night was deal with another rich, pompous ass who was going to play the name game and tell him how to do his job. After a few initial tense moments, the detective came to realize Hunter was not the typical rich playboy type. His genuine concern for Emma was overwhelming. Months later, Hunter almost made the ultimate sacrifice in Hardwicke, which Detective O'Reilly had the utmost respect for.

"Alright, Ryan, walk me through what you found and why you think there was a break-in."

Ryan carefully recounted what he found earlier, leaving out no detail. When he was finished telling his tale, Ryan pointed out the knicks on the cabinet and physically walked the detective to the panic room closet.

"I was careful not to touch more than I needed to and to wear gloves on the off chance there are any fingerprints. Which, by the way, I highly doubt. Given this person's skills, they aren't going to pull an amateur move like not wearing gloves."

The detective walked the room one more time, examining every inch. Hunter and Ryan watched the detective crouch down on the floor just outside the main closet door. Taking a small flashlight out of his jacket pocket, Detective O'Reilly looked closely at the carpeted floor in front of him.

"Ryan, let me see the bottom of your right shoe."

Ryan had a puzzled look on his face but did as he was asked.

"Okay, I thought so. Your soles are smooth since they are what I like to call 'office shoes.' They won't leave a distinct pattern on carpeting, soil, or grass. Come here."

The two men crouched next to Detective O'Reilly and looked at where his flashlight was pointing.

"Can you see the slightest outline of a boot here?"

Hunter and Ryan nodded, although it was extremely tough to see.

"And you can just about see how there is this checker-box pattern," the detective mentioned, allowing his flashlight to highlight what he was talking about.

"How in the hell did you see that?" Hunter finally asked.

"I would like to say that it was years of experience, but I think, in this instance, it was shit luck." Detective O'Reilly laughed. "There is a technique I can use to try to get an image of the footprint. I need to go back to my office to get a few things. While I am gone, please don't walk in this area over here," the detective told Ryan as he pointed to the area from the file cabinets to the closet.

"Got it. So, you don't think I'm crazy?" Ryan said with a wink.

"Well, I can't comment on your state of mind, Ryan. I'm no shrink. What I can tell you is I believe

Wicked Nemesis of the Hunted   275

you. Someone besides you was here this morning. A very, very clever someone. I'll be back in a jiffy."

"Sounds good. I will take you back upstairs and wait for you next to the pond," Ryan responded.

"Thank you, detective. I know this is not in your general purview. We needed someone we could trust to handle this with discretion," Hunter commented.

"I understand. Never a dull moment with you boys, is there?"

"There doesn't seem to be," Ryan confirmed.

"If I may. I have been doing this type of work for more years than I care to count. This building is remarkably high-tech. My instincts tell me you gentlemen have an insider involved. If that is the case, you need to be extra vigilant and not take anything for granted."

The men nodded in unison and escorted the detective back to the lobby. Once the detective left the premises, Ryan and Hunter made their way to one of the park benches. Hunter rarely sat in the lobby, partly because of his jam-packed schedule.

"I have to say, besides the charity event and the wedding, I am rarely down here. It really is peaceful. Even with the number of people coming and going."

"I know what you mean. So, I had a sort of epiphany when I was here a little bit ago, waiting for our good detective to show up. I agree with Detective O'Reilly somewhat about his inside-job comment."

"How did I know you were going to say that?"

"But I have a slightly different scenario. While I was on this exact bench earlier, I noticed the distinct types of people coming through here. And one type stood out to me. The type that would generally go unnoticed. The type that would be expected to be here at various times during the day. And the type that blends in so much no one would question their presence."

"Enough with the preamble, Ryan. Spit it out, for God's sake."

"A deliveryperson!" Ryan exclaimed as if he just said the winning answer on a game show.

Hunter sat back and thought about Ryan's suggestion.

"Hunter, it makes perfect sense. Not all deliveries are left at the front desk. And honestly, who would question a deliveryperson if they were in the same type of uniform plus carrying a small package?"

"You might be right. Part of me hopes that is the case. I really *do not* want to imagine any of our employees are part of this."

"The challenge will be finding this person. Since they are only posing as a deliveryperson, there would be no record of packages being dropped off or anything like that. I was too rattled this morning, so I only checked the surveillance footage of the security area and my office. What I need to do next is examine the footage outside the building."

"I know you installed more than enough cameras along the entire perimeter of the building, so hopefully we will get lucky."

"Right now, we need a little luck. This is really starting to piss me off." Ryan cursed.

For the next twenty minutes, the two of them sat in silence, watching the myriad of people traffic moving through the lobby.

Ryan contemplated all the happenings these past few weeks and how he could have prevented them. In his mind, he had lost the edge he had spent years cultivating. And if that were the case, how was he going to get his edge back to ensure the safety of those around him?

Hunter was amazed no one either noticed him or recognized him, which caused him to feel invisible. He always thought he was a good leader and knew his people. These few minutes were an epiphany for him to spend more time with the people who kept this company moving forward.

Before either Ryan or Hunter could do any more reflecting, Detective O'Reilly approached them. Hunter and Ryan stood to greet the detective for the second time that morning.

"Detective. Did you get what you needed?" Ryan inquired.

"All set," the detective replied as he patted the duffel bag he was now carrying on his left shoulder.

"Let's head downstairs. Do you want coffee or anything?"

"I'm good. Thanks, though, Ryan."

Once back in his office, Ryan closed the door to prying eyes behind them. Detective O'Reilly did not waste any time. He pulled out the various pieces of equipment he needed and got to work within seconds. Dusting the file cabinet inside and outside plus the doors and knobs for fingerprints produced no tangible results. Next, he got down on his knees close to the footprint without compromising it.

Ryan and Hunter watched from a safe distance so as not to disturb the detective or the area around him. Ryan had seen similar techniques used in the aftermath of some of the assignments he had been on. After using a special camera like the ones that can identify impressions made on paper, Detective O'Reilly moved on to employing the electrostatic dust-lifter technique.

This process detected any dust or residue on surfaces potentially tracked in with the person and subsequently left behind. If done correctly, the outline of the shoe impression would be formed on the special film. The film itself has two sides—one black and the other aluminum-coated. The black side is placed against the shoe impression. Then a high-voltage charge is applied to the film, which causes the dust and residue to transfer to the film.

After several tense minutes during which the three men almost held their breaths, Detective O'Reilly stood up and tried to work the kinks out of his aging joints.

"Geez, it has been a while since I have done crime-scene work like this."

"What's the verdict?" Ryan asked anxiously.

"I think there is at least a faint outline. It should be enough to, at least, get us an estimated shoe size and even the type of shoe. In my opinion, it looks like some sort of boot and men's size ten," Detective O'Reilly responded while he wiped the dust from his pants.

"Alright. What's the next step?" Ryan asked, with hesitation in his voice.

"I am going to have one of my techs look at this. I will keep this as quiet as I can, but this is not my area of expertise. And I know you don't want just answers; you want the right answers."

"I get it. Let us know what you find out. And thank you. There was a moment this morning where I thought I was losing my mind," Ryan admitted, managing a smile.

"Ryan, did you ever think you would need to be playing spy games working for Hunter?" The detective let out one of his famous belly laughs.

Hunter chimed in. "I am beginning to think I wouldn't have all these issues if I hadn't hired Ryan."

"Very funny, both of you. You should take your act on the road. Hit up Vegas. Let's go, detective. I don't want you missing out if they brought in donuts this morning." Ryan bantered.

The three men, once again, took the elevator back up to the lobby. After saying their goodbyes, Ryan and Hunter went back to the same indoor park bench.

"So, what do you think?" Hunter asked.

"About this whole insane mess? Or just life in general?"

"Does the general footwear description ring any bells?"

"Hunter, I am sure there is a slew of people in this building who are wearing some sort of boots. Does it narrow it down slightly? Of course, it does. We can rule out any women working here or delivering anything. And on average, a man with a size ten shoe is under six feet tall. Beyond that, I have no frigging clue."

Hunter heaved himself off the bench and strolled toward the private elevator, leaving Ryan sitting by himself on the bench.

CHAPTER 29

Once Ryan was back in his office, the place he used to think of as a sanctuary, he requested the video footage for all the outside cameras on and around the building during the time frame in question. While waiting for the files to be sent to him, Ryan reflected on the fact that both his apartment and office had been breached. There was no longer a place he did not feel violated. The more he reflected on this, the more irritated Ryan got. And the question remained if the same person was the culprit.

Before Ryan could completely dive into that particular black hole, the email with a link to the surveillance footage showed up. There were almost twenty wide-angle cameras focused on each doorway plus the parking garage and streets surrounding the building.

After an hour, Ryan stood up, without learning much more except the fact there were a lot more people around than he thought during the early morning hours. Although only halfway through the footage, Ryan needed a break. Given the weather was not conducive to outdoor running, he opted to hit the treadmill in the gym instead.

When Ryan reached his predetermined ten miles, he took a quick shower and retreated to his office to finish reviewing the videos.

Ryan hit pay dirt on the last video. At approximately 4:45 a.m., a figure could be seen walking toward the loading dock, where several trucks were waiting to offload produce, bread, and meat for the cafeteria.

Based on the physique, Ryan determined the figure was male and approximately six feet tall. Ryan's eyes remained glued to the screen like he was watching an intense movie, afraid to look away for fear he might miss something. Next, the man could be seen wearing a dark jacket and khaki pants. He innocently grabbed one of the boxes of produce and proceeded up the loading dock steps to where other workers were quickly unloading their goods before disappearing out of the camera frame.

The excitement overtook Ryan, causing him to almost fall out of his chair. Quickly, Ryan saved these ten minutes of video and sent the encrypted file to Hunter's email. Knowing Hunter would more than likely immediately come down to him, Ryan started tracking this mystery man on the cameras inside the building, now that he knew the point of origin.

Suddenly, Ryan stopped the video tour of the Logan headquarters and went back to the previous footage. Thirty minutes after Ryan witnessed the unknown intruder entering the building, the trespasser could be seen leaving the same way he had come. What Ryan saw next wasn't something he anticipated or expected.

Once the man cleared the loading dock area, he looked straight up at the camera and gave a salute with a smile. This well-lit area showed the intruder clear as day. To Ryan's shock, it was unmistakably Greg Smythe. Greg sauntered down the street toward Atlantic Avenue as if he didn't have a care in the world.

"That rat bastard! Guess that clears that up!" Ryan roared.

"Clears what up?" Hunter asked when he entered Ryan's office.

"Why don't you take a look for yourself and let me know if you see anyone familiar," Ryan said with a fevered stare.

Ryan sat back in his chair, his heart pounding, and observed Hunter. Within the span of a few minutes, Hunter's calm demeanor transformed to rage.

"Are you fucking kidding me? This asshole is back?" Hunter abruptly stood up with clenched hands, causing the chair he was occupying to fall over backward.

"I thought that would get your blood boiling. I have to say, *not* something I was expecting. I honestly hoped since we haven't seen or heard from Greg Smythe, he was either dead or on a beach somewhere lying low," Ryan remarked through gritted teeth.

Hunter picked up the chair and sat back down, trying to calm the multitude of emotions circulating through him. Not wanting to ever turn out as evil as his father, Hunter had tried to make a conscious choice to be empathetic and understanding. Greg Smythe was a completely different story—the man had stalked, tormented, and kidnapped Emma— and for that, Hunter wanted to see him suffer an excruciating demise.

"At least we now know who one of the players we are dealing with is even if we still don't know who is paying our good friend, Mr. Smythe." Ryan hesitated. "Or know who helped Greg get into an ultra-secure area of the building."

Hunter blinked rapidly in response to Ryan's last words.

"Hunter, the security office requires a special keycard to get in here. These cannot be faked. It is looking more and more like he has inside help. Which is disturbing on so many levels."

"I don't know how to wrap my head around all this, Ryan. I am going to say this out loud to you and only you. If I get the chance, I will kill this man with my bare hands if I must. He won't be allowed to inhale another breath if I can help it."

Ryan was stunned by Hunter's declaration, although he felt the same way. "I completely understand and am right there with you. Let's make a deal. Let me be the one to end his miserable life. Trust me, you don't want that on your conscious."

"I will agree to give you the first crack at him. If you can't finish the job, then I will," Hunter replied, leaving a chill in the air.

"Let's switch tactics for a few minutes. I'm still trying to understand how all this fits together. We are still missing some large pieces of the puzzle. And I am wondering if there are some red herrings that have been strategically placed in our path to make us inevitably run around in circles."

Hunter stared at Ryan with a baffled look.

"What I mean is there are fresh players involved, and to our knowledge, they weren't involved previously."

A small smile formed on Hunter's face. "Gotcha. You are referring to your lady friend."

"Yes, my lady friend seems to be part of this. You know how I don't believe in coincidences. My former colleague shows up out of the blue. Greg Smythe pops back up and breaks into this building. All of this is around the time we found your father's secret hideaway.

"I would also strongly suggest you increase the security around Emma now that we conclusively know Greg is back in Boston. He leveraged her once to get to you—let's make sure that opportunity is taken away from him this time around."

Hunter pulled his phone out of his pocket and texted a quick note before responding to Ryan.

"Done. I have doubled the amount of security around Emma. And before you bring this up, I'm still not ready to tell Emma about any of this. She has been so relaxed since the honeymoon and enjoying life. I don't want to spoil her bliss and cause her to be in a panic or paranoid. This is non-negotiable, Ryan."

Ryan knew from Hunter's stern tone there would be no changing his mind.

"Your call, buddy," was all Ryan could respond.

"Thank you, Ryan. Where do we go from here?" Hunter urged.

"I need to focus on the third file cabinet. I don't know what the contents were of the yellow folder Greg stole, but I'm hoping the other files might at least give me a clue. As I mentioned previously, I don't think the color coding was arbitrary. Philip never did anything random—it was always calculated and with precision. Each color means something. I just need to figure out his thought process and the pattern. Then, it might give us a clue as to why that specific folder was so important."

Wicked Nemesis of the Hunted 287

"What you said makes sense, but a few minutes ago you thought some of these things might be red herrings to throw us off the real trail. Would it be plausible this is one of those instances? Mind you, I know nothing about spy games."

"This is the problem, Hunter. I just don't know. But I do know if we dismiss it and something happens, it won't be good for any of us. My first order of business is to find out more about Mr. Smythe." Ryan rubbed his chin and leaned back in his chair.

"Find out more? I thought he was an mystery?" Hunter questioned, clearly perplexed.

"I may have a few new resources at my disposal that were unavailable the last time this asshole came into our lives."

"I do not want to know what you're referring to, do I?"

"That is affirmative. Let me do a little additional research to see if anything interesting surfaces."

"Okay. Keep me informed." Hunter stood up and meandered out of Ryan's office with less confidence than when he entered.

After Hunter was enclosed in the elevator, Ryan locked his office door.

Opening the secret compartment in his desk drawer for the second time, Ryan retrieved the appropriate cell phone and selected the only number contained in the contacts.

Two minutes later, that same cell phone vibrated, causing Ryan to have some angst.

"To what do I owe this pleasure so soon after our last conversation, Ryan?" asked Carolyn in a genial voice on the other end.

"I was hoping to avoid making this call, but circumstances have changed."

"Interesting how you seem to need me now more than previously."

"I need information. And I need it quickly." Ryan hated the see-saw game, which always had been a part of these conversations.

"Of course, you do. What's the matter? Your top analyst on vacation?"

"You are in a good mood today. I wonder why that is," Ryan remarked cautiously.

"It is always a good day when one of my top agents calls me for assistance. Gives me a sense of gratification."

Ryan tried not to show his irritation and knew he had to play along to obtain the information he needed.

"Oh, Ryan, you used to be more fun than this. Lighten up a bit. A deal is a deal, and I will provide any assistance I can. Let me guess what it is you are looking for."

"How about I just tell you? I am not in the mood for guessing games."

"Does it have anything to do with the little breach in your office last night?"

Wicked Nemesis of the Hunted   289

Ryan was stunned into silence.

"As I have told you on many occasions, we keep tabs on our former employees and anything interesting happening in their lives," Carolyn continued smugly.

"I should have known. Did you bug my office? Or is it my email or phone? Or all the above?" Ryan rapidly tapped his fingers on the desk.

"Ryan, you always were the paranoid one. I just wouldn't want anything to happen to you. How about you tell me what, specifically, it is you need?"

"Fine. I need anything you have on Greg Smythe."

"Ahh, the suspect in Emma's kidnapping and stalking plus many other misdeeds. And the same person who broke into your office—if I am not mistaken."

Ryan inhaled sharply before responding, "Yes. We know that 'Greg Smythe' is an alias. I need to know his true identity plus anything else, including financials. He is too skilled to just be another thug for hire. In fact, he has some of the same skills your company teaches its new recruits."

"Are you implying he is one of ours, Ryan?"

"I am not implying anything, Carolyn. Just making an observation. Maybe he took a few online courses in entering top-security buildings undetected," Ryan said, seething with sarcasm.

"The name does not ring a bell, although there have been so many employees who have passed through these doors over the years. It is awfully hard to keep track." Carolyn tried to sound thoughtful.

"I thought you told me you keep track of your past employees."

"Well, we keep track of the *important* employees. Those who did not meet our lofty standards, for instance, are not worth wasting resources on," Carolyn replied.

Ryan tucked this tidbit of information away.

"How quickly do you think you can get me the information?" Ryan grew impatient.

"I will see what we can do and hopefully have something to you by end of day today. Ryan, it is always a pleasure speaking with you. Stay in touch," Carolyn expressed before disconnecting.

Ryan wanted to smash the phone with his bare hands when the call ended. A flood of emotions erupted through him, resurfacing memories from a time in his life he had worked hard to leave in the past. He knew he was dancing with the devil, which meant he was once again their asset to do with as they pleased.

CHAPTER 30

Around three o'clock, Ryan's desk drawer vibrated. Unlocking the special compartment, he noticed a text message with a file attachment on the secure cell phone. Ryan hesitated before finally opening the file. Part of him was afraid of what he may learn.

Ryan strode over to his open office door and peered into the bullpen, referring to what the team called their open area workspace. Everyone was caught up in their work and did not notice Ryan observing them. Gently, Ryan closed his office door and locked it.

Satisfied he wouldn't be disturbed, Ryan maneuvered back to his desk and opened the attachment. Ryan plugged his phone into his laptop and uploaded the file for easier viewing.

With a deep breath, Ryan began digesting the multiple pages of information in front of him. An hour passed and he hadn't moved an inch. He had been completely enthralled with the information the file contained.

"It would have been nice to have this information when all this shit started," Ryan commented to an empty office.

Ryan learned Greg Smythe and he had indeed been employed by the same company. And the two overlapped for a couple of those years, although Greg was never specifically part of any of Ryan's operations. Greg was part of a specialized technical team, which is where he learned his exceptional breaking-and-entering skills. Ryan also learned Greg's code name was "The Fox," which Ryan assumed was due, in part, to his perceived cunning nature.

Leaning back in his chair, Ryan tried to mentally organize what he had uncovered about Greg. The information would help the team, although he wondered how much of the report had been redacted by his former boss.

Ryan decided he needed to take a long overdue break and ran upstairs to grab a coffee and snack. Opting not to dive into the protein bar on the short walk down to his office, Ryan decided to wait instead of trying to balance both the steaming hot black coffee and opening the wrapper at the same time.

Once back in his office, Ryan placed the coffee on his desk and attacked the chocolate-and-peanut-butter energy booster. With no napkins in sight, Ryan wiped his hands on his pants before awakening his laptop.

The screen came to life with the same report he had been scouring before his mini break. Blowing on his coffee to cool it down before he burned his mouth, Ryan tried to absorb what was on the screen in front of him.

Greg spent most of his early days in and out of foster care until he turned fifteen, when he was placed in a group home until he became an adult. The foster care reports were all basically the same. Greg was a troubled child, with little regard for the other children in the home. He preferred to be isolated and had trouble interacting with others the same age. One report noted how Greg would never look anyone in the eye—he would always turn away if someone were speaking to him or look downward.

Reading on, Ryan noted Greg had started with his manipulation abilities early on. Another report stated Greg appeared to treat people like they were pawns in a game, to do with as he pleased. There were instances where some of the other children he was in contact with would end up with broken bones or other minor injuries. No one could positively attribute it to Greg, but shortly after an incident, Greg was moved to another foster family.

Ryan leaned back in his chair with his arms clasped behind his head. Letting out a sigh, he wondered if Greg was born this way or a result of his upbringing. Either way, Greg had been at this an exceedingly long time and wasn't going to stop any time soon. Since Ryan now had a better understanding of Greg's mental state, he hoped it would give them a slight edge. The challenge would be how to use this information against Greg.

Putting this thought to the side for the moment, Ryan perused the remaining content in the file. After Greg graduated from high school, he went to college in Boston on a computer science scholarship. Ryan wasn't surprised Greg excelled at subjects like computer programming or math. From what Ryan had witnessed throughout this nightmare, Greg was very calculating. It was as if his brain functioned like a computer program's algorithm.

After graduating in the top ten percent of his class, Greg started working for Ryan's and his mutual company. Ryan rubbed his chin in deep thought. Similar to Ryan, the agency recruited Greg in his twenties. It was a bit clandestine how the company went about the recruitment process.

Ryan was led to believe he was applying for a security job at a large corporation. During the initial interview, Ryan was subjected to a battery of psychological tests before a grueling two hours of questions from a panel of what he thought were company executives. His future handler was one of those taking part in the interview.

After a half day of this, Ryan was brought into a small conference room. Across the table sat Carolyn, who motioned for him to take a seat. Ryan recalled how he was mesmerized by her beauty but also her stature. She had both an authoritative presence and warm nature, simultaneously.

Ryan closed his eyes and felt like he was back in the bland-looking room, staring into Carolyn's hazel eyes. He could remember every word of the conversation like it had happened yesterday.

"Ryan, please let me introduce myself. I am Carolyn, an assistant director here. Can I get you any water or something to eat? I know it has been a long, grueling morning for you."

"No, ma'am. I am fine. Thank you for asking," Ryan replied, trying to sound confident.

"Very well. I would like to congratulate you on passing the interview process. Your scores were off the charts in several areas—something I must admit I have not seen in too many candidates over the years. You are quite an impressive, young man," Carolyn said warmly.

"Thank you, ma'am."

"Please, call me Carolyn. I think after today we can dispense with the formalities."

"Very well, Carolyn," Ryan acknowledged, trying to calculate the end game of the conversation.

"I would like to explain a little more about this job. It is more than a job—it is a way of life. I notice that you are not married, nor do you have any children. Is that correct?" Carolyn asked, reading the file in front of her.

"Yes, that is correct."

"That is particularly good. This line of work is not for everyone and is even more difficult if you have attachments who could potentially become liabilities."

"I must ask, Carolyn, exactly what type of job is this? I thought I had applied for a security role."

"This is, indeed, a security role, but not corporate security. This is national security."

Ryan's jaw fell open while he gaped at Carolyn.

With a jovial laugh, Carolyn responded. "I can see you were not expecting to hear that. That means we have done our job well.

"Ryan, we are a specialized area of the US government tasked with stopping incidents from occurring on foreign soil that would ultimately impact our national security. There are a lot of people out in the world who do not like or approve of our way of life. They do not believe in freedom or democracy. And as a result, our freedom is always at risk if we do not take measures to protect ourselves."

Ryan swallowed hard and let Carolyn continue.

"If you accept this position, you will have the opportunity to help protect our freedom from any of these threats. You will travel all over the world to accomplish this. Admittedly, not in the most desired locations."

"So, I won't be staying at the Ritz is what you are saying." Ryan joked.

A smile formed on Carolyn's face. "Yes, that is what I am saying. I think you have the qualities we are looking for. The qualities we need to be successful in this never-ending fight. Most Americans never know the number of threats against us every day… and that is how we want to keep it. We want the American people not to fear going about their daily lives. They shouldn't have to worry about going to the grocery store or driving to work, wondering if they will come home alive to their families."

Carolyn looked Ryan squarely in the eyes before continuing. "I think you have what it takes to make a difference, Ryan. The question for you is: Do you want to make a difference or be part of the oblivious population?"

It was Ryan's turn to smile. "I don't want to be sitting at a desk watching computer monitors in a corporate lobby somewhere. I applied for this job because I need to pay my rent, not because it was my lifelong dream."

"Excellent. I knew I was right about you, Ryan. Your past military experience will be the edge we need to win this war as well. Based on your test scores, you have a unique ability to calculate outcomes and risks on the fly. That skill will be most valued in this position."

"Upon entering this room, I began calculating the end game of this discussion. Within the first five minutes of the psych tests, I knew this was no ordinary job interview. About one percent of me thought of walking out, but ninety-nine percent of me was intrigued to see where this would lead."

"And what do you think now, Ryan? Want to help us save the world? Or at least our little piece of it?"

"Count me in!" Ryan replied with enthusiasm.

"Like I said, I had a good feeling about you, Ryan. I have been watching you for a little while now. You are destined for remarkable things here."

Ryan couldn't hide the incredulous look on his face in response to Carolyn's comments.

Carolyn smirked and stood up. Ryan stood up as well.

"It was a pleasure to meet you today, Ryan. I look forward to seeing how you progress," Carolyn said with her hand outstretched.

Shaking her hand, Ryan replied, "Thank you for the opportunity, Carolyn."

"Someone will be in shortly to escort you back to the lobby. You will receive a package in the next couple of days with your training schedule and other pertinent information."

Carolyn left Ryan in the room by himself, although he had the distinct feeling he was being watched. Within two minutes, a security guard came to escort Ryan back to the lobby of a company that didn't exist in the real world.

Before Ryan could continue further down memory lane, Hunter appeared in his office doorway.

Wicked Nemesis of the Hunted   299

Taking his usual spot, Hunter commented, "Why is it every time I pop down here it always seems like I am waking you up from a nap?"

"Funny, Hunter. Your sarcasm does not become you, by the way," Ryan stated, rolling his eyes.

"That is what Emma says. If I didn't know any better, I would say you both have been conspiring against my unique form of humor."

"To what do I owe the pleasure of your company, Hunter?"

"I looked at the clock and noticed it was time to head out. Since I haven't heard from you in recent hours, I wanted to make sure you didn't fall asleep on the job."

"Nope. No sleeping on the job. Just doing a little reflecting and soul-searching."

"Okay, that sounds a bit ominous. I am going to kick myself for asking this, but here it goes. What is it you are searching your soul for?"

"Just remembering the good ole days long gone from my previous line of work."

"You will need to provide a bit more information, Ryan. Does this have anything to do with what is happening in the present?" Hunter had a long day of endless contracts and negotiations and was quickly regretting his detour down to the depths of the building.

"Yes, it does." Ryan sighed. "I was finally able to find out more about the elusive Greg Smythe.

Specifically, his past."

Hunter's eyes bulged. "What? How? When?"

"You forgot where and who in your response."

"Don't be a wiseass, Ryan. Start at the beginning. Please."

"Fine. I contacted someone who would be able to get this information, and they did. I am sure I wasn't given the complete story, and some of it was left out, but it's a hell of a lot more than we had yesterday."

Ryan proceeded to tell Hunter what he had learned about Greg's upbringing and college years.

"So, in a nutshell, it sounds like Greg was a sociopath from early on. Which makes complete sense. That had been my feeling from the beginning. Nice to have it finally confirmed." Ryan finished.

"If you say so, Ryan. I can tell you are holding something back. Spit out the rest."

"The cherry on top or icing on the cake, whichever you prefer, is Greg and I previously worked at the same company. In reality, we were there at the same time for almost two years. I don't recall ever knowing him. And, to my knowledge, he never provided any, let's say, technical support for any of my projects."

"Let me get this straight. A sociopath worked at the same place with you for two years, and you never crossed paths? Yet one day he miraculously appears out of thin air in Boston. At the same time, need I remind you, we are on the brink of an enormous discovery? Do I have that correct?" Hunter was exasperated.

"About sums it up. But regarding your Boston reference, Greg did go to college here. He may like the Boston vibe or these lovely winters."

"Umm, isn't it you who says there are no such things as coincidences?"

"Not sure. I am sure I may have said it one time or another."

"How can we use this information to send this asshole to hell where he belongs?"

Ryan was taken aback by Hunter's demeanor. "Hunter, as I have told you. I will be the one to 'send him to hell.' I understand your frustration, anger, and fear. Trust me when I say, you *do not* want this on your conscience. This isn't like in the movies. It will weigh on you until it destroys you."

Hunter logically knew Ryan had a point, but he couldn't shake the hatred coupled with fear slowly consuming him.

"Understood. Just know I will do whatever it takes to protect my family."

"I get it, buddy. I still have several more pages from the report to comb through. These would be the post-recruitment years. I will see what else I might be able to gather from them. But it can wait until tomorrow morning. Time for us to call it a night after the day we've had."

Ryan packed up his belongings, locked his desk drawers, and practically pushed Hunter out the door. Before leaving, Ryan made double sure the office was secured.

The two men walked in silence up the flight of stairs to the parking garage. Within minutes, each of them was behind the wheel of their respective cars and exited the garage.

CHAPTER 31

Dusk overtook the city with its golden hue radiating off the concrete-and-glass jungle. Ryan often wondered if this was what purgatory was like—not bright or dark but somewhere in between. Shedding just enough light but with a menacing backdrop.

As Ryan was parking his car at his apartment building, a text message arrived. His pulse quickened slightly when he saw the sender's name. Ryan struggled with his recent decisions and knew he was now past the point of no return. The darkness was about to swallow him whole again. It was like he was standing in quicksand, with no way out.

Ryan fumbled with his keys when he stepped off the elevator to find Sue leaning against the wall.

"Hi, Ryan. I hope you don't mind me waiting for you. Although I wondered if you were coming home at all."

"I didn't know I had a curfew. I am surprised to see you here, Sue."

Opening the door and disarming the alarm system, he held the door open for Sue. While she glided her way to the living room, Ryan could not help but notice her features once again.

"Ryan, stop looking at my ass. We have business to discuss first."

Ryan cocked an eyebrow and followed Sue, intrigued by her insinuation this might not be all business tonight.

"I'm not sure what I have in the way of dinner. I can order takeout if you would like," Ryan said casually.

"Let's get the business out of the way first, Ryan."

"I get the distinct impression you are under some sort of deadline. What is it you need to ask me?"

"Rumor has it you have been in contact with Carolyn about a specific individual we would both like to locate."

All of Ryan's senses were immediately on alert. How in the world did she know this? He only received the report today. It has been less than twenty-four hours since Ryan even made the request.

"Ryan, I can tell from your hesitation you are trying to calculate, in your almost nonhuman way, how much I know and from whom I have learned this information. Then you are doing your usual risk assessment to determine how much you should tell me to satisfy my employer, whom you are still

Wicked Nemesis of the Hunted   305

trying to confirm." Sue relaxed on the couch and, once again, crossed her long legs in the salacious way only she could.

"I hate it when you do that."

Sue gave her best "who me?" look in Ryan's direction.

"You seem to know a lot for someone who is no longer employed at our former company."

"Nice try, Ryan. I cannot confirm nor deny that I am employed at any company."

"It was worth a shot. No pun intended, of course." Ryan replied with a wink.

"Ouch. I thought we had gotten past that small indiscretion of our relationship."

"I am not going to rehash the fact you shot me. I just couldn't pass up an opportunity to remind you."

"Ryan, you are right. I am under a bit of a time crunch. How much do you know about Greg Smythe? You show me yours; I'll show you mine. Tit for tat. All's fair in love and war."

"Stop! Please. I get your point."

"So, are you willing to trade information?"

Ryan opened the refrigerator and grabbed a Guinness for each of them.

"Fine. We can share information."

Ryan knew they both would not be totally forth-coming and guessed she already knew most of what he had been privy to.

"Greg started his sociopath career at an early age in foster care. Exceedingly high IQ. Graduated in the top ten percent of his college class with a degree in computer science. That is all that I know as of right now," Ryan said, withholding the fact he had more of the report to read through.

"Makes sense. And I can't say I'm shocked. Were there any details about his days in foster care?"

"Most of the reports were the same. He was isolated and manipulative. There were always accidents with the other children in the house, which generally led to Greg being uprooted and placed somewhere else."

Sue thought about this information carefully before responding. "Okay. That plays into what I know so far. He is callous and without any regard for human life. He is a machine without emotion but one that can play the part he chooses to get the job done."

"Why the urgent interest in Greg?"

Sue did not immediately respond. "I think he is trying to kill me."

Ryan gasped. "Are you sure? I was under the impression you two didn't know each other. Was I wrong?"

"Our paths crossed briefly around the time you left our last assignment."

"You mean when you shot me."

Wicked Nemesis of the Hunted   307

"Yes. After I shot you, some things happened in that godforsaken place. You were taken to safety, which was my plan for you."

"Did I just hear you correctly? You shot me to protect me?" Ryan gulped his beer.

"In essence, yes. Ryan, I was working on something slightly different than what the rest of the team was assigned. I am not going to go into details. Just know shooting you was the hardest thing I have ever had to do. You were in far more danger than you realized, and I needed to be the one to save you."

Ryan glanced at Sue with a blank stare.

"I think I was fairly capable of taking care of myself," Ryan scoffed.

Sue looked directly at Ryan. "I know you were. I just couldn't take the chance of something happening to you. I need you to trust me when I tell you this was the only way. Look, we are getting off track here."

"At this point, I don't know what track I am supposed to be on!" Ryan exclaimed.

"Greg was the analyst, for lack of a better description, assigned to me during our mission. None of the rest of the team knew. It was need to know only. Unfortunately, after all hell broke loose, I knew we had been compromised. And the only person who could have done it was Greg Smythe."

"I am not sure I even want to know more about this. You are saying I crossed paths with Greg, unknowingly, and what? He was targeting me back then?" Ryan finished his beer and braced himself against the counter.

"Yes. That is exactly what I am saying. Greg is a hit man for hire. But you already know that. I am still trying to figure out the connection between back then and now. As you drilled into me when I was working with you…there is no such thing as coincidences. This is a big neon sign coincidence."

Ryan rubbed his face, grabbed a second beer, and plopped next to Sue on the couch. They looked like a normal couple discussing the events of their respective days. Ryan acknowledged nothing could be further from the truth.

"Let's forget about the link to the past for a minute. Why do you think Greg is trying to kill you in the here and now?"

"There have been some unusual events recently. At first, I thought it was just my current employer being careful. Now, I am not so sure."

Ryan looked at Sue with questioning eyes.

"I found several listening devices in my apartment. For the last week, I have been followed on more than one occasion. And before you ask me, yes, I change my routine daily. I started receiving text messages and emails calling me by some of my aliases."

"Definitely creepy. But why do you suspect Greg?"

Wicked Nemesis of the Hunted   309

"Ryan, think about it. My life, like yours, is more secure than Fort Knox. We use encrypted messaging. We are trained in avoiding detection. And I know for a fact Greg is in Boston right this very minute."

Ryan almost choked on his beer. "How do you know?"

"Again, let's skip the 'how-to' portion of this conversation. But yesterday I caught a glimpse of him."

"Where?" Ryan shouted.

"Calm down, cowboy. I was getting off the train, and I saw him across the platform."

"Are you sure it was him?"

"Very sure. He waved at me." Sue threw off her shoes and wrapped her legs underneath her on the couch.

"Interesting."

"Ryan, you don't seem as outraged as I had anticipated." Sue paused. "You knew he was in the city, didn't you?"

"Well, I saw him on a security camera. He waved at the camera."

Sue burst out laughing, causing Ryan to join in.

CHAPTER 32

After ordering and inhaling a primo pepperoni pizza, Ryan and Sue relaxed in bed, watching a movie until Sue drifted off to sleep. Ryan's body complimented the curves of Sue's naked body, fitting together like a jigsaw puzzle. Softly caressing her butter-soft skin, Ryan mulled over what he had learned. When Sue stirred slightly, Ryan stilled hoping he did not inadvertently wake her.

Throughout the night and into the early morning, the couple seemed to take turns sleeping. When Sue was awake, Ryan was asleep, and vice versa. Ryan's mind drifted from the Amazon rainforest to a train platform and then to his office. Each time, Greg Smythe was in the shadows, just out of focus, but Ryan could sense him lurking. It was like Greg was haunting Ryan in his dreams and in real life.

Dawn stayed hidden behind the ripples of clouds, creating the illusion of Bermuda's pink sands in the sky. Rolling over, Ryan watched Sue sleeping. Her breathing was rhythmic and tantalizing. Ryan felt a small pang of guilt for what he was about to do. He wasn't sure the last time she had slept this soundly.

Delicately, he ran his fingers down the side of Sue's body, causing goose bumps along the way. Exploring as he went, he could hear quiet gasps from the woman sharing his bed. As the sun rose, so did the activities under the covers.

Exhausted and perspiring, the couple lay on their backs in bed, trying to catch their breaths.

"Well, that was fun," Sue said, propping herself up on her elbow and looking at Ryan.

"Indeed, it was. I think I need some more fun before I start the day, though."

Without another word, the couple once again succumbed to their most carnal desires.

Losing track of time, Ryan strolled into his office, humming a melody two hours past the time he normally got to work.

"Someone is in a good mood for being two hours late," Hunter remarked.

Ryan nearly jumped out of his skin, not expecting Hunter to be outside his locked office door.

"Geez, Hunter. You, once again, almost gave me a heart attack."

"Well, the funny thing is, I own the building. Therefore, I can wait outside any office I please," Hunter replied.

Ryan unlocked his door, and the lights magically illuminated the space. Hunter situated himself in his usual spot while Ryan unpacked his messenger bag. Examining his desk, Ryan felt like something was missing.

Hunter rolled his eyes. "Looks like you forgot your usual coffee and muffin."

"Damn! Not sure how I could have forgotten the two most important things to start my day," Ryan groaned.

Hunter cocked an eye in Ryan's direction. "Gee, I wonder what had you so preoccupied this morning."

"I decided to have a bit of a lie-in this morning, as you Brits say. No big deal," Ryan tried his best to brush off the inquisition he knew was headed his way.

Hunter snorted. "Sure. Just needed a little extra sleep. My question is: With whom did you need this extra sleep?"

Ryan dodged the question. "Is there something you wanted this morning, your highness?"

"Ah, the old changing-the-subject ploy. I have used it many times myself. Alrighty. If you wish for this lady to remain nameless, so be it."

Ryan crossed his arms across his chest. "Again, I will ask, is there something you needed?"

"Nope. Can't I just drop in unannounced to see my pal?"

Wicked Nemesis of the Hunted   313

"As you stated, you own the building, so what is mine is yours."

"That is very philosophical of you."

"It is my softer side coming to the surface. Let's switch gears because this conversation is exhausting."

"Fine by me. I wouldn't want to tucker you out any more than you already are," Hunter agreed and smoothed the front of his shirt.

Ryan proceeded. "Any news from the researchers?"

"No, nothing concrete since our meeting with them. I am going against my nature and not pressuring them too much. But I really wish we would get a breakthrough soon."

"Well, finding those plants in Hardwicke was a blessing and a curse."

"How so?"

"It is a blessing in the sense we have something more tangible to study. And a curse because they probably aren't viable enough to replicate. It's like the proverbial carrot on a stick—close enough to almost touch but not close enough to grab it."

Hunter let Ryan's synopsis penetrate his thoughts.

Ryan paused for a moment before continuing. "I am still curious about what's in the file Greg removed from here." Ryan pointed to the infamous file cabinet.

"I agree. Why was only that *one* file taken?" Hunter commiserated.

Ryan stared in deep thought at the file cabinets lined up to the side of his desk while simultaneously watching Hunter out of the corner of his eye.

"Ryan, I know that look. You are mulling something over in your calculating brain. And if I were to take a guess, I would put my money on you uncovering more information."

Ryan remained silent.

"Your silence signals I am on the right track. Let me continue. I think this information may have come from your lady friend."

Ryan shrugged.

"I think I am two for two. Here is the third and final piece of this scenario. You are contemplating whether to tell me what you know. You are doing your typical risk-and-reward analysis."

Ryan shifted slightly in his chair, unnerved by how well his best friend understood how he thought.

"Your body language just confirmed I am correct on all counts. Ryan, you know I will never ask you to divulge any information you either don't want to or can't. I just need to know if this latest information ups the ante for this game. Or is it a draw?"

Ryan chose his words carefully. "For now, I think it is a draw."

"Can you elaborate? Even a little?" Hunter probed.

"I don't think I am ready to completely divulge what I have learned…*yet*. There are some details I need to work out first. And, Hunter, this isn't me trying to keep information from you. This is me making sure this isn't a wild goose chase. All I can say is there aren't any *new* players involved, to the best of my knowledge."

Hunter immediately picked up on Ryan's emphasis on "new players" and knew Ryan always selected his words wisely and purposefully.

"I understand. I know this goes without saying, but I am going to say it anyhow. Please let me know as soon as you can. I want to be prepared."

"Of course, Hunter. I wouldn't have it any other way."

Hunter rose and started for the door.

"Hunter?"

He turned and responded, "Something else, Ryan?"

"I would strongly recommend you start having Jared driving you to and from wherever you go. I noticed you have been driving yourself since you returned from your honeymoon."

The reality of Ryan's suggestion, along with his cryptic responses this morning, was a wake-up call to Hunter. It felt like someone had slapped him in the face. Although Hunter had already prepared for this possibility, hearing Ryan say the words sent a chill down his spine.

"If you think it is necessary, Ryan, I will do as you ask."

"Thank you for not fighting me on this, Hunter. I would feel better knowing that when I can't be there, someone is watching both you and the lovely Emma."

"And the mention of Emma means she is to be driven wherever also?"

"Yes. I would rather be safe than sorry. And we both know Jared is an excellent driver."

"You are correct. He proved his driving skills back in the Hardwicke debacle. We were lucky to have him there with us."

"I wholeheartedly agree. Hunter, start this today. Please call Emma and let her know. You can blame it on me being paranoid or overly cautious."

Hunter walked out of Ryan's office feeling an additional weight resting on his broad shoulders.

Once Hunter was securely tucked into his office high in the sky, he let out the deep breath he had been subconsciously holding. Staring out at the expansive ocean, Hunter knew what Ryan was trying to tell him—the threat from Greg Smythe had escalated. Tension started to infiltrate Hunter's neck and shoulders at the thought that the man who kidnapped and almost killed his wife was prowling in the shadows of Boston while waiting to strike.

Hunter slumped on the leather couch facing the horizon. A relaxed smile formed on his face while he reminisced about the first time Emma was in his office. Wanting to impress her, the duo had used his office for their initial meeting to plan the gala. They drank a bottle of rose wine from Holloran Vineyards. The pair dined on Caesar salad, thinly sliced tenderloin beef, asparagus with béarnaise sauce, and red roasted potatoes, finishing with crème brûlée.

After their lunch, Hunter remembered how proud he felt to have the most beautiful woman in the world on his arm as they toured the Ares Logan headquarters. He recalled Emma was in awe of the space and thrilled as her vision for the gala began to form. Her infectious smile at that moment would be forever etched in Hunter's mind.

Hunter confessed that shortly after, the world as they knew it began to implode. If he could, Hunter would give up all his worldly possessions to go back to the exact moment when he and Emma were carefree, and the greatest problem was finding entertainment for the gala.

Pushing himself off the couch, Hunter grabbed his cell phone from his desk.

Jared answered on the second ring. "Yes, sir, how can I be of assistance?"

"I know I have been driving myself lately, and Emma has been doing the same. I will need for you to resume driving us wherever we go, starting today."

"Of course, sir. Shall I pick up Mrs. Logan first

or you this evening?" Jared requested.

"How about you drive me to her office to get her?"

"Very well, sir. Do you have a time in mind, or would you like to get back to me with a departure time?"

"I will call Emma to see what time she might be ready to head home and then text you."

"Absolutely, Mr. Logan."

"Thank you, Jared." Hunter ended the call without waiting for Jared to respond.

Hunter knew the next call was going to be a much trickier conversation than this last one. Jared was his employee, and Hunter knew Jared would never question or argue with Hunter's request. This would not be the case with his wife. Her incredibly independent nature precluded her from accepting what anyone told her she had to do.

Without a viable excuse to procrastinate any longer, Hunter hit the speed dial for Emma.

After the third ring, Emma cheerfully answered the call, "Hello, my sweet."

"Hi, kitten. How is your day going?"

"The usual. Full of meetings. Is anything wrong?"

"Can't I just call to hear your lovely voice?" Hunter inquired.

"Yes, but there is usually more to it. Hunter, spill. What is going on and should I be concerned?"

Hunter flinched slightly, knowing he was going to give his wife half-truths once again.

"Now, why is it you always think I am up to no good?"

"Stop deflecting, Hunter. You hardly ever call me during the day unless there is a reason."

"I missed you."

"I'm waiting for a more plausible reason. I know you miss me as I miss you."

"I thought I would pick you up from work tonight so we could spend more time together."

"Uh-huh. Something is going on, isn't there?"

Hunter bowed his head, wishing Emma wouldn't challenge his request.

Hunter snapped. "Emma, for once, can you just go with the flow?"

"Whoa. Dial it back, Hunter. Now I know there is undeniably something going on."

"I will tell you about it tonight when we get home. I just need to know what time to pick you up at your office."

Emma could feel the tension through the phone and decided not to continue pushing for answers right now.

"My last meeting should end around four p.m., so I could be ready by four-thirty. Or, I have plenty of work to keep me busy until you get here. Whichever is better for you is fine with me," Emma said, trying to be agreeable.

"I will see you at four-thirty in your lobby. Do *not* wait for me outside," Hunter responded, more forcefully than he meant to.

"Hunter, you are starting to scare me."

"That is not my intention, kitten. I never want to scare you—only protect you."

"Not sure that makes me feel any better. Look, I have to run to my next meeting, so I will drop this for now. But, Hunter, I expect you to tell me what the hell is going on when we get home. And I mean all of it. No leaving anything out. Or I will call Ryan, and we will have a little meeting of our own. Is that clear?" Emma stated, with her own fierceness bubbling to the surface.

"Yes, kitten. Crystal clear. I love you."

"I love you too."

Hunter walked over to the wall of windows, noticing a large sailboat on the horizon. Tonight's conversation was going to be difficult and one Hunter had been dreading. Since Ryan confirmed Greg Smythe had officially rejoined the game, Hunter's options were limited. His primary goal was to protect Emma and the life they were building together. He had made the conscious decision to leave her out of the latest developments, to try to protect her from the evil which was again seeping into their lives. Hunter prayed Emma would understand and forgive him for his questionable choices.

CHAPTER 33

With Jared driving the Mercedes, Hunter's car pulled up in front of Emma's office building at precisely four-thirty p.m. Almost hopping out of the car before Jared came to a complete stop, Hunter dashed inside the building to find Emma waiting by the security desk. Emma's facial expression said it all—she was not in the mood for subterfuge. Hunter would have no other choice but to tell her the whole truth.

"Hello, Hunter. Looks like you are back to having Jared driving you around," Emma commented, nodding in the direction of the car waiting outside.

Hunter softly kissed Emma on the cheek, hoping to melt some of the ice she was protruding. Without saying a word, he grabbed her bag in one hand and held her hand tightly with the other. The setting sun was hidden behind the clouds like smoke plumes from a raging fire below.

Jared was waiting with the door to the backseat open when the couple exited the building.

"Good evening, Mrs. Logan. I hope you had a pleasant day," Jared said while offering his hand to help Emma in the car.

"Hi, Jared. The day was good. Thank you for asking," Emma responded as she slid into the car.

Hunter nodded to Jared and entered through the same side of the car as Emma. Within a few minutes, Jared merged into the early stage of Boston rush hour traffic. The passengers sat in silence for the twenty minutes it took to arrive at their penthouse.

Upon entering the penthouse, Emma kicked off her shoes and dropped her bag in the foyer. Without warning, she spun around, catching Hunter off guard, and causing him to stumble backward a few feet. The fury in Emma's emerald-green eyes bore a hole into Hunter's soul.

"Emma, I know you are upset with me, and rightfully so. Let's sit down. I promise to tell you everything."

Without a word, Emma stomped to the couch and sat down so hard the cushions made a groaning sound. Hunter swallowed hard, knowing he was about to face Emma's wrath. When they got married, Emma made Hunter promise not to withhold information or keep secrets from her. She felt so strongly about it that she added it to their wedding vows. Hunter knew it would be nearly impossible to keep this vow but made the promise anyhow. Now he was going to deal with the consequences.

Sitting on the coffee table in front of the couch where Emma had situated herself, Hunter stared into Emma's fiery eyes, briefly remembering it was her eyes that first attracted him to her.

"Emma, I need you to understand that everything I do is out of love for you and our life together. I would move heaven and earth to keep you safe. And would give up all of this just to be a part of your world," Hunter said with sincerity.

Emma could tell Hunter spoke from the heart and responded in kind. "Hunter, I have never doubted your love for me. And I know there will always be some things you keep from me from a business perspective. I've had a feeling for a little while you and Ryan were keeping secrets."

Hunter could not hide his surprise. "You did?"

"Contrary to your belief, I know you better than you think. I have been trying to give you the time and space you needed to sort things out. And assumed those things had to do with the episode in Hardwicke."

"For the record, Ryan told me to let you in on all this...*repeatedly*."

"Ryan is a very smart man. The smartest I know."

"Ouch! Okay, that stung a bit, but it was well deserved."

"Stop evading the subject, Hunter. *Please* tell me what is going on. I am not a child who needs protecting." Emma pleaded while gently resting her hand on Hunter's knee.

"I know. I know." Hunter inhaled and exhaled. "Greg Smythe is back in Boston."

To Hunter's astonishment, Emma kept her composure.

"I figured this had something to do with that wretched creature. Tell me the story from the beginning. And don't you dare leave anything out!" Emma demanded.

For the next hour, Hunter recapped the details, including how he and Ryan found the secret vestibule at the Hardwicke estate and the break-ins at the Ares Logan headquarters. Once Hunter finished his tale with all the twists and turns expected in a suspenseful thriller, he moved to sit next to Emma. Without hesitation, Emma wrapped her arms around Hunter.

They sat in silence for a few minutes while Emma processed the deluge of information from Hunter. Slowly, she unraveled herself from him. For a moment, Hunter panicked, thinking for a split-second Emma was going to bolt. Instead, she cupped Hunter's face in her hands and kissed him. Hunter responded although somewhat confused.

Emma grinned. "Hunter, I love you more than the air I breathe. This is a lot to take in, and I am trying to process everything. Especially why you feel this inherent need to protect me. You, of all people, should know secrets don't stay buried—no matter how hard you try."

"You are absolutely correct about secrets. And for the record, I was going to tell you when I thought the time was right."

"I believe you. Let me make this a little easier for you. I would like Jared, or whomever you choose, to drive me for the foreseeable future."

Hunter was completely dumbfounded and realized he should have had more faith in Emma— something he would need to work on.

"I must say this is not the reaction I expected. Mrs. Logan, you continue to astonish me every day," Hunter commented and kissed her hand.

"That is my job—to always keep you on your toes. You had better call Ryan to let him know you are still alive and that I have agreed to the extra security measures," Emma stated before heading to the kitchen to begin dinner preparations.

Hunter watched Emma enter the kitchen before calling Ryan.

"Hey, buddy."

"Did I interrupt anything?"

"Nothing except rummaging through the refrigerator looking for anything that could remotely pass as dinner."

"Emma is in the kitchen doing the same thing."

"I am sure she will have better luck than me. Guess it will be another night for takeout. But I am assuming you didn't call to find out what I was having for dinner."

"You are correct. I just wanted to let you know I told Emma everything."

Ryan stared at the phone before responding, "And you're still amongst the living? How the hell did you manage that?"

"It was touch and go for a while and then, in only the way she can, Emma amazed me with her level-headedness."

"Emma? Your wife? Are we talking about the same person who's like a volcano erupting when she gets pissed off?"

Hunter chuckled, "Yes, one and the same. She said she has known for a while you and I were keeping secrets."

"I hope you told her I have been the one trying to reason with you to let her in on all this insanity!"

"Yes. I told her. So, you are in the clear."

"Phew! I still want to be a knight in shining armor in her eyes."

"I would not say shining but more dinged-up armor," Hunter countered.

"Funny. At least she knows. Is she going to be alright with the extra security?"

"Actually, she mentioned it before I could even get to that part. I already spoke to Jared about sticking to Emma like glue. Since Emma will be in good hands, there is just my personal safety to contend with. That is where you come in."

"Oh boy. Can't wait to hear this."

Wicked Nemesis of the Hunted   327

"You get to chauffer me around wherever I want to go."

"What you're saying is you want to carpool? I guess it is more environmentally friendly."

"Think of it however you must. You will need to be at the ready—day or night. I have a nice uniform for you to wear as well."

"Hunter, do I need to remind you of all my various skills? If you want to continue breathing, you will never bring up my being a chauffeur or wearing a uniform again." Ryan partially joked with a steely tone.

"Fine. It was worth a try. Do you think you could manage not to sleep in tomorrow morning? I would like to get to the office by seven a.m.," Hunter teased.

"I will pick you up at six forty-five a.m. And Hunter?"

"Yes?"

"I am glad Emma knows everything. You know I thought it was for the best. She is very astute and doesn't miss a trick. And that could be to our advantage."

"I know you are right. I just wanted her to be in an eternal world of bliss without any of this ugliness touching her."

"I get it. Unfortunately, she *is* part of all this. We will get to the bottom of everything. Then you two can live the fairy tale happily ever after."

"Have you been watching the *Hallmark Channel* again?"

"No! Now go help Emma with dinner. I will see you bright and early tomorrow."

Hunter helped Emma prepare baked chicken with rice for dinner. The couple spent the remainder of the evening relaxing on the couch watching mindless TV. For the first time in weeks, Hunter felt some of the weight on his shoulders dissipate. He hoped each day would bring more sunshine instead of dark storm clouds.

CHAPTER 34

Ryan showed up at Hunter's on time and crawled in the morning traffic to their destination. It was another drizzly morning, which caused cars to inch along the Boston streets. Amid horns playing an out-of-tune symphony in the Seaport District, Ryan could hear rolls of thunder in the distance. Just before the Mercedes pulled into the parking garage, a large bolt of lightning slammed into the Atlantic Ocean in front of them.

"Holy shit! Did you see that?" Ryan shouted while he parked the car.

"That was a little freaky. Hope it isn't an omen about how the day will go."

"You and your omens. First, it was the black crow from the other day. Now it is a lightning bolt."

Hunter shrugged and exited the car.

Riding the elevator in silence to Hunter's office, the two men contemplated the current situation from their own vantage points. Ryan focused on how to bring down his nemesis while trying not to lose his soul to the devil. Hunter's thoughts were occupied with protecting his family, at any cost, including the lengths he would go to if necessary.

Stepping out of the elevator, Ryan noticed Hunter's assistant was again suspiciously absent from her usual post. She normally guarded like Hunter was the King of England. Hunter unlocked the door to his office and headed toward his desk to drop his bag. Casually, Ryan surveyed the room in the manner he was trained to do.

"Ryan, you don't need to be looking for unwelcome visitors up here," Hunter remarked while unpacking his bag.

"Sorry. Old habits. And may I remind you— good thing or else we wouldn't have known Mr. Smythe broke into my office."

Hunter ignored Ryan and called his personal chef to deliver freshly made muffins and coffee.

"I know you diverged from your routine this morning, so the least I can do is provide you with caffeine and nourishment. Take a seat. It will be a few minutes."

Ryan did as he was told and sat across the desk from Hunter. While the pair waited for breakfast to be delivered, Ryan asked and pointed to the door, "Where is your guard lately?"

"She had some personal business to attend to. Why? Do you miss her?"

Ryan pursed his lips. "Just curious. She usually guards you like you were royalty."

"She said something about a sick aunt out of state and requested a few weeks off."

"Okay. The timing seems a bit odd, that's all."

"You can't be serious, Ryan. She's been with me for years. And my father before me."

Ryan's eyes bulged. "She was your father's assistant?"

Hunter stopped what he was doing and looked at Ryan. "Shit."

Before they could continue with their conversation, a knock on the door signaled breakfast had arrived. Instead of the chef, a young woman in her twenties materialized when Ryan opened the door.

A sly smile formed on Ryan's face. "Please come in. And who might you be?"

The woman bowed her head slightly while her cheeks flushed. "I am sorry for the intrusion, Mr. Logan," she said in Ryan's direction.

"That grumpy gentleman over there is Mr. Logan. I am Ryan. It's nice to meet your acquaintance, miss——?"

"Sorry. My name is Kimberly. Today is my first day," she responded shakily.

"You may put the coffee and muffins on the table in front of the couch, Kimberly. Welcome to Ares Logan. What is it you do besides save my life by providing the caffeine I desperately needed?"

A giggle escaped from Kimberly before she caught herself. "I am an assistant in the kitchen. I do whatever the chef needs me to do. Will there be anything else, Ryan or Mr. Logan?"

Hunter jumped in before Ryan could continue with his flirtation, "Thank you, Kimberly. That will be all for now. And, welcome to the company."

Without another word, Kimberly disappeared out the door and into the elevator. Ryan closed the door and poured himself a cup of black coffee before relaxing on the leather couch.

"Does Emma know about Kimberly? I would guess she would be none too pleased to know that a beautiful, young woman is catering to her husband's needs."

Hunter shook his head and strode across his office to pour himself a cup of coffee.

"As usual, you are completely delusional, Ryan. This morning was the first time I even met the girl. And I am shocked you didn't know every detail about her life, given you are the security guru... supposedly."

Ryan took a sip of the steaming coffee before indulging Hunter with a response. "Now that you mention it, I am disappointed with myself. Hmmm, must be because I've been so preoccupied with all your crap. I've made a mental note to make sure I do a thorough background check on her."

"Just remember the sexual harassment policy, tiger. I really don't want to have to fire you."

Ryan feigned shock and put his hand on his chest. "Who me? I am looking out for you. Can't be too careful these days."

"Alright, this conversation is going downhill fast. Why don't you take your breakfast to go and start doing some work this morning? It is what I pay you for."

Ryan stood and wrapped two muffins in some napkins, threw his bag over his shoulder, and stared at the Wedgewood coffee cup in front of him. Even Ryan knew he was not agile enough to make it down to his office without dropping or spilling the coffee. Before he could contemplate his options any longer, Hunter thrust a "to go" cup with a lid in front of Ryan.

"Gee, thanks."

"I swear you are like a child sometimes, Ryan."

"Funny," Ryan said before opening the door to leave.

Downstairs in his subterranean palace, he situated himself to start the day. His first order of business was to see what he could find out about the intriguing new employee he met in Hunter's office. She did not give off any malicious vibes, but Ryan learned a long time ago looking innocent does not mean somebody necessarily is.

It took Ryan the time to devour one of the

muffins to find the personnel file on the enticing Kimberly. She went to one of the top culinary schools in the country and graduated at the top of her class. Moved to Boston after graduating to find her dream job in one of the five-star restaurants, only to have those hopes put on hold due to lack of experience. The rest of her file and resume was like any other young college graduate. The background check also did not show any red flags.

Ryan closed the file on his laptop and considered this a non-threat to Hunter or the company. Kimberly was all she said—someone trying to get experience to further her career goals. Ryan secretly wished all research was open and shut like this one. Lately, there had been too many head-scratchers, and Ryan was struggling to keep up.

With Greg clearly back in the picture, Ryan needed to double his efforts. There was no telling what plotting and scheming Greg had been up to these last several months. Given Greg's past training and his sociopathic tendencies, Ryan needed to be ready for anything. The question remained about how this venomous reptile was going to strike next. And if this was just another fragment of the diabolical master plan or the finale.

Ryan paced around his office, staring at the file cabinets that had started to collect a light layer of dust. Hunter and Ryan mistakenly thought this ordeal had ended in Hardwicke. Ryan could not

Wicked Nemesis of the Hunted   335

afford to make the same mistake again. Especially if the next episode was more explosive than Hardwicke.

Wearing a pattern into the industrial carpet, Ryan decided to review the video footage one more time from Greg's escapades. Three minutes into the video, Ryan's laptop flickered and the lights in his office dimmed for approximately ten seconds. Immediately Ryan phoned Hunter.

Without any preamble, Ryan asked, "Did your lights dim or flicker?"

"Just for a few seconds, why?"

"I think I am being paranoid but, after the last incident with the power which still has no explanation, and now this one, I am wondering what is going on."

"Ryan, need I remind you there is a whopper of a thunderstorm going on right now?"

"And when was the last time a thunderstorm affected the power in this building, Hunter?"

Hunter paused before answering. "I can't recall."

"Exactly! The answer would be *never*. Our backup generator is military grade and comes on instantly."

"I am not doubting what you are saying, but Ryan, you saw the crazy lightning this morning."

"I need to make a few calls. We've had a lot of peculiar stuff happening lately. I want to be sure it really is the New England weather and not a cyberattack."

336   *Tracey L. Ryan*

"I am all for you being overly cautious. Let me know what you find out." Hunter disconnected and moved on with his morning.

The first call Ryan made was to his analyst to have her look into any anomalies either internally or externally with the power and network. Next, Ryan called the leader of his cybersecurity team to do the same. Figuring it wouldn't hurt to have two teams working on this, Ryan logged on to the power company's website to verify if any buildings in the surrounding area had reported any outages.

Satisfied he had covered all the bases to the best of his ability, Ryan dove into the second muffin. He had shoved the last quarter of the muffin in his mouth when a knock at the door startled him. Wiping crumbs from his face and brushing off his shirt, Ryan opened the door to see Jared standing in front of him.

"Jared, to what do I owe this visit to the basement?" Ryan asked and ushered him into his domain.

"Ryan, forgive me for the intrusion." Jared looked around the surroundings, realizing he had never been to Ryan's office previously.

"What can I do for you? Please have a seat," Ryan said, waving his hand toward one of the chairs in front of him.

"Did you notice a brief power fluctuation?"

Ryan automatically went on alert. "Yes. It lasted for a couple of seconds. Why?"

Jared fidgeted slightly in the chair. "Do you know what caused it?"

"I am going to guess it was a result of the storm we are in the midst of. Is there any particular reason why you are asking?"

"Ryan, I am sure we each have the same basic facts about one another. With the events both past and present, including the fact there was another similar incident a few weeks ago, I thought it wise to seek information. And I thought you would be the best person to provide it."

Intrigued by Jared's cryptic request, Ryan answered, "I see."

"I know you are the chief of security, and I am only a driver. I just don't believe in coincidences."

Ryan chuckled. "I think we both know you are more than just a driver, Jared. You obviously have expert training based on how you handled yourself in Hardwicke."

"It was a lucky shot," Jared responded.

"Lucky shot? You killed Ashley with one bullet dead center in her forehead. I would not call that lucky. I would call that expert."

"If you say so, Ryan. Look, I just wanted to find out if there is anything I should know, given the increased security for Mrs. Logan." Jared began to stand up, realizing he may have made a misstep.

"Sorry, Jared. I didn't mean any offense. I was grateful you have the skills that you do. Things could have ended up very differently that fateful night. Please. Sit down."

Jared sat back down and waited for Ryan.

"Look, there isn't much to tell just yet. Do I believe there is a possibility—and I do mean possibility not probability—the two power incidents are related? Hell, yes! But what I don't have is any proof at the moment. I have a few folks working on it to see if there was anything out of the ordinary during those periods. I can keep you apprised of what I find out if that helps."

"Thank you, Ryan. And I apologize for being a bit defensive. I just don't like to discuss my skills as you call them. I would like for my past to stay in the past."

"Hey, I get it. A word of advice? The past rarely stays as hidden as we think it is. Just look at all the secrets Hunter's mother was keeping. Those secrets destroyed the woman. She is now a shell of the strong-willed person she was previously."

Jared ignored Ryan's commentary. "Thank you for your time, Ryan. I would appreciate it if you could keep me in the loop so I can be better prepared."

Both men stood up, and Ryan walked Jared to the door. Before leaving, Jared turned to shake Ryan's hand and then disappeared into the elevator. Ryan stood in his office doorway for a few minutes, looking nowhere in particular before heading back to his desk.

"That was unexpected and a bit baffling," Ryan muttered.

"You do know talking to yourself is a sign of senility?" Hunter asked.

"Hey, did you send Jared down here to find out about the power flickering?" Ryan asked with a furrowed brow.

"No. Why would I do that? I would either call you or come down here like I just did."

"Hmmm."

"Can you elaborate more than that?"

"Jared has never once come down for a visit before today. Then he asked me about the power and if I knew what had caused it."

Hunter's eyes widened. "That is a bit odd. Why would he do that?"

"He said it was so he could be better prepared, given the need for increased security. It seemed very out of place. But you know him better than I do, Hunter."

Hunter shrugged. "I guess. I mean I know what he's capable of, but I don't really *know* him."

"I have never asked you but now I am going to, Hunter. What do you know about Jared's past? I tried to allude to it with him just now, and he got all squirmy. Said he wanted his past to stay in the past."

"Well, a lot of people would rather not dredge up the past. I am speaking from experience, of course."

"I know. Something was off with the whole conversation. Hunter, what is his deal?"

"Look, Ryan, what I can tell you is Jared has an exemplary background. Which I believe he proved in Hardwicke. If he wants to forget about his past, then it is not up to me to reveal it."

A heavy sigh escaped from Ryan. "Hunter, I understand you want to keep his confidence, but I am not trying to gossip about the man. I am trying to figure out what the hell is going on around here! Within minutes of a potential cybersecurity breach, I have your driver coming down here asking me if this incident and the one a few weeks ago are related. So, forgive me if I don't let you off the hook that easily."

"Fine. I will tell you the basics. Anything beyond that you will need to get from Jared himself. Deal?"

"If that is all I can get for the moment it will have to do."

"Jared is former military. From what he told me, he quickly showed he had some natural talents they were looking for. A specialized group within the military took him under their wing and cultivated those talents. You will never find any documents on any of the missions he was part of, but I have no reason to doubt what he told me. Satisfied?"

"It will do for now. Based on what you just revealed, it sounds like Jared was part of a black ops team. It would explain his expert marksmanship. I won't push any further unless it becomes necessary. But Hunter?"

"Yes?"

"When I tell you it has become necessary, then I expect all the details."

"Alright. I promise to give you the information if there is no other way to move forward. Now, where are we with the little power fluctuation we had?"

"My team is still looking into it. I did contact the power company, and no other buildings in this area have reported power outages or fluctuations of any kind. Also, the team is not only looking into this building but all our other buildings."

"What is it, Ryan? You have that look on your face."

"This all feels like how a caged animal will test the electric fence looking for weaknesses."

"Well, that is a pleasant thought." Hunter jumped up from his chair and strode to the door. Turning back to look at Ryan, Hunter said, "Let me know as soon as you can confirm or deny this is anything to be worried about."

"Of course."

Ryan did not know where to go from here. He knew they were being hit from all angles, which made his entire body tense.

CHAPTER 35

R yan gave up on this team being able to uncover anything beyond a random power fluctuation from a thunderstorm. Rolling up his sleeves, he decided to concentrate on the mountain of files in the cabinets in front of him. Although he had previously reviewed every file, this time he decided to read them word for word versus just skimming for context.

A text arrived when Ryan pulled open the second drawer. The text told him what he already suspected—no other companies within the Boston city limits had any issues during the specific time frame in question. When this blip occurred, the firewalls were unavailable for less than one second. A full scan was run on all systems and no threats were found. A further review of all Ares Logan buildings, including the cancer-prevention-drug research lab, showed the same power fluctuation at the exact same time.

Ryan reread the text several times to make sure he understood what it meant. There was no cyberattack, but a weakness was identified. It was like how a tiny chip in a car windshield didn't seem like much at first until someone drives over the first pothole and suddenly there is a spiderweb of cracks.

Deciding not to tell Hunter until he had more information, Ryan packed up his belongings to head home.

The team was working on plugging the hole in their firewall, along with retesting the entire system, to try to identify any other entry points.

If someone were to circumvent the firewall, they would have carte blanche to not only wreak immeasurable damage but, more importantly, steal the cancer-prevention-drug research. And Ryan knew the perfect sociopath with the necessary programming skills to accomplish this. The question would be how Ryan and his team could prevent the unthinkable from happening.

After a quick dinner consisting of Chinese take-out, Ryan spread the files he took home across the coffee table in his living room. Deep down, he knew clues were waiting to be found in the papers.

After two hours, Ryan had three color-coded piles of varying height displayed in front of him. The blue folders contained dates and times of plant growth presumably from the hidden basement at the Logan estate. The red folders focused on formulas and more scientific information Ryan didn't understand but hoped the scientists would. Finally, in Ryan's mind, the yellow folders held the jackpot.

Not only were there dates but also coordinates with locations. Ryan was buzzing with what he saw in front of him. Before getting too excited, he consulted his phone to test out his theory.

"Hot damn!" Ryan yelled.

Without wasting another minute, Ryan called Hunter.

"Dude, I found something in those files! Specifically, in the yellow ones." Ryan rambled without taking a breath.

On the other end, Hunter had to hold the phone away from his ear due to the volume of Ryan's voice.

"Slow down, Ryan. And please, no shouting. I think the residents of Waltham heard you."

"Sorry. I took some of the files home from the office and have been plowing through them for two hours." Ryan paused to take a breath. "You won't guess what was in the yellow files!"

"Ryan, stop squealing like a schoolgirl. How about instead of guessing you just tell me?"

"There are locations for the plants."

"That's it? I thought you had already determined that."

"No. You don't understand. The earlier files had rough locations. *These* files have actual coordinates."

"So now we know exactly where the plants are in the Amazon?"

"Sorry. Everything in my head is moving faster than my mouth can work. Not the Amazon…Florida!"

Hunter fumbled at Ryan's discovery and almost dropped the phone.

"Say that again? Did you say Florida?"

"Yes, Hunter. Florida. Southern Florida, to be more precise."

Hunter was silent on the other end.

"Hunter, are you still there?"

"Yes, I am still here. Just trying to wrap my head around the fact you just told me we may have an easier path to getting live plants. And the fact you also confirmed the test results Dr. McGrady provided to us were not an anomaly."

"I know! Totally unexpected, to say the least. I need to do a bit more investigating to narrow down the locations. I have general areas right now."

"Do you think you will be able to get the exact coordinates?"

"Nothing is absolute, but there is a chance. The only caveat is the missing file Greg helped himself to."

"I hate to be a downer, but are you sure these coordinates are legitimate? I mean, my father would go to any lengths to cover his tracks. It seems a bit odd he would just have put this information in these folders."

"I understand your hesitation. Just don't forget

that we found these in a hidden room in your house. A room that no one in the family knew about. I would say it is safe to say Philip didn't intend for anyone to ever know about the room or its contents."

Hunter rubbed his chin. "Although you make a valid point, Ryan, what about the most recent files? We still have no idea how they got there."

"Let's not get ahead of ourselves. I'll try to narrow down the search radius a bit more. I can show you what I have tomorrow morning at the office."

"Alright. Thanks, Ryan." Hunter felt lightheaded.

The men disconnected to continue with their evenings. Ryan resumed digging through the content in the yellow folders for more specifics related to the potential locations of the plants they desperately needed. Hunter chose to forget about plants, soil, and the rainforest so he could finish enjoying dinner with Emma, which concluded with attentively satisfying his wife for dessert.

More hours passed, with Ryan becoming more absorbed in his reading materials. Stretching his arms over his head to try to relieve his neck and shoulders, Ryan pushed himself off the couch. For the last several hours, he had been hunched over in the same position. As soon as Ryan moved, his muscles shrieked in agony.

Ryan packed up the piles of paper on the coffee table into some semblance of order and placed them into his laptop bag. Once in his bedroom, he stripped down to his boxer briefs, and after inspecting the bed for unwanted creatures, he fell into the plush cotton sheets.

Within minutes, his mind went into sleep mode. Dreams came and went throughout the night. Some focused on adventurous carnal activities with Sue while others were more mundane. At one point, Ryan rolled over in the middle of the night and spooned the empty pillow next to him.

CHAPTER 36

A little after five a.m., Ryan groggily opened his eyes. When the room came into focus, Ryan's dreams from last night faded quickly. Lying on his back with his hands clasped behind his head, Ryan tried to replay the images of Sue in his head.

A chirp on his phone brought him back to reality. Reaching over to where his phone was on the nightstand, Ryan smiled when he saw who had texted him.

He quickly typed his response. "Lying in bed thinking of you."

Sue was just as quick to respond. "Same here."

"What should we do about this?" Ryan replied.

"I have some ideas."

Within a few seconds, Ryan's phone started playing "With or Without You" by U2, signaling a video chat request.

"Good morning, sunshine. You are up early today," answered Ryan's silky voice.

"I was dreaming of you, so thought I would see if you were awake," responded Sue's sultry voice on the other end.

"I was very lonely here this morning after some delicious dreams of you last night."

"That is what I like to hear. Care to share?"

"I would rather show you."

"Me as well. Unfortunately, I don't think I could wait twenty minutes to drive to your apartment."

For the next fifteen minutes, the lovers relived their uninhibited fantasies in vivid detail over video.

Still panting, Sue said, "Well, this was an unexpected pleasure."

"I have to say it was a first for me and it was incredible," Ryan replied, wiping sweat off his brow.

"Hopefully, next time we can do this in person."

"I would like nothing more," Ryan said, still breathing heavily.

"How about tonight? I could bring dinner. We will need our nourishment. Lots of protein."

"I do believe I would thoroughly enjoy that. Say seven o'clock?"

"I will be there. You might want to take a nap today, Ryan. You won't be getting any sleep tonight."

"I will keep that in mind. See you later."

The pair disconnected, leaving Ryan alone with a multitude of visions racing through his head. Before this went on too much longer, he hopped out of bed and into a cool shower. Ryan hoped the cool water would clear his head so he could begin what was going to be the longest day in history. Thankfully, Jared was driving the power couple to their respective work locations this morning, giving Ryan a reprieve from Hunter's predictable inquisition.

By the time Ryan reached his office after his standard stops along the way, last night's dreams and the morning's reality were a distant memory. Ryan knew Hunter would be down to his office first thing to discuss the findings from last night, and he wanted to be prepared.

Within minutes, Hunter magically appeared in the doorway to his office. Without saying a word, Hunter took his usual seat and crossed his legs, staring at Ryan.

"Good morning, Hunter. I've been wondering when you would materialize in my office."

"Materialize?"

"It is a bit strange how no one ever hears you coming and then—poof! You are in the room."

Hunter shook his head. "You are in an odd mood this morning, Ryan."

"No more odd than usual."

"If you say so. Anyway, what else were you able to find out after our call last night?"

"In fact, quite a bit. I am still doing some research, but I feel optimistic."

"Optimism is good. Care to share?"

Wicked Nemesis of the Hunted   351

"I spent several hours last night combing through the information in all the yellow folders I brought home with me."

"And?" Hunter huffed narrowing his eyes at Ryan.

"*And*…there is not one but *two* potential locations of these plants in the United States."

"What?" Hunter exclaimed, almost jumping out of his seat.

Ryan pulled up an assortment of the coordinates he found in the folders on his laptop and turned the screen around so Hunter could also see the visual.

"Keep in mind this is only a sampling. But all these coordinates are located either in southern Florida or northern Puerto Rico."

Hunter's mouth dropped open as he stared blankly at the screen.

"So, what you are saying is we may not have to take an expedition to the Amazon?"

"As I said, I still need to do more research, including reviewing word for word all the other yellow folders. That was the other revelation last night—the color coding of the files does mean something as we suspected. Yellow has been all about locations while the others are more of the science stuff."

Hunter sat back in his chair to absorb this new evidence while Ryan waited patiently for a response.

"How long do you think it will take to give me a more definitive answer?"

"I am going to spend today mapping out all the coordinates I've found so far. Now that I know to focus on the yellow folders, hopefully, it will go more quickly. I'll check in with you by mid-afternoon with a progress report."

Hunter pushed himself up from the chair he had been occupying and headed toward the door.

"Hunter, this may be the break we need. I don't want to get too excited, though. We need to keep in mind the actual key to unlocking the whereabouts of live plants may be contained in the one folder we are no longer in possession of."

Hunter nodded and disappeared out the door, leaving Ryan with the monumental task of identifying every coordinate mentioned in the sea of yellow folders. Ryan took a sip of his lukewarm coffee, trying to decide the best way to organize all of them. Deciding the job was too big for just himself, Ryan called in some reinforcement to help with the data analysis.

Each time Ryan identified perceived map coordinates, he would pass along the information to his analyst to plug into some sort of algorithm that was beyond his comprehension. Ryan was out of his league when it came to the programming miracles his analyst was able to perform. What would take Ryan hours, if not days, only took her minutes.

Wicked Nemesis of the Hunted   353

By noontime, Ryan and his analyst had mapped out exact areas to focus on in both Florida and Puerto Rico. Ryan never knew these rainforests even existed within the country.

The only tropical rainforest managed by the US Forest Service was in Puerto Rico. Boasting almost twenty-nine thousand acres, the rainforest had an abundance of wildlife not found anywhere else in the United States, along with colorful plant life. From what Ryan could find online, this was a mountainous rainforest and home to some of the highest quality water, providing picturesque natural cascades and pools. Ryan winced at the flashback of his dream around the waterfall and pool he almost drowned in.

Shaking the memory from his mind, Ryan concentrated next on the Florida locations. There were several areas on both sides of Florida that were noted in the files. The Key West location stood out purely due to the number of additional notes in the files. The Key West Tropical Forest & Botanical Gardens only spanned about eight acres and dated back to the 1930s. It was home to a plethora of endangered fauna and flora native to the region, with three of the last freshwater ponds in the Florida Keys. Minus the waterfalls in Ryan's dream, everything else seemed to fit.

Ryan was not a botanist, so he was going purely on instinct, based on what he had been able to decipher from his online research. The only surefire way to know if the elusive plants existed was to survey both locations. Ryan needed to think about a course of action in more detail before discussing it with Hunter. Showing up at either location with a group of research and security people would raise some eyebrows. Especially if certain unknown individuals were keeping close tabs on Ryan's comings and goings, as he suspected.

By mid-afternoon, Ryan had developed a reasonable plan. To jump start things, Ryan decided to head up to Hunter's office. The elevator deposited him in the waiting area outside Hunter's office and, once again, his assistant was presumably still on leave.

Behind a slightly ajar door, Ryan heard two raised male voices. He had forgotten to consult Hunter's online schedule before his quick ride to the top floor of the building. Unsure of the proper etiquette, Ryan gently knocked as he slowly opened the door.

Ryan did a double take upon entering. Jared was in the midst of a mildly heated conversation with Hunter before they noticed Ryan standing in the doorway.

"Sorry to interrupt. I can come back later," Ryan said and began to retreat.

"No need, Ryan. I have said what I needed to say to Mr. Logan," Jared snarled on his way to the elevator.

"Do I even want to know what that was about?" Ryan asked and sat on the couch.

Hunter shook his head in exasperation. "Jared is displeased with some of my decisions regarding security."

"I thought security was my gig."

"It is except for certain tasks Jared is better suited for."

"Call me intrigued!" Ryan flashed a smile in Hunter's direction.

"Never mind. I am guessing you have information for me." Hunter bristled.

"Fine. We'll move on to the business at hand. Yes, I have more information. Based on what I was able to decipher, I narrowed it down to El Yunque National Forest in Puerto Rico and the Key West Tropical Forest & Botanical Garden."

"And your confidence level in either of these locations?" Hunter asked coolly.

"It is presumably fifty-fifty. Both fit the bill when compared to the Amazon. The enormous question is if your father went to the Amazon *after* researching these places *or* before."

Hunter tilted his head at Ryan.

"If your father went to Puerto Rico or Florida before the Amazon, then we could conclude he didn't find what he was looking for. If he went to either place after his initial trips to the Amazon, then it might lead us to believe there may be something worth looking for in these locations."

"But he supposedly died in the plane crash in the Amazon. Wouldn't that suggest he found nothing in either Puerto Rico or Florida?" Hunter rubbed his forehead.

"Possibly yes and possibly no. I know you want clear-cut answers. Unfortunately, I just don't have any…right now."

"I gather you have a plan, Ryan?"

"Indeed, I do. I still need to work through some details, but I would recommend we start with Key West. Then, if there is nothing there, move on to Puerto Rico."

"Okay. What do you need from me?"

"I don't want to show up in either location with a caravan of people in tow. It would attract some unwanted attention. We will need to create some diversions."

"Diversions? Why do I feel like I have been dumped into a James Bond movie?"

Ryan chuckled. "Well, it's kind of like that. I will need to make a couple different plane reservations on commercial flights for myself to destinations nowhere close to where I will be heading. I will also need you to file flight plans for the Ares Logan jet to some boring corporate location and list some random executive as a passenger. In midflight, we will change the flight plan to the actual destination. A little unorthodox but it needs to be this way.

Oh, and the commercial reservations will be made for a day or two after my actual departure on the corporate jet."

Hunter's eyes glazed over slightly, trying to comprehend all the cloak-and-dagger routines that came naturally to Ryan.

"Hunter, do you understand?"

"Yes, I think so. It should concern me this comes so easily for you."

"Well, if you've had the years of training I have, it would become second nature to you as well. Don't sweat it."

"Why Key West as the first choice?"

"Both places are nice this time of year, so it was a tough choice. Sandy beaches, beautiful women, umbrella drinks."

"I am not in the mood, Ryan," Hunter commented tersely.

"Tough crowd today! I think Key West will be the easiest since it's much smaller than the national forest in Puerto Rico. And I am hoping, with a colorful tropical shirt, I will fit in as a tourist."

Hunter rolled his eyes. "What you said actually sounds logical. Not the part about your attire."

"Let me work through some of the logistics and then start making reservations." Ryan hesitated. "I was going to ask if you wanted me to take Jared along on this fact-finding mission."

"If all you are going to do is go down there to take a look, then I think Jared is better suited staying here to keep an eye on things."

"Your call, boss man."

"Ryan, I don't need to remind you how important this is."

"I know, Hunter. You don't need to remind me. My plan is to go to Key West for no more than three days."

"And if you don't find what you are looking for?"

"Then I will go to Puerto Rico directly from Key West, unless there is a reason back here preventing me from doing that. It will be easier, with less time wasted flying."

"Seems reasonable. You have my approval to make all the necessary arrangements."

"I'm on it. I should be able to nail down everything and fly out in a couple of days. Fingers crossed we are finally making some progress."

Ryan left Hunter staring out at the deep blue ocean, wrapped up in his private thoughts. While on the rapid elevator ride down to the basement, Ryan pondered what the riff was between Hunter and Jared. It was the first time he had ever witnessed a confrontation between the two men.

Before Ryan could contemplate the multitude of possibilities, the elevator doors sprang open, and he was once again back in his domain. Closing the door to his office, Ryan began the painstaking process of creating fictitious flight information. His first commercial flight was to San Diego where there was a small Ares Logan office. The next flight was going to Dallas, where one of the subsidiaries occupied a large office park. If anyone checked, they would see Ryan had visited both locations numerous times over the last few years and shouldn't raise any red flags.

Ryan knew Hunter always kept the corporate jet at the ready, so he decided to wait until the last minute to alert the flight crew. They were paid to follow instructions, not to ask any questions, which helped put Ryan's mind at ease.

CHAPTER 37

Noting the time, Ryan packed up his belongings so he could rush home to do a bit of cleaning before his highly awaited guest arrived. A sly smile crept onto his face when he thought of being with Sue tonight. The hard part would be not letting his travel plans slip out. Luckily, Ryan didn't talk in his sleep, and he knew rest would not be the focus of the evening.

Ryan speed-cleaned every room in his small apartment and even changed the sheets on the bed in anticipation of his overnight guest. At six forty-five p.m., a knock on the door signaled Sue's arrival. Ryan's heartbeat hastened slightly in anticipation when he opened the door.

Sue stood in front of him in a long trench coat, with bags in both arms. Looking at her from head to toe, Ryan noticed how she looked exotic and intoxicating. Her brown eyes made his inner animal stir. Grabbing her overnight bag before it slipped, Ryan held the door for Sue, allowing her to enter.

"Thanks. I wasn't sure what you would be in the mood for, so I went to the Italian deli on the corner. Did you know they have an incredible selection of premade dinners?" Sue asked, placing the paper bag on the counter.

Ryan whirled Sue around to face him and intensely kissed her. She wrapped her arms around his neck, wanting the kiss to last.

"Hello," Ryan whispered as he tucked a loose strand of hair behind Sue's ear.

"Hello. That was quite a welcome, Ryan."

"I thought I would set the mood for the evening."

"It looks like we both had the same idea," Sue commented. She unbuttoned her coat to reveal she was wearing nothing underneath except her silky skin.

Ryan grabbed her hand and almost ran to the bedroom where, for the next hour, they went on a deep exploration. Relaxing on their backs without sheets anywhere in sight, the couple held hands in silence. Ryan turned and leaned on his elbow, facing Sue's direction.

"What do you say we get some nourishment and then decide what we want to do for dessert?" Ryan nuzzled Sue's neck.

Sue playfully pushed him away. "Go get dinner started or else we will never eat!"

Ryan grabbed his boxer briefs from the floor before heading to the kitchen, leaving Sue lying in a blissful state. A few minutes later, she joined Ryan in the kitchen wearing one of his T-shirts that barely covered her assets.

Once dinner was successfully reheated and consumed, the lovers decided to continue their discovery on the couch before heading back to the bedroom where Sue fell asleep in Ryan's arms. For the next few hours, the couple each relived their fantasies in dreamland.

Around four a.m., Ryan was kicked awake. Startled and immediately on alert, Ryan observed Sue had been the culprit. Sue's face was contorted, and her legs were thrashing about like she was running in her sleep. A soft moan escaped her. Ryan wasn't sure if he should wake her or if this dream would pass in the next few minutes.

Sitting up as gently as he could, Ryan watched Sue intently, wondering what pain she was reliving. At that moment, he would do anything to take Sue's agony away from her if he could. As quickly as her dream started, it seemed to dissipate. Sue rolled over with her back toward Ryan, and her moans became even breaths. Ryan slid back down and wrapped his arms around Sue, trying not to wake her.

When the alarm suddenly announced it was time to begin the day, Ryan almost had a heart attack.

"Holy fuck!"

"I guess this means we have to get up," Sue said through a yawn.

"I am so sorry. Apparently, I forgot to turn off the alarm last night. I will blame you since you were distracting me," Ryan teased.

"Do I even want to know why you have the alarm set so early in the morning?"

"I usually head to the gym and stop at the corner store for coffee," Ryan said, slightly embarrassed.

"You need to be up at the crack of dawn to do that?"

"I guess not. I never really thought about it. It has been my routine for years."

Sue rolled over and put the pillow over her head.

Ryan leaned over, letting his fingers wander, and whispered in Sue's ear, "Since we are both obviously awake and in all the right places…" Ryan let his voice trail off.

After a steam-filled shower and light breakfast, Ryan decided to prod a little about Sue's apparent nightmare. He silently said a prayer he wasn't going to regret asking Sue about it.

Facing her, Ryan went for it. "Sue, last night you had a nightmare. You don't need to tell me about it. It just got me a little worried."

Sue managed a small smile and responded, "Ryan, everyone has nightmares at some point while they are sleeping. I think it is sweet you were worried. But there really isn't a need to be. I honestly can't recall any of my dreams last night. Did I talk in my sleep or something?"

"No. Nothing like that. You kicked me rather hard, and I am sure there will be a bruise on my shin." Ryan flashed Sue a wide smile.

"Well, at least I didn't injure any important body parts. That would have been a real shame."

Sue stood directly in front of Ryan and kissed him. He broke away after a minute with the distinct feeling Sue was trying to deflect the conversation.

The couple engaged in the same pattern of activities for the remainder of the weekend, stopping intermittently to regain their strength. By Sunday evening, Ryan felt completely at ease with Sue being in his space. What started out purely as satisfying his carnal needs was beginning to burrow deeper within him. He was still torn by their past and what the future could look like. And neither completely trusted the other and likely never would.

For the longest time, Ryan watched a serene Sue sleeping next to him. Thoughts of her past crept into his mind. Ryan believed it didn't serve any purpose to expose all one's secrets to a partner—some things should just be left concealed in the past. In this specific case, was that the best course of action?

Glancing at the clock on the bedside table, Ryan saw he only had a few hours before the alarm was going to interrupt the sound of relaxed breathing next to him. A slight pang of guilt struck him when he least expected it. When the alarm sounded in the morning, Ryan knew he would begin a new set of lies even if they were lies of omission to Sue.

Ryan burrowed under the covers and held Sue tightly as he drifted off to sleep. Little did he know that Sue had her own lies of omission, which would inevitably collide with his mission. And this could have deadly consequences for both.

While the satisfied couple was enjoying what could be their last hours of blissful slumber, a shadow lurked outside Ryan's apartment building. The high-tech equipment in Greg Smythe's hands showed two reddish-orange figures in what he assumed was the bedroom.

A sly smile formed on Greg's face at the thought of literally killing two birds with one stone. A small explosive device strategically placed in the building would reduce the bricks and mortar to a pile of rubble. Unfortunately, Greg had orders from his employer not to bring any more suspicion their way before the mission could be completed. Once finished, Greg was free to do whatever he wished with his nemesis and the bitch who caused him so much humiliation at their former employer.

The moon was bright and provided enough light to illuminate Greg's walk back to his car parked several blocks away. Delight overtook his emotions, knowing he was able to get exceptionally close to his enemies without them having a clue. This feeling would need to hold Greg over until he was able to dispose of them properly. His current employer and mentor of sorts had taught him how to explore his sociopathic tendencies and turn them into an advantage.

The cool night air reminded Greg of his time in the unforsaken desert land of the country's enemy. He had watched triumphantly, from a safe distance, when Ryan was shot by his lover as they tried to evacuate. The only thing that would have made the moment better was if Ryan had been killed. The moments following the chaos bubbled up all the anger again.

Greg had been fooled into helping the provocative female agent who portrayed herself as a traitor. During their clandestine meetings before that fateful day, Greg thought he had found his soul mate. Someone who had the same qualities as he did. Someone who he did not have to suppress these traits around and with whom he could truly be himself.

Zipping up his dark-colored, lightweight jacket to shield himself from the ocean wind playing hide-and-seek around the buildings in Boston, the fury continued to rise to an atomic level. Shortly after that day in the desert, Greg figured out he was being set up as the scapegoat in an award-winning theatrical performance. Greg struggled to remember how he caught on to this fact but was thankful his inner psyche had told him something wasn't right with the situation.

The day of the epiphany was the day Greg decided to offer his skills to the highest bidder once he completely disappeared from his old identity. It was always his hope and dream to one day come face to face with those who wronged him. He had so many plans for Ryan and Sue. Greg wholeheartedly believed that once these plans were put into motion, there would be no stopping him.

Greg reached his car, looked in all directions to confirm he had not been seen by anyone, and drove off in the direction of his lair. Even if someone had noticed him lingering outside of the apartment building, Greg knew he was a chameleon. The person would be described as the opposite of what Greg looked like. And even then, the people who saw him would be wrong. No one really knew what he truly looked like or who he was.

Dawn slowly made her presence known while Greg drove the short distance to the Seaport District. After he parked his car in his assigned parking spot in the garage, Greg quickly changed his appearance to the person who lived one floor below the newlywed couple, Hunter, and Emma Logan. Checking his appearance in the rearview mirror one last time, Greg exited the car and proceeded to the elevator to bring him within feet of the precious couple.

Nothing would please Greg more than being able to dispose of these arrogant socialites, but his employer was adamant nothing was to be done to them. They were an important part of the larger plan to acquire the cancer-prevention drug. The same drug could ultimately be used as a weapon, resulting in many enemies of the United States paying unimaginable sums of money to acquire it.

Greg exited the elevator at his floor, which was shared with one other condo. The Logans' condo occupied the entire top floor of the building whereas the other less expensive condos each shared a floor. Inside, Greg went about his normal routine, pleased with himself for tonight's escapade.

It was time to move to the next phase of the plan. Unbeknownst to Ryan, Greg had managed to clone both his phone and computer. Greg was aware of every keystroke Ryan made, including the feeble attempt at subterfuge with the multiple plane reservations to various mundane locations.

Greg smiled while he lay in bed. He just needed to wait until Ryan and Sue found the much-needed plants. Little did the lovers know, but they were going to be doing all the dirty work for him. Greg just needed to watch and wait. This thought, amongst other more nefarious ones, helped Greg fall asleep immediately.

Special Thanks

I WOULD LIKE TO GIVE SPECIAL THANKS TO MY family, friends, and readers. Your support and encouragement continue to make this journey more fulfilling than I ever could have imagined. I hope you have enjoyed this next installment of the series and that it provided a little fun escape from reality.

Although the story was fiction, there were some real aspects weaved in that I hope made the tale come to life. Having the opportunity to put my hometown in these books continues to be amazing. I encourage you to visit Hardwick if you get the chance. You will find a pristine, rural town that holds a peacefulness hard to find in today's world.

I've also enjoyed being able to feature some excellent small businesses owned by friends of mine in these books. I encourage you to check these out to help support the local economy. I promise you won't be disappointed.

It has been an exciting experience meeting new people during the many events I have been part of. I love hearing from readers and fellow writers, so feel free to drop me an email through my website. Keep reading and be on the lookout for the next book in the series.

OTHER BOOKS FROM THE SERIES BY TRACEY L. RYAN:

Wicked Game of the Hunter
Wicked Shadow of the Hunter
Wicked Storm of the Hunter

Visit TraceyLRyan.com for more information about including tour dates.

Made in United States
Troutdale, OR
07/05/2024

21029451R00216